QUIETLY *waiting*

Printed in Australia

Cover by Melinda Childs @studioorchard

Internal design by Book Burrow www.bookburrow.com.au

First printing: August 2024

RICHFOX BOOKS Pty Ltd

www.justinfoxauthor.com

Paperback ISBN 978-1-7637492-0-7

eBook ISBN 978-1-7637492-2-1

Hardback ISBN 978-1-7637492-1-4

Distributed by RICHFOX Books

RICHFOX BOOKS acknowledges the traditional owners of the land and pays respects to the Elders, past, present and future.

A catalogue record for this work is available from the National Library of Australia

QUIETLY

waiting

Justin Fox

For my mother Evelyn, who encouraged me to write.

For Meg, Nicholas, Hayley & Charli.

For my friend Pete, who helped, encouraged and believed.

'An unwavering source of support.'

The story begins at the end.
History repeats.

Tanya 1.1

TANYA CHECKED HER watch for the hundredth time, then for the thousandth time that day, she thought of him. *Where was he? Was he alright? What was he doing?* She clutched a tissue in her right hand, intermittently dabbing at her eyes. Tears had become a constant companion. She was expecting a phone call, that was now well overdue. *There must be an unexpected delay,* she thought.

'He'll call soon,' she reassured herself. 'Delays were nothing to worry about,' she kept reminding herself. 'Focus on the positives,' she repeated to herself.

This had become her mantra. It helped to keep the scarier thoughts at bay. This was no normal situation they were in; it wasn't as if he had missed the bus or just caught a later train home from the office. She was an emotional wreck.

It hadn't always been this way; she had not always been so easily aroused to this level of anxiety. Her surroundings didn't help. She was all alone in a wing of an enormous country house, a place she knew well but only as a visitor and only recently as a place to call home. It had been in her family for more than 120 years and was currently under the custodianship of her aunt, who had taken it over from her grandparents. She had been lured there with the offer of a job. Her aunt had approached her at a very vulnerable time, she suspected the involvement of her mother.

The job was to research, then write the biography of one of her relatives. It seemed plausible; however, her cynical side suspected its sole purpose was to keep her occupied while her husband was away. The house's vast empty spaces exacerbated her anxiety, there were too many ghosts lurking in the shadows. Haunting pictures stared down from the walls; secrets were hidden everywhere. The servants, of which there were many, kept a discreet distance. Perhaps they had been instructed to do so at the direction of her aunt, under the false assumption that she wanted privacy. The loneliness weighed heavily on her. At these times, her work was the only thing that could distract her, but in this moment of uncertainty, she couldn't concentrate for long enough to immerse herself in it. All she could do was be patient, think of him, pray that he was safe and wait for the phone to ring.

Tanya 1.2

MEETING HER SOUL mate had not been in her plans. As her aunt would later tell her, it only ever seemed to happen when you least expected, or even wanted, it to. Her brother was to blame. He was passing out from the Royal Military Academy, Sandhurst, where he had been training to become an officer in the British Army. It was a family event, one that she was unable to get out of.

She had never envisaged her brother as a soldier; she still wondered at his decision to become one. Well, the truth was, it wasn't all his decision. He was guided, no, perhaps pushed was the correct word, in that direction by their mother who, after consulting friends, was convinced it was just the thing to end his listlessness. With her father gone and her aunt her only other close relative, travelling abroad, it would be just her and her mother making up the party to celebrate her brother's great achievement.

She had tried to come up with an excuse to avoid it, started to think of one, then memories of her father had surfaced, memories of a promise made on his death bed, that she would look after her mother when he was gone. It was a powerful memory, a solemn commitment. It was enough to guilt her into accepting the invitation, regardless of how precious her weekends were.

Tanya was coming to the end of the university phase of her life, as she deemed to term it. These were the final opportunities to spend time with her friends, fellow students and teachers, to live the life she had come to enjoy so much. Yes, of course, they would see each other again over the years to come, probably many times for some of them, but it would never be the same. They would change, she would change. What they were experiencing together would not come again. She cherished it. It was sentimental, still it was hers, something she had earned. So that was that, out of feelings of guilt, love and family togetherness, she had agreed to go.

Boys. What do you do with boys? Especially, what do you do with restless, directionless, rich boys? Send them into the military, of course! Just as in days of old, the tried-and-true method, give them a place to burn away all that excess energy. Give them something worthy to focus on, then before you know it, they will be back home, ready to direct their energies into the family business or a decent respectable career. Tanya found the idea repulsive.

So, it had been arranged for her brother Harry, even though it was not supposed to be possible in this modern equal opportunity age. At the orchestration of her mother, emails had been sent, petitions made, a word or two in the right ear from distinguished family friends and eventually, a place had been offered. Wealth and privilege were still, it seemed, able to provide their own avenues to success.

Tanya had been forced to admit, though, that her brother seemed to be excelling in the army. Monitoring his progress closely, from what she could see, he was relishing the lifestyle, rising successfully to the many challenges. It needed to be remembered that it was only training. However, it unlocked something in him and now, forty-four weeks later, he was passing out as an officer, with a career ahead of him. An amazing transformation.

Tanya, busy focusing on completing her studies, had allowed the event to creep up on her. She found herself late on the Friday night, prior to the ceremony, alone in her flat, packing. A frantic unscheduled call to her mother revealed that the expected dress code was conservative, garden party wear. She wasn't completely sure she knew what that was. In the end, she packed the only two outfits she owned, that she thought might match this description, hoping for the best. They were having dinner with a friend of Harry's back at the hotel in the evening after, so Tanya packed a black dress for what would probably be for her, a boring affair. She would travel in jeans and a t-shirt. *No use in going over the top for riding in a car,* she thought. To that end, she decided to leave her jewellery case at home. Why make the effort?

The alarm drew her out of a deep sleep at 6:30am on the following morning, Saturday. She stepped straight into the shower, the water helping to wake her up. Making little effort beyond brushing her teeth and drying her hair, she ate a simple breakfast consisting of two rounds of toast with strawberry jam and a hot mug of tea. When she finished, she was fully awake, feeling ready to conquer the world, or at least deal with her mother. As an afterthought she decided to pack a pair of fancy, black high heel shoes for the dinner. She pulled on her jeans and t-shirt and was ready to leave with twenty minutes to spare. As soon as she walked out of her building, she spotted the big silver car parked waiting, the driver standing ready.

As soon as he saw her, walking across the courtyard with her suitcase, handbag, and backpack, he came running across to help. *Was she that helpless?* she asked herself. At that moment, a female acquaintance, emerged with a similar amount of luggage, a child in a pram and another holding her one free hand and headed for the bus stop. There was nobody to help her!

Sheepishly, she half-heartedly waved at the woman who stared at her, as the uniformed driver relieved her of all but her handbag, carrying them apologetically to where the large Bentley waited. The older she got, the more her family's wealth embarrassed her. *Well, I have given people something to gossip about over their coffees,* she thought. The driver held the door for her as she climbed into the back seat and smiled, thanking him. He nodded in return. Her mother was in the car, half asleep and barely acknowledged her. Tanya leant across, kissing her on the cheek, then reached into her bag retrieving a book. They travelled in silence as the world around them came alive. Immersed in her reading, Tanya saw none of it.

Tanya 1.3

$\mathcal{S}$ITTING ALONE IN her room, the memories of that day were so clear. She re-lived, not just the imagery, but the emotions that all came flooding back, leading to sensory overload. Tanya tried to distract herself, picked up a book then put it straight back down, checked her phone, her watch, took some tissues from the ever present box. Though it had not begun that way, it was now remembered as one of the happiest days of her life. The memories were comforting; they remained fresh, allowing her to retreat into them whenever she wanted. She sat back down in an armchair closed her eyes and let them wash over her.

Tanya 1.4

THE JOURNEY WAS uneventful. They only stopped once at a service centre so the driver could stretch his legs; the two women never left the car. It was only when the car turned into the long drive that led to the hotel where they were staying, that Tanya looked up from her book. The hotel was built upon the ruins of a former stately home, the grounds still showed signs of the estate's former glory. It interested her. They drove past high garden walls and immaculately trimmed hedges, an enormous fountain lay defunct but, in its day, would have been very impressive. The main house was newly renovated, after being left vacant and derelict for many years. She had read an article about it; the building had been completely gutted before being rebuilt. She wondered if this fate awaited any of her family's properties. As it came into view, she was impressed, even more so on entering the foyer.

On the outside, it looked old, the historical sandstone façade had been restored. Inside, it was completely modern, with only a few traces of the past remaining. The foyer was topped by a large glass dome that filled it with light; the walls were lined with Scandinavian oak panels; a white marble staircase stretched to the floors above, an opulent relic from the distant past.

To the left of the foyer was the restaurant. The wood panelling in there was darker, giving it a more intimate feel. Each table was cleverly screened from the others, providing individual spaces and privacy. It had a French bistro feel that reminded Tanya of somewhere she had eaten in Paris, though she couldn't remember the exact location. There were four private dining rooms, one of these had been reserved their dinner party later that evening.

They were met in the foyer by the manager, who personally welcomed them. He led them past the assembled staff, who were lined up to welcome them, causing Tanya more embarrassment, then personally showing them to their suites on the top floor. There was no check in. They passed the marble staircase in a glass lift. Up close it made for an elegant sight.

The graduation parade was scheduled to begin at 3pm. Tanya had already decided to forgo lunch as there would be refreshments after the ceremony. With two hours until they had to leave, she slipped off her jeans, set the alarm on her phone, then laid down on the king size bed with her book to rest.

It was while lying there, the thought occurred to her, that perhaps she was a little jealous of her brother. Harry had done well; he would pass out of the officer training school, then after three weeks leave, join his regiment ready to begin his new career. A clear path laid before him. The next few years were mapped out, a lot of hard work lay ahead, but there were rewards, fulfilment. It could take him anywhere; he was off and running. In comparison, she had no idea where to begin. Finishing a degree was one thing, but what next? She had been avoiding these thoughts. The clock was ticking though and soon she would need to confront them.

Tanya had taken a two, that had turned into three-year, break from study after leaving school. During that time, she had travelled, searching for something to become passionate about, trying to find somewhere she could make a difference, adding some value to the world. Then her father had died unexpectedly after a short illness. The shock of this event led her to go wandering around blindly for another year, before deciding that it was time to study.

Study was an escape, but one with a purpose. She immersed herself in the things she loved: literature, art, journalism, all the while earning a degree. Now that stage of her life was coming to an end.

Tanya dreaded the thought of becoming lost once again. Of retreating within herself, living a life with no real purpose, trying to find ways to fill her days as she slowly slipped into insanity, dealing with the endless boredom. There were practical things to consider, like, where would she live? She had been avoiding that question for months. Moving back in with her mother was not something she could bear contemplating; she loved the house where she had grown up, but it was different now that her father was gone. She just didn't get along with her mother. Their bond was strong, but they just couldn't live together.

She had learnt to restrict her interactions to the things they enjoyed doing together, to avoid, at all costs, the things that triggered conflict. She knew she needed to work harder at making it work; she was determined to do so, but it was hard. Realising that she had been focusing on the negative aspects of the day ahead, she shifted her focus. Here, she reasoned was an opportunity to spend time celebrating her brother's achievements, enjoying time with her family, creating memories. With those more positive thoughts, she drifted off to sleep.

The alarm was brutal. She moved quickly to turn it off, then went straight into the bathroom. As she flicked the light switch, an exhaust fan sprang into life, followed by what seemed like a hundred lights that illuminated the room, battering her senses. She took her time getting ready, choosing carefully from the clothes she had packed, regretting the decision to leave her jewel case at home. Admiring her work in the mirror, she liked how the navy-blue suit hung on her.

When they met in the hotel foyer, she could feel her mother's eyes give her the once over and was not convinced the smile she offered was approval. Her mother, excited by the occasion more than her, was now more awake and wanted to talk. This was difficult for Tanya, who had no interest in how her mother spent her days, no interest in the small talk of who, where and what was happening. The criticism of her outfit was subtle and came early.

'Did you forget to bring a skirt, or do you not own a suitable one?'

The suit she was wearing had cost a fortune, yet the way her mother spoke, you would have thought she found it in a ditch by the side of the road. Tanya didn't bite, returning her mother's smile.

'Did you bring a gift for Harry?' her mother asked, searching for another thing to criticise. Tanya was ready.

'Yes, some cuff links and a tie.'

Tanya had made a special effort researching, then buying from, the Army and Navy store. The conversation continued in this style as they drove the final leg of their journey. Tanya showed great restraint, allowing her mother a great deal of latitude. As they arrived at the academy, the advantages of a chauffeur driven car were obvious. It gave Tanya more cause to cringe. They were directed to a VIP area where they were met by a General Sebring. When they asked him if he was the course director he said, 'Good heavens no.'

He was, however, a mentor to the cadets. Yes, he knew Harry, knew him well, outstanding young man, he would host their party, as well as appearing as the Queen's representative.

Her mother seemed to know this man, though he had introduced himself as if he were a stranger. Her mother was more comfortable with the VIP treatment than Tanya, who could only wonder who greeted the parents of the cadets from less affluent backgrounds. The British Army was an institution, rooted in hundreds of years of tradition. How do you change that? The officer class was still there, even though all the cadets would be officers after today. Still, it seemed to her, there were "officers" and there were officers. Tanya didn't like that train of thought, it led to anger threatening her mood and, in turn, the day itself.

They were led to a podium to view the afternoon's events, her mother looked fit to burst. She leant close to Tanya, whispering, 'What do you think of your brother? I never thought I would see the day; his father would have been so proud, don't you think?'

Tanya smiled. It could have been a very different story. Her brother loved the beaches in Ibiza, the French Riviera; he could easily have remained a playboy, lived off his trust fund, idled through life. She had not appreciated before, how much this must have troubled her mother, seeing her brother directionless. His life had been one endless party, it must have given her more than the odd sleepless night. *There was much to be thankful for on this day,* she thought. Soldiering was, and always had been, a dangerous business, she reminded herself. Soldiers die. There was fighting in Afghanistan. Harry would more than likely be facing danger at some point, that possibility was very real.

When the parade began, Tanya watched the cadets carefully. She was envious as they marched proudly past in their smart uniforms. Again, a touch of jealously appeared in her thinking; she had been as directionless as her brother, though without the partying. Harry had once been snapped by the paparazzi cavorting on a beach with a famous model when the latter was topless and wearing a string bikini. Why had nobody intervened in her life, placed her on the straight and narrow?

The general spoke well. He remembered, just as if it was yesterday, what it was like standing as they were, listening to speeches, how privileged he was to be standing before them today. How many times he had been thankful for the lessons he had learned as a cadet while attending the academy. How in the bleakest moments this training had kicked in, saving not only him, but the men under his command. He told them how he looked out upon them at the start of their careers, while his own was coming to an end, with envy. How he wished that he was starting again, that he was certain they would enjoy as successful and varied careers as he had. Tanya tuned out when, as he began to speak of duty and service, having spotted Harry, she wanted to wave, then decided that it would, under no circumstances, be appropriate.

With great fanfare, the parade ended. Tanya looked across to her mother who was bursting. It had been years since she looked this happy.

It pleased Tanya as it made the trip worthwhile. The general led them off the podium and after a short walk, for which he apologised, he led them into a marquee for refreshments. They sipped on champagne while they waited for their hero to arrive.

Tanya had goose bumps just thinking about what happened next. Recalling again her aunt's prophetic words, about meeting someone at the wrong time, her aunt had further added that Tanya was one of the lucky ones, for most people it never happened. 'True love,' she had stated, 'was rarer than anything known.' Therefore, by her reasoning, it needed to be respected. Tanya understood this. *And when it happens,* she thought, *nothing no matter what it is will ever be as important again!*

He appeared as just a glimpse through the crowd, walking next to her brother. Her mother, incidentally, stepped in front of him, blocking any closer view as she gave Harry a hug, before passing her brother over to her. She hugged Harry tightly excited to see him.

'Hello,' he whispered into her ear, 'I'm glad you came.' Then almost as an afterthought, 'Oh, I almost forgot,' moving aside, 'this is Evan.'

Tanya almost fainted as the thunderbolt struck her. He was standing in front of them with his hand outstretched, her mother shook it. When it was her turn, all she could say was, 'Yes.'

'Yes,' she said again, then stood there speechless.

They all turned, staring at her; she was saved by the arrival of General Sebring. *Wow!* was the only word that occupied her mind. She reminded herself that she was a strong-willed, independent woman; she didn't need the arrival of Prince Charming types, but here he was, squeezed into a uniform with polished buttons. A uniform that barely hid his muscles, that enhanced his beautiful face and bright blue eyes, instantly reducing her to a babbling idiot.

Tanya had to stop for a moment, wiping the tears from her eyes. She struggled to compose herself, feelings of happiness that she was helpless to avoid, overwhelming feelings she struggled to describe. *Something is wrong,* she thought. *I know it is, take a hold of yourself.* It was the voice of her father: stern, loving. Calm down! The voice was as clear as if he were in the room, returned from the grave. It had the desired effect, but only for a moment. In her mind she could see herself there, but with no memory of what they were talking about. She spent the entire time looking at Evan, captivated by him. When Harry and Evan excused themselves to go and collect their things, she snapped out of it, watching carefully as he walked away. Her mother was chatting to the general, who she learned was now joining them for dinner.

'What do you know about him?'

'Who, darling?'

Both the general and her mother turned to face her. 'That young man with Harry?'

'Evan, he's a friend of your brother's.'

'Absolutely first-class young man,' the general added. 'Where's he from, how old is he, is he married, engaged?'

The general and her mother exchanged glances, then stared at her with expressions of amusement.

'He's from London, no, he may have grown up in Wales originally, I'm sorry I really can't remember. As far as I can recall, he's unattached, most of the young men, who come here, are.'

'You can ask him yourself darling, he's joining us for dinner this evening,' her mother added.

'Yes of course.'

She felt like a teenager, giggly, like when someone she fancied winked at her, in her long-forgotten youth. How could this be? She was not normally affected like this. She had dated other men but nobody had ever aroused feelings like this within her. She felt tingly all over, her skin ached, she could feel her blood as it flowed through her veins, she wanted to shout, yell, chase after him. What if he needed something, some help or assistance, something only she could provide? Could this be happening to her, could your life change in an instant? Yes, she thought almost giggling, then doing it again covering her mouth, this time as she attracted the stares of those around her.

'Tanya, please excuse us, I want to introduce your mother to the minister.'

She waved them off, watching as they weaved their way through the crowd. Had they not realised that she had just fallen madly in love, to admit it was scary but admit it she would. Here was the man she would love forever and then some, for whom she would do anything, and she was certain he felt the same in an instant life changed. Was it that simple?

Standing alone, she knew how true that feeling was. How definite she was she had met her perfect match, her soul mate, in that moment. That perfect moment, forever frozen in her mind, she knew what her life would hence forth be about. *Control yourself, take things easy,* she reminded herself. What if he is married or has a girlfriend or boyfriend, a million things. *No,* she thought, *he has nobody, he has been waiting for me as I have been waiting him, now he is here, it's perfect. He will be mine.*

She stood for a long time, holding a glass of champagne but not drinking. How long had it been since she had been happy? Truly, madly, emotionally happy. She could not remember. The world around her melted away as she basked in the joy, the purity of the moment. When her mother and the general returned, she was standing in exactly the same spot, transfixed, staring into space.

The general walked Tanya and her mother back to their car. Harry and Evan arrived soon after them. Her heart, once again, was set a flutter. Her mother sat in the front allowing the three young people to occupy the rear seat. Tanya sat in the middle and this position provided her certain opportunities. While her brother chatted with their mother, she could make small talk with Evan. She could also make some covert contact with him under the guise of car movement. She would make small talk without losing too much self-control.

Things like, 'Where did you grow up?' 'What do your parents do?' 'Can you take your shirt off?' That sort of thing.

She learned that he had been born in Wales, that his father had been in the army then joined the police force rising to the rank of detective inspector. They had moved to London when he was eleven. He had been a promising snooker player in his youth, his parents were alive but were away visiting his sister who lived in Florida. His sister had just had a baby, the first grandchild. He did not have a girlfriend, he smiled while answering this question. A wry conspiratorial smile. Harry had invited him to join him on leave, but he had decided to find a nice quiet place, buy a few good books then settle in. Unless, of course, something better came up. He smiled once more as he said this and his hand, accidentally on purpose, brushed her leg on a straight road with no bumps.

Tanya leaned into him on a gentle corner with no internal car movement, her senses were on high alert. *My god, he feels it,* she thought. Something was pulling them together. She leant into him again. He met her in the middle. It was electrifying, the car ride became a testing ground where each would instigate something, then judge the reaction of the other. Evan had been studying psychology at university when he was accepted into the army. He had plans to finish his studies one day; he would like to be a detective like his father had been. All too quickly they were back at the hotel.

She reluctantly left Evan and the rest of them in the hotel lobby, then almost ran up to her room. There was much to do. She placed a call to the concierge and soon everything was organised. The spa was full, but they arranged a hairdresser and beauty specialist to visit her in her suite.

She showered, then the hairdresser washed her hair. The beauty specialist went to work, before the hairdresser moved back in to finish the job. Turning her attention to her wardrobe, she had little choice but to settle for the black dress she had packed. It would do. It hugged in all the right places. She was thankful that she had the impulse to pack the high heels.

The only jewellery she had with her was her Rolex watch and a diamond bracelet, both gifts from her late father. In desperation, she had no choice other than turning to her mother for help. Tentatively, she knocked on the door to her mother's suite. To her surprise, it was opened by General Sebring. He ushered her in without a word, her mother was seated on the sofa a large silver tea tray sat before her.

'What is it darling?'

Her mother looked up at her with those dark green eyes that Tanya had always found fascinating. There was something different about her, a look of excitement, of happiness, a certain contentment she wasn't used to seeing displayed. It was too easy not to think of her mother as a living breathing human being, not just her mother. Then it dawned on her, that she was imposing on them, intruding on an intimate moment perhaps, oh dear, she blushed at the thought.

'I just um, well I didn't bring my jewellery case, I wanted to,' she stammered. After composing herself, Tanya spoke clearly. 'I thought that perhaps you might have some jewellery, I could borrow.'

Her mother spoke, directing her comment towards the general, rather than her daughter.

'Young people these days, never think ahead. Please excuse me for a moment, Henry. Come darling, let's see what we can find.'

She led her through to the bedroom where Tanya was surprised to see three, large jewellery cases on the dressing table. She opened each of them.

'Now let me see, oh I have just the thing. This was a present from your grandfather, a family heirloom.'

She rummaged around in the bottom of one of the cases and pulled out a large velvet bag. Inside was a three-layered gold chain. In between, each of the finely woven gold links were encrusted with precious stones: rubies, emeralds and diamonds beautifully set into the gold. At the front, each chain was separated by a gap of a few centimetres. It was antique; the artistry and skill used to make it, incredible.

'Here, sit,' her mother commanded. There was real affection in her mother's voice. She was enjoying this more than she would allow herself to admit. Her mother noted the change in her daughter, knowing instantly this man meant something more to her, that he was important enough for her to want to visit her mother and borrow jewellery, something that was very out of character. She wondered at life, marvelled at it. *It never ceases to surprise you,* she thought.

Tanya sat at the table, lifting her hair to allow her mother to place the necklace and fasten it. It looked heavy, but she could barely feel it.

'What do you think?'

'It's beautiful.'

The gold shimmered brightly against the black of her dress, the precious stones sparkled.

'Now, what else?' her mother said, clearly thinking the necklace was not enough. She rummaged around in the cases again, this time taking out a smaller blue velvet bag.

'I bought these for myself when I was just a little older than you are now.'

They were gold and diamond earrings. Tanya carefully put them on, her mother smiled at what she saw. Gently, she placed her hands on Tanya's shoulders. Tanya took her left hand and placed it on her mother's.

'You look spectacular.' Tanya stood to go.

'I've imposed myself enough on you. Thank you for your help.'

'Hold on a moment. Here take this one.'

She handed her daughter another velvet bag. This one was green and larger than the others, but lighter.

'You can put that one on in your room. After all, a woman doesn't ever have to be completely naked.'

She smiled and winked. Tanya took the bag and went back to her room. When she had closed the door, she opened it. Slowly, she removed what was inside with a loud gasp.

'Mother!'

They were five for dinner. The general, Harry and Evan looked handsome in their dress uniforms as they met in the bar. Tanya was the last to arrive. She could not only feel Evan's, but all of their eyes, on her. It made her blush. She looked stunning.

She had put on her mother's surprise final piece of jewellery. It added to the sensuality that she was feeling. She had managed to calm herself down, that was, until she saw him.

The general took charge as soon as Tanya arrived. He summoned the head waiter with a wave of his hand, then they were shown into their private dining room. It was an elegant, intimate space with soft mood lighting. The chairs were red and extremely comfortable, the colour offset the beautiful mahogany dining table.

The table was laid with crisp, white linen placings and napkins, the porcelain crockery accentuated by the antique silver cutlery and servers that shone brilliantly. The ladies were seated first, then the general. They paired up, with Harry the odd one out at the head of the table. Her mother was wearing a tiara that had been a gift to one of the ancestors by a Russian Tzar. Evan, to her great delight, sat next her. They should have found someone for Harry, but then it wasn't meant to be a date night. There were three waiters, dressed in gold embroidered white uniforms. Linen napkins were carefully placed upon each person's lap, the atmosphere was formal, the menu modern.

Tanya hung off Evan's every word, she quickly noticed he, in turn, hung off hers. All five of them sat bolt upright, watching their behaviour carefully in the initial stages. As the meal progressed, they became more relaxed. By meal's end there was a feeling of casualness.

The general was a great host, relishing in the role. He had lived an interesting life, the son and grandson of former soldiers, he grew up in Surrey. After the war his father worked as a banker providing well for them, he had a sister who was younger. His mother didn't like boarding schools, so he went to a co-educational day school close to their home. He played cricket, rugby and enjoyed a game of tennis. Life was good. He started studying at university, then after two semesters decided he wanted some adventure.

The army in the late 1960s was not the most appealing of careers. When he arrived at Sandhurst, it had been at a time when numbers were down and society was asking questions about military expenditure. There had been a marriage once but that had not been a success, there were no children, his only regret. He had a million stories. Tanya liked him. Maybe he was stepfather material. This hurt, but those feelings weren't fair on her mother, who was the happiest she had seen her in years.

Evan had been assigned to his regiment; Harry was still waiting. The general promised to find out what he could to expedite things. Evan expected to find himself in Afghanistan inside of a year. He politely kept this out of the conversation and after dessert he excused himself.

When he left the room Harry leaned across whispering to his sister, 'What do you think?'

'He's very nice.'

'He's a good man. I have got to know him well over the past year.'

When Evan re-entered the room, Tanya moved her leg so it was touching his. He smiled. Coffee was served and she could feel the heat of his body through the material of his uniform. After coffee, her mother and the general mercifully excused themselves. The three remaining members of the party decided to move out onto the terrace. Finding a comfortable nook, they ordered cocktails. Harry left them with a smile after two rounds. It had become obvious to him that he did not exist in their world.

Tanya and Evan had two more rounds; both were more than a little lightheaded. Their combined energy continued to build. When they finished their drinks, Evan stood, offering Tanya his hand without a word. Tanya took it without hesitation; his touch was electric. There was a deep underlining meaning in accepting Evan's hand, both of them understood this it was private, personal. Tanya fully aware, had accepted willingly without hesitation.

The hotel had several beautiful tranquil walled gardens, each with a different theme, that were connected by gravel paths that wove their way through each garden then onto the next, eventually winding their way back to the hotel. It was now late into the evening, but it was still warm enough and light enough for a late stroll, nothing unusual about it. They may even encounter others.

In silence, he led her along the path through the entrance into the first garden. As soon as they walked through the entrance, he drew her to him. Falling into his arms, their lips met for the first time. His hands dropped to her waist, lifting her dress slightly. After what seemed like hours, she opened her eyes, staring into his that were wide open.

This garden had a Japanese theme. Tanya spotted a pavilion that had a very Japanese look. She pointed towards it and it was now her turn to lead the way, Evan was happy to follow. It was darker inside the pavilion than it had been in the garden. There was a wooden bench that looked out onto a koi pond; water ran out of a fountain made from bamboo. It was the only noise, other than their breathing, just for a moment they each considered whether they were moving too quickly! They had already gone beyond the point of no return.

Quickly they succumbed to their overwhelming desires. Standing near the bench, kissing passionately, their hands began exploring each other's bodies. Evan's fingers lightly pressed against the fabric of her dress. Tanya was hesitant at first, but as her desire rose, she became more daring. His hands cupped her buttocks, then they were under her dress. When he touched her bare skin, she gasped. He lifted her dress and their movements became frenzied, frantic. He pulled her underwear down by the sides and moved his lips to her neck. Tanya moved back against a column; his hands were on her bottom. She jumped, wrapping her legs around him. It was intense. They were completely lost in the moment; with total abandon they consumed each other. Tanya cried out biting her lip.

Tanya was sitting on Evan's lap, facing him. Basking in the afterglow, their lips met again savouring the most intimate moment of their lives.

The memory burned forever into her mind.

Tanya 1.5

TANYA FOUND THE vividness and intensity of the memory overwhelming. Even here, a million miles removed, she could still taste it, feel how she felt, his touch, the roughness of his hands like sandpaper on her skin, indelible, imprinted forever. It was so intense that she needed another short break. The phone remained silent and she ached for him. The air in her lungs seemed to freeze as time stood still. It was torture, the not knowing, the endless waiting. Tanya looked for something, anything that would distract her. Finding nothing she paced around her room. She looked out the windows, thought briefly about food, then gave up, sitting back down, retreating once more into her memories.

Tanya 1.6

THEY FELT A little embarrassed walking back through the hotel lobby. It was as if everyone could see what they had been doing, written on their faces. Like naughty children who had been caught, they ran up the staircase, laughing. Happy, they fell into her suite; she turned around, her back to the door, and kissed him. It was a long, wet, passionate kiss, with hands all over each other's bodies. Neither wanted to be the first to stop; they clung to each other intensely. Tanya conceded first, retreating to the bathroom. Evan looked around the luxurious room, catching his image in a mirror, he smiled.

'Look at you, boyo, who would've thought eh?' His strong Welsh accent cutting through the silent room.

'Huhummm.' It was Tanya, she was completely naked except for a gold belly chain. She beckoned to him with her finger, backing out of the room. Shaking, he followed her into the bedroom.

When Tanya woke, she found Evan wrapped around her, his body pressed tightly up against hers, his arm draped across her chest. Neither of them had ever experienced anything like they had over the past few hours. There were moments so intense, she cried out as the feelings shuddered through their bodies. In the moments in between, they whispered softly to each other in the dark. Private whispers, whose meaning was only known to them. Exhausted they fell into a deep contented sleep. The room was still dark, she couldn't tell if it was still night, or if the curtains were particularly good at keeping out the light. His warm breath blew gently down the back of her neck. At that moment, there was nowhere in the world she would rather be. Unable to move, she strained to catch a glimpse of the bedside clock. Five fifteen, there was plenty of time. They were meeting everyone for breakfast at eight and were departing at eleven thirty. She thought they might skip breakfast.

Tanya could feel Evan stirring. She giggled at the absurdity of how quickly her life had turned around, her desire slowly built once more, filling her body, overcome with unbearable longing, she succumbed.

The decision to avoid the group breakfast and call room service instead, was an easy one. After they finished, they went for another walk around the gardens. Tanya was buried in his side, his arm wrapped tightly around her. There were too many people around for a repeat of the previous night's performance, but they didn't care, it was enough to be together.

'What are your plans for the next three weeks?'

Her voice quivered as she asked him, slightly giving away how nervous she was about his answer. She had debated with herself when the right time to ask might be. At that moment she couldn't bear being parted.

'I was just going to head to the coast find somewhere quiet by the sea, visit a bookstore, choose a few, then hide from the world until it was time to leave.'

Tanya's heart sank. 'That sounds lovely.'

'That was until I met you of course,' he laughed. She leaned harder into him; he bent his head kissing her. 'Now I just want to spend that time with you.'

She was instantly filled with joy; the dreaded goodbye was postponed. 'Instead of dropping me at the station this morning, I'll say my plans have changed. I'll ask if I can travel back to the city with the rest of you.

When we reach the university, I'll say I'm getting out with you. As far as anybody will know, I'm just catching the train from there.'

Tanya laughed. 'We may create the illusion of that, but unless they have gone blind since last night, they will know the moment they set eyes on us.'

'Well at least everyone will save face,' Evan offered, slightly embarrassed that his brilliant plan was flawed.

Back in her room alone, she packed her suitcase whilst Evan did the same in his room. She was still wearing the belly chain that she was hoping to keep. Tanya was also hoping it would be the last time she would be alone, for a while anyway. She drank from a cold bottle of sparkling mineral water. Her lips were swollen, bruised, the cold bottle and the near freezing liquid helped ease the pain. The realisation of what had made them sore, made her laugh. She wondered where all of this was going. Did she dare to dream?

The negative feelings she had been experiencing just a day before, were completely gone, replaced by a new optimism and hope. Aching to know what was coming, she could hardly contain her excitement. It was just like reading a novel you couldn't put down, she wanted to keep turning the pages. Whatever had been missing from her life was now there in abundance, bringing with it a new energy, a love so strong, something that she had never felt existed, was enveloping her. Everything she had been doing, or thinking, was swept aside, sensations, emotions that had lain dormant were awakening. All she now thought about was her future life with Evan, that and nothing else.

There was no answer at her mother's door when she went to return the jewellery. In the lobby, when she tried, she was told to keep them, attracting nothing more than a conspiratorial wink. It was Harry who saved them from any embarrassment over the change in travel arrangements. After everyone had assembled, he made his suggestion.

'Evan, why don't we drop you off at the university with Tanya; she can help you organise your journey from there?'

And just like that, they were saved. The general had left after breakfast, her mother informed them that she had enjoyed a lovely walk through the gardens with him prior to his departure. Tanya caught Evan's eye; both were blushing.

The dull drive back was exciting because he was there. They held hands surreptitiously, Evan making small circles in her palm with his finger, as her brother dominated the conversation with talk of Ibiza partying. Tanya tuned out completely when the discussion turned to money, investments, and the country estate her father had jointly left them. Lunch was in a roadside café; the final leg of their journey was the longest. They were dropped in the exact spot she had been picked up just a day earlier. They stood watching together as the car disappeared.

Tanya would always mark this moment as the commencement of their life together.

Tanya 1.7

NO PHONE CALL. Becoming distraught, she went to make tea in the small kitchen. The worst was the unknown. If you knew about something, you could deal with it; not knowing what you might be up against, reduced you to helplessness. Out of fear of loss, she couldn't stop the memories, couldn't allow the replays to end. What if they faded or became weaker, or heaven forbid, disappeared completely? Right now, she could enter that world whenever she wanted to. If they stopped, what was she left with? They continued on in an endless loop. Her room was on the third floor of the house and she had the entire wing to herself, but didn't need so much space. She was not overly fond of it. Despite this, she had managed to find a few favourite places. One was the window seat that overlooked the gardens below. She made herself comfortable, her phone close at hand, a mug of steaming hot tea sitting on the windowsill, then let her mind carry her away.

<h1 style="text-align:center">Tanya 1.8</h1>

THAT EVENING, AFTER they had been dropped off, had been special. There were many fond memories for her to replay in her mind. She could clearly remember the anticipation and excitement when they were planning their holiday. Sitting at the table in the kitchen of her tiny flat, side by side, making the bookings on her laptop.

'We can go anywhere, do anything,' she told him. Evan had looked at her, a serious expression on his face. 'Really?' he had said nervous uncertain. 'Really,' she had responded.

'I can't afford–' He stopped, seeing the disappointment creeping into her expression, not wanting to say the truth. It was a pivotal moment.

'We can,' she said resolutely. There was deeper meaning here. He looked at her carefully, as the meaning of what she had said, sunk in. He leaned across kissing her.

'I have some savings we could -' She cut him off.

'Let's keep that for later, my ancestors can pay for this.' There was an edge of seriousness in Tanya's voice. An, "I won't take no for an answer" message in her eyes.

'I've always wanted to visit the Greek islands.' She visibly softened as he said this, the muscles in her face relaxing, the madly in love Tanya had returned. *That enchanting smile,* he thought.

'The Greek islands it is,' she said taking his hand in hers. He started making the circular patterns in her palm again with his finger, the same as he had been doing in the car.

'Not now, we need to finish booking our trip.'

He tightened his grip on her hand, pulling her into his lap. She sat facing him, their eyes locked together. She held onto either side of his face, kissing him, their mouths forming a connection as the electricity swept through their bodies, grinding against him as he fumbled with her clothes. They entered their newly found private world, where nothing else existed and everything outside could wait.

They booked first class tickets to Santorini; they would then travel by private helicopter to their island paradise. They would split their time between a luxury hotel and a private yacht. To pay for it all, she needed the special credit card with the high limit that was kept locked away in a small safe in her bedroom. While she was retrieving it, she added the gifts from her mother to her jewellery box. All except the belly chain, which she continued wearing. Evan closed his eyes as the totals for the trip appeared, which made her laugh. For once, she was happy to be able to spend money so freely.

Having set the ground rules early, it was her hope they could overcome some of the awkwardness her wealth aroused. A lifetime of experience had taught her the effect money had on people, how damaging it could be to relationships. She was instinctively cautious, wishing to avoid hurting his feelings or bruising his ego. She wanted them to share, knowing her wealth was protected, that technically it could never be that they could share.

They left the following morning, a luxury car service took them to the airport, where Tanya shopped while Evan relaxed in the lounge. She was more certain about him than she had ever been about anything. Everything they did felt special, held meaning.

The suite in the hotel where they stayed, was set high up on the cliffs above a beautiful, white sandy beach, reached via a special elevator.

The sun shimmered off the blue sea that twinkled like precious stones. They had their own private pool, but preferred the beach. They sipped cocktails under a cabana, then swam before walking to a restaurant for lunch. In the afternoon they drank beer on the beach in between more swimming, then retreated to their room, before dinner.

Tanya wore a bikini flirting with Evan every chance she could; he seemed to always find an excuse for taking his shirt off. After five days of sheer bliss, they were picked up by a huge motor yacht and it wove its way through the islands, with no particular destination in mind. The crew were well trained and extremely discreet. They had private lunches on little islands, lay naked on pristine beaches, swimming in crystal clear waters.

At night, they dined on sumptuous meals, prepared by the resident chef on a table on the bow of the ship. The yacht travelled long distances while they slept. Each morning, they woke up in a new location, ready to explore. They were surrounded by a bubble of happiness and joy that neither wished to burst.

Back on their island paradise, they continued living as if tomorrow would never come, wrapped up completely in their own world. More serious discussions were avoided, not a bad word was exchanged between them. The times she enjoyed the most were when they were sitting alone, either on the beach or in their room reading. She would look above her book at him and couldn't avoid smiling, so happy, so contented.

Evan suggested one night over dinner that they should build a house and live somewhere sunny, preferably on a beach, a beautiful house of their own design where they could one day raise a family in the sun. Tanya was touched. This was the first time Evan had spoken of the future, of what he wanted from life. He became animated, enthused.

'We could do it. We can live anywhere, do anything. Let's do it,' he exclaimed, 'Create our own life.' It boosted her spirits at a time when they were starting to flag.

Left largely alone, except for a few text messages from family and friends, Tanya had started to wonder if they could hide away from the world forever. As time passed though, the outside world, with its obligations and commitments, started calling. Each could feel the pull back to reality that was looming large before them. Tanya showed it the most, slipping into melancholy. Evan worked hard to raise her spirits without discussing it directly. He was matter of fact about any deployment he may be facing. A few months, he reassured her, then they would be together forever.

They had only been together two weeks, the happiest of Evan's life. There was a case, a very strong one, to say, 'Let's slow down, everything's happening too fast, take a breath, step back.' The problem was, doing that took time and time was a luxury they didn't have. Call it instinct, call it anything when you know you know. He wanted to spend the rest of his life with Tanya, however long that might be. He asked himself if he was being selfish, asked himself many things. In the end it came down to one thing, was he certain? The answer was yes!

Once that decision was made, then if she was in agreement, and he was sure she would be, then he wanted forever. Their forever, however long that might be, was to start immediately.

With the help of the hotel's concierge, he put a plan into action. Waking at 4am, he dressed silently, then slipped out of their hotel room, leaving a note explaining that he would be gone for the day and that it was a surprise. She was to meet him for dinner at 6pm sharp. The pain of being parted the moment he stepped out of the hotel, was accompanied by dark thoughts, the origin of which he couldn't explain, feelings of impending doom, premonition like. These feelings were kept secret from her. There had been dreams, haunting dreams where he was falling into a dark pit falling with no end! He stopped himself from thinking like this. Wasn't today meant to be a happy day?

A helicopter ride took him back to Santorini where a car had been arranged. They drove for an hour, winding through the streets in the early morning. He looked out the window watching everything as the day began. The shop was in a laneway that could only be reached on foot. It was an old shop and the concierge had assured him the jeweller was a master craftsman, renowned for his work. His family had been jewellers for generations.

He said his name was Marcos and invited Evan to have some breakfast with him. They sat at a small table just outside the front door. As the sun began to rise, they drank coffee and ate. Evan put the man's age at mid-fifties. He had weathered skin, was dressed simply but Evan could not place his nationality, though his origins were not Greek.

'What brings you here young man?' His English was perfect, cultured.

'I need an engagement ring.'

'When?'

'Today, I've been told you're the man to see, if you need something quickly.'

He smiled, acknowledging the compliment.

'I have some, I could quickly re-size or did you have something else in mind?'

'I was hoping, perhaps you could make me something special.'

'Today?'

'By this afternoon.'

Marcos eyed him carefully. 'You can pay?'

'Yes, whatever it costs.' A lump formed in his throat as he said this. 'Alright. I love a challenge, who is it for?'

'My girlfriend, Tanya. I can show you a picture.'

Evan took out his phone and he showed him a picture from the dinner on the first night they had met.

'Interesting, that necklace is exquisite. How did she come by it?' 'It was a gift, been in her family for years.'

'The work looks familiar.'

He looked carefully at the picture, He wanted to know more but there was work to be done.

'Okay let's get to it.' He picked up a sketch book and pencil. 'You know the young woman's size I take it?'

Evan handed him a ring he had borrowed from Tanya's collection. All that morning and into the afternoon Marcos worked while Evan hovered around. All the work was done right there in the little shop. The end result was stunning. There was little left from Evan's savings, but it had been worth it. He said goodbye to Marcos and headed back to the hotel, changed and was ready to meet Tanya at precisely 6pm.

Everything was organised to perfection, as he stood nervously awaiting her arrival, he looked around taking it all in. The venue was a cave next to the beach. It was private, the table surrounded by candles. A candle lined path led down to the beach. A soft breeze was blowing, red roses in vases were everywhere. It was private, intimate. An unseen chef was preparing the food, discreet waiters also out of sight would serve them. As she entered, his heart skipped a beat. She was wearing a white dress that enhanced her newly tanned body, her eyes lit up as she saw him. They embraced.

'I missed you today,' she whispered.

A waiter appeared as they took their places. The meal was intimate and they were completely wrapped up in each other. When they had finished, they kicked off their shoes, wandering slowly hand in hand down onto the sand with a bottle of champagne.

When they reached the water's edge, Evan fell down on one knee. Tanya at first thought he was opening the champagne. Noticing the small box in his hand, she gasped, her own hand went to her mouth. Evan said nothing, she shuffled her feet excitedly. Shaking, she nervously held out her hand. He placed the ring on her finger. She placed her hands on his cheeks, kissing him deeply, while still on his knees. Their lips remained locked together as he stood, holding her tightly around the waist. Her eyes closed, slipping into a world of sheer bliss imagining their life together.

Evan's feelings were different. For him it was all about the moment, the future was promised to nobody. He held her now and he never wanted to let go. They stopped kissing for a moment just as the moon emerged from behind a cloud. She looked at her ring, her heart melted. Evan opened the champagne and poured it into a single glass that they shared. He handed her the glass then swept her off her feet carrying her into the water. He waded in until it reached his waist. Tanya was giggling the entire time. She held the champagne glass up to his lips.

'You're crazy. I'm engaged to a crazy man.'

They kissed again, as he effortlessly held her in his arms.

Tanya 1.9

ALL GOOD THINGS, Tanya thought, as they lay beneath the sheets on their final morning. The future was uncertain, yet she fought to remain optimistic. Evan held her tightly. He loved these times, savouring every moment. Everything felt new and fresh, it was like being reborn. They took their time over breakfast and lunch then, after a final swim, it was time to leave their island paradise.

Their plane touched down on a rainy evening at Heathrow. The dark city streets dampened their mood as they travelled to the hotel. There were only two days until Evan had to report for duty and their precious time together was quickly evaporating. They needed help; they needed to see her mother.

They woke early, going straight to her mother's house in Belgravia before breakfast. The house was an anomaly occupying three walled in acres in the middle of the city. Surrounded by lush gardens, the four-storey mansion was more like a palace her mother called their oasis. The butler, who had known Tanya all her life, welcomed them at the door. After exchanging pleasantries and introducing Evan, he showed them through to the breakfast room.

Evan stared in amazement as they were led through the house. Everywhere he looked was something else to wonder at: works of art covered the walls, antique Furniture, precious Ming vases stood next to statues and hand-crafted wooden display cabinets held porcelain and other exquisite objects. There was a wall of photographs in gilded frames and he recognised everyone from prime ministers to presidents and celebrities. All the pictures looked as though they were taken in the house or gardens. There was even one of Queen Victoria standing with another woman in the garden. When he opened the door to the breakfast room, they were greeted by, not only Tanya's mother and her aunt but General Sebring, who they both were surprised to see.

The news of their engagement prompted celebratory embraces and heartfelt words of congratulations. After they sat down at the table, they explained their dilemma. They wanted to get married straight away, only Evan had to report to his regiment. General Sebring, or Henry, as he now insisted he be called, sprang into action.

'Is that all? Allow me,' he said as if it were nothing.

He phoned Evan's regimental commanding officer, who just happened to be a friend. By the time he put the phone down he had negotiated an extension of Evan's leave by three weeks. He also asked to pass on his congratulations.

After breakfast, the planning began. Tanya's mother called on her personal assistant and they went to work. Pausing only for a celebration lunch, the work continued. Tanya watched as her mother, aunt, the assistant and the general worked the phones. Her and Evan's input was limited to questions of what they wanted. It struck Tanya as odd that nobody doubted, nor thought to question, the urgency of the wedding. It discomforted her, because it confirmed her greatest fear, that the unavoidable, uncertain, dangerous future was looming. Nobody, it seemed, wished to deny them this brief period of happiness.

Five days later, the guests gathered, for the most unexpected wedding of the decade. The venue was the family estate "Land's End", the current home of Tanya's Aunt Selena. The estate had been transformed for the occasion. Everywhere you looked was evidence of all the hard work that had gone into organising the wedding. The chapel was decked out in roses, a pavilion was erected on the bluffs overlooking the ocean. It was a huge structure, complete with polished wooden floors for dancing, chandeliers and comfortable lounging areas. The tables in the dining section were elegantly decorated. There was a real sense of fun, while maintaining a romantic atmosphere. The gardens did not escape the hands of the decorators as there were fairy lights and ribbons and the maze was lit up like a Christmas tree.

Four of Tanya's closest friends served as bridesmaids. None of them had expected the wedding announcement but they were happy for her, while at the same time being amazed at what they were seeing. Tanya's friend, Jenny, who she had known since pre-school, was her maid of honour. She was the most surprised of all. Tanya had always been conservative with her feelings, cautious, giving little away. She had a strong will and was independent. Jenny had never expected to see her like this, head over heels in love with a man. *You just never knew,* she thought.

Tanya was enjoying a moment alone before the ceremony, her hair and make-up had just been finished. She was sitting in front of a mirror wearing a white silk robe, taking a few moments to gather her thoughts, while her friends had the finishing touches done to their hair and makeup in the room next door. The large parlour room had been transformed into a salon for the wedding and resembled nothing of its usual appearance. Her aunt really didn't like the older parts of the house, spending her time in a new wing she had built specially. Tanya was taking a few moments to compose herself and was deep in thought when her aunt stopped by on her way to the chapel.

'You look beautiful.'

Tanya blushed, 'Thank you, Aunty.'

'I have to keep pinching myself, I can't believe we are here, of all the things I could imagine you doing, you surprised me!'

It was a nice compliment. Honest. 'You've been a great help, Aunty.'

'I'm happy for you and so is your mum. Your dad, although I think he would be surprised, he would've been happy for you as well.'

Tanya felt a warmth in her stomach, she was missing her father a great deal.

My wedding day, it's my wedding day, she thought closing her eyes for a moment, to focus on the emotion swelling inside.

'Surprised, yes I suppose he would have?'

'It's a happy time, you are so in love, Tanya. It's written all over your face. I spotted it the moment you came to your mum's house. Was it really only a week ago? What else do we need to know? I just never thought you would be open enough to experience it, not in this way, not so head over heels. You've always been so; I'm lost for words. I just think it's wonderful to see you like this, happy.'

Tanya couldn't think of anything to say. She bowed her head, then as sincerely as she could said, 'Thank you.'

'I want to ask you something. Do you ever think about the builder of this place, the one who laid the foundation for all that we have?' her aunt asked.

It was an interesting question. If Tanya was honest, she rarely did, this brought a feeling of guilt, she took way too much for granted?

'Dad used to tell me stories, I know a little, not much, far from enough.'

'Well, I'd like to find out more, I think that we owe it to her,' her aunt replied, 'Do you have any plans after graduation?'

'No.'

'Well, I was going to suggest that you come and stay here, conduct research and then write an account of her life, a biography. Something that can be a legacy, perhaps we will publish it, share it with the world. 'It would be a paid job, one that has been almost waiting for you to

be ready to write it, the timing is perfect. It will help keep you occupied and take your mind off things.'

That hung in the air. Each knew the heartache that was coming, though neither wanted to acknowledge it openly. Tanya considered it.

It would solve many of her problems, give her something to focus on, for a short time at least. It was an intriguing idea and quickly started to take hold.

'I'll do it,' Tanya said with a smile.

'It's settled then, I'll prepare everything. After you graduate, you can move in and begin. Now, let's put that and everything else aside and enjoy the day.'

Tanya stood and they hugged, her aunt left her. She sat back down and continued looking at her reflection in the mirror. She smiled; things were going so well. Jenny came into the room and walked over to where Tanya was sitting. Standing behind her, Jenny could only think that her best friend looked fantastic.

Tanya was grateful to her friends. She knew she was not the closest, most affectionate person. She wanted to get better at this, better at letting people around her know they were appreciated.

'Hey Jen, you look stunning.' Jenny smiled.

'So do you.'

'It's almost time to start getting dressed. Nervous?'

'Yes, but good nervous.'

'Come on, I'll give you some help with the dress.'

Tanya stood up and let the robe fall to the floor showing she was wearing her gold belly chain. After being helped into her dress, the others joined them. They fussed around Tanya until it was perfect. Two flower girls had been found amongst the relatives, along with a page boy in a miniature version of the men's military uniforms.

When everyone was ready, they headed to the chapel. The guests were waiting, the party assembled in the chapel foyer. Evan, his best man and groomsman were standing in front of the altar. Harry was the last to arrive. He also cut quite the figure in his uniform. He smiled at his sister.

'You look beautiful.'

He offered his arm to his sister. Tanya lowered her veil, she closed her eyes, took a deep breath, an attendant opened the door and Harry led her down the aisle. Halfway down, Evan, unable to wait any longer, turned to look. Their eyes met and the first tear of the day escaped.

Tanya 1.10

$\mathcal{S}$TARING OUT OF the window, these memories brought more tears, as her phone sat silent. Evan's call was now long overdue. One day, Tanya would tell her granddaughter how handsome Evan had been in his uniform, how brightly the lights shone. She had felt like a princess in a fairy-tale. She would go on to tell her how, when her brother escorted her down the aisle, every head turned to look, but that she only had eyes for one. As the happiness radiated through the chapel, the archbishop blessed them and the choir sang. Now, she was surrounded by enveloping loneliness, the cold was setting in fast and she shivered.

Tanya 1.11

THE WEDDING DAY flashed by so quickly, they hardly had the chance to take it all in. It was wonderful to spend the day surrounded by friends and family, to feel their love. It was well after midnight when they farewelled the last of their guests before retreating to one of the estate's guest houses. Evan helped her out of her wedding dress, a task filled with laughter. Tanya tried to ensure its preservation, draping it over a table before tackling him onto the bed.

'I love you,' Tanya whispered to him in the early morning.

She loved this time of the day, loved waking in the pre-dawn to be with him, while the rest of the world slept.

'I will love you for the rest of my life.'

As he said it, Evan knew he would never make a more truthful statement.

After spending their wedding night on the estate, they caught a helicopter, then private jet, to Spain for their honeymoon. They wandered the streets of Madrid and Barcelona, played on the beaches of Majorca. They went everywhere arm in arm, shopping in markets, spending long lazy afternoons doing nothing. It was while laying on a beach in Ibiza that Evan once again surprised her. Out of the blue he turned to Tanya and said, 'I could definitely live the rest of my life here.' Tanya smiled. He never made long term plans; she had come to accept his moment-to-moment form of existence. She decided to be daring.

'Do you want to look at some houses?'

She was wearing a black bikini, lying on her side facing him.

'I don't have–' he stopped, realising what he was about to say. She lowered her sunglasses, looking at him over the top of them. It was a look tinged with disdain, a 'Really?' look. It pulled him back into line.

'I mean, yes, I would very much like to look at some.' She moved closer to him, rubbing him on the chest.

'If we find something we like, something we decide we want, I'll make a phone call to our business manager and solicitor and they will do the rest.'

'We have a business manager and a solicitor?'

Evan had never used a solicitor and didn't really understand what a business manager was. Tanya didn't respond. He touched her hand smiling. This was her world, she could handle the details, he didn't want to be difficult in any kind of way, didn't want to spoil things. He knew that all Tanya wanted was the best for them. Why not enjoy life?

It was the third villa they had visited. They knew without a word being spoken that they had found it. It was white with a huge swimming pool that faced their own beach where they were assured a large yacht could be moored. With eight bedrooms, ten bathrooms and countless other rooms, size wouldn't be a problem. It was modern, sleek and came with a large piece of the land that surrounded the secluded bay.

Tanya made the call; her instruction was simple. 'Buy it.'

They were at dinner when the text message from the solicitor arrived.

'It's yours.'

They spent the following days there making plans, before continuing on their honeymoon. They were on a private jet, when Evan announced that he thought they should buy their own place in London, a penthouse, one with multiple levels right in the middle of the city. He also said they should have a fancy car and driver.

'Anything you want, I'll buy you the moon.'

She sat in his lap as he wrapped his arms around her waist, kissing him deeply. She placed her hands on his cheeks. They were madly in love. He had accepted who she was, now Tanya needed to do the same, but that was harder. His acceptance meant the things that worried her, her wealth, her strength and independence were all gone. She now had to find a way to come to terms with the fact that he was a soldier. She needed to find a way to accept the life he had chosen, just as he had accepted her. He had found a way, now it was her turn, but she wasn't quite ready. Not yet. She stayed in his lap; the air hostess kept a discreet distance. Still, the idea of being caught heightened their arousal. Unable to contain themselves, Evan reached for Tanya's skirt.

All too soon, the honeymoon had ended. Tanya was back at university; Evan had reported for duty. The separation was harder than either of them had ever imagined. Tanya carefully planned the little time they spent together, ensuring that every minute was meaningful.

Keeping her eyes peeled on the real estate in London, one Saturday morning over tea and toast, she spotted the penthouse of Evan's dreams. It was spread over three levels with a swimming pool, hot tub and gym. It had a huge garden terrace with spectacular views. The building was near the Thames, had its own private elevator and came with apartments on one of the lower floors for guests or servants. Six months earlier, she would never have considered buying it. She phoned Evan who had just come in from a morning run. He quickly went online and took a look. All he could say was, 'Wow.'

By the afternoon it was theirs, Tanya hired people to decorate and furnish it.

Her graduation was gratifying, but not exciting. Evan wasn't there, but her mother, the general and her aunt tried to make up for it. They booked a nice restaurant while the removalists loaded the truck with her belongings. The majority of the furniture, all except a few sentimental pieces, would be given to charity. Tanya was headed for her aunt's estate. They hadn't discussed the job much since her wedding day but she now wanted nothing more than to immerse herself in it. Her aunt handed her an envelope that she said contained instructions, then announced that she was traveling to Switzerland. Tanya would be returning to the big house on her own.

'Have you heard the news?' Her mother was excited about something and wouldn't be denied. 'Harry has moved to the operational support unit. He's being trained in IT and will be leading a team in modern warfare.'

Tanya bit her lip. Her heart sank. She decided this would not upset her. The hypocrisy, no, she would be happy for her brother. The general looked meek, complicit. Had her mother bullied him into it? Had she used her subtle techniques to influence him? Why would he not do the same for Evan? Surely he could find Evan a nice safe job. She put this aside. She no longer agreed with the way restaurants were being used by the family, to somehow pay you off or improve your mood.

Her mother handed her a carefully wrapped package containing three rare first editions. Her aunt's gift was in a jewellery box, two necklaces: one diamond, one pearl. They looked very old. *There was a story there,* she thought, *there is history inside this gift.*

She smiled, leaned forward and kissed her aunt; she then turned and kissed her mother.

'Thank you, all these are wonderful gifts.'

Remaining civil was hard; she didn't like this aspect of her personality that was emerging. She was coming to terms with too many things. How could it be that the man she loved was at this very moment training to leave for war? It was unthinkable, a crime of some sort was being committed that her beautiful man would soon leave her for the cruel, unforgiving world of the battlefield.

To compensate, she drank a little too much wine and was more than a little drunk, as the conversations continued around her with little involvement from her during her own celebration. As they left the restaurant, the triage of limousines pulled up: her mother's silver Bentley which carried away her mother and the general; her aunt's sleek black Mercedes Benz, taking her to the airport and the last was her and Evan's dark navy blue bespoke Rolls Royce.

It was a long, lonely drive. Her spirits lifted only as the car turned into the long driveway of the estate. It brought back memories of visiting as a child. She remembered the excitement of arriving for their visit, the days spent happily exploring and playing in the gardens with her brother.

The house was set a long way back from the road, the oak trees that lined the drive were planted by men who had never sat in their shade. The house was built in a small valley near some bluffs that overlooked the ocean. It was shielded by three magnificent gardens, a maze and several outbuildings. There was a cricket ground that had not been played on for fifty years, a private beach, rarely used, below them. It was reached by following a winding stone path. Her aunt was originally going to assign Tanya to the same guesthouse she had stayed in for her wedding, then thinking better of it, she gave her an entire wing in the main house.

Tanya wandered through the halls. There was a coldness to the vast open spaces; it had felt warmer when decorated for her wedding. She started to understand why her aunt had built her own sanctuary. The library would be her workspace, it rivalled the one at her university for size. Tanya opened the door, stepped inside then closed it behind her. Selena, her aunt, told her everything that she needed was inside. In the middle of the room was a large, long table, the size of perhaps four or five full-size billiard tables. Around it, the rows of books stretched along the walls, rising three stories above her to the custom glass roof. No matter how many times she came into this room, it always amazed her, the sheer size of it. It was set in another time, a time of wood, brass, and leather. Rich Persian rugs lined the floors, the hand-crafted bookcases held thousands of volumes, many beautifully bound in leather, a vast number of wooden filing cabinets held documents, collectibles, as well as family records that traced her family history back to the beginning or what they perceived it to be, for history has no end.

On the large table were a series of large leather-bound volumes, each had a gold etching on the front and side: Karam Journal 1, Karam Journal 2 etc. There were also document files neatly laid upon the priceless table that was protected by a starched white tablecloth. A laptop computer still in the box, a pile of A4 notepads and pens were neatly stacked next to a leather desk mat. The room, like the rest of the house, was cold, not just in temperature. There were fireplaces, however they were serving simply as decoration, not having been lit in decades. Temperature was controlled by a custom system that kept the books safe. The rarest volumes were kept behind glass and handled with gloves.

Brass reading lamps, with green shades, sat at intervals on the table that was surrounded by comfortable green leather chairs. The walls were covered in family portraits and works of art. The portraits stared down with dour expressions, the cold dead eyes following around the room, lending their cold ambience to the overall feel. One of the portraits of a child, was most haunting. The brass plate declaring a death in childhood, his expression colder than the others. Sad, he looked on the verge of tears. A brass plaque on the frame read, 'Drowned so his brother could live.' A strange inscription, Tanya thought.

The art was a mismatch of styles. Each generation had added to the collection, obviously to her, their tastes varied wildly. It wasn't the only gallery in the house, many of the better works hung in the more public spaces. There was a phone, more for ordering from the twenty-four-hour seven-day kitchen than anything else.

Tanya wondered how rich they were. She had no idea the extent of her family's wealth. She had never been interested. Her aunt was single, had never married, had no children and ran the business on her own since Tanya's father had died. She did most of the work prior to his passing as well. His interests were different. He had wanted to create something new, something of his own. He built a second empire of his own. Tanya had seen newspaper reports claiming he was a billionaire but he had never talked about it. Tanya suspected that the reports were true.

Her brother told her things about oil and coal interests that they had sold because he didn't like the effects of these businesses on the environment. Harry handled all of that, but there was little involvement from either of them. Perhaps if there had been more, her brother wouldn't have needed to join the army. But their father had not wanted that, he had not wanted them to be tied down by his business interests, wanted them to find their own way. One day this huge estate would belong to her and her brother. She shivered at this thought. She had been close to her father, it was said that nobody had a stronger bond with him, not even his wife, now he was gone. The tears came quickly, he would know what to do, what to say. *People die,* she reminded herself.

Tanya 1.12

TANYA PICKED UP her phone. Nothing. Feeling nauseous, she crossed the room to her bed. She changed into a jumper, removed the jeans she was wearing, then slipped beneath the covers. Curling up, she drifted off into a troubled sleep.

She woke disoriented. It was dark, cold outside of the covers. Her face felt cold and she searched through the fog of her mind. Slowly it came to her, she had been dreaming, the remnants remained, but they were fading fast. It had been vivid; her dreams always were. She struggled to hold onto the strands. She had been on a tiny street somewhere exotic, Japan maybe, then in an instant it was gone, all traces were erased.

She remembered Evan. In a panic, she reached for her phone. It had not rung, there were no missed calls. She felt colder now. She pushed back the covers but didn't climb under them. Sitting on the edge of the bed she decided it was time to turn up the heat; she did this from her phone and put on some track pants. Hungry, she phoned the kitchen, even though it was after midnight.

She finished eating, then with a drink in hand, she found her way to a comfortable armchair. She noticed the envelope her aunt had given her when she first arrived, on the side table and her mind drifted back once more.

Tanya 1.13

TANYA REMEMBERED HOW different things had been on her first night as a resident at Land's End. University was behind her, the joy of finishing tinged with the sadness of saying goodbye. She remembered how strange it had felt, coming to live in the house rather than just visiting. All her possessions had been carried up to her wing by the servants. She had been too embarrassed, after the years of independence at university, to allow them to unpack for her. Many of the boxes remained unopened still. Although she was hungry after the journey, she had felt too embarrassed to phone the kitchen to order something. *Why?* she wondered.

When she visited as a child they had loved calling down at all hours of the night for ice-cream or anything their hearts desired. Back home they had servants and a chef of their own, but not round the clock service. At least not for the children. Back then, it was a great thrill.

Her aunt had been on her way to Switzerland. For the first time, the loneliness had encroached in on her. She remembered switching on a lamp then struggling with the climate controls. Giving up, she'd sat sipping a glass of wine from a bottle she had brought with her. The house was certainly a step up from her small flat, yet it lacked the charm of that place. Maybe she should have gone to their penthouse, worked from there, but she wanted to enjoy that with Evan. It wasn't the same when he wasn't around.

Searching for distraction, she turned her attention to the envelope her aunt had given her, back then it had been pristine, not the ragged state it appeared in now. Inside were the instructions for her project. In theory, it sounded simple enough.

As they had briefly discussed, she was to research the life of Karam, an ancestor who had travelled to England in the late 1800s. She would need to gather information from any source available, learn whatever she could, seek to sort fact from legend, then write Karam's story.

There was a lot of existing material. Karam had kept journals from her early teens until the end of her life, many survived. She was educated, to a degree, which was unusual for the time. The journals were all written in Hindi and had been painstakingly translated. Her aunt wanted to know who Karam was, wanted more than the dead-eyed pictures that lined the walls, the very few photographs. They were living in the house Karam had purchased then had remodelled, but how much of her was left now? Her aunt wanted to know. She also wanted to know why she came here, wanted her relationships analysed, who was who in her life? There was a fascinating story here somewhere, her aunt could feel it. Tanya was sceptical.

'Unravel all the secrets,' her aunt had urged her. 'Search for the truth.' The project was very close to her aunt's heart; she just didn't have the time or skill to bring it to life. She added, as a note, that there were other family diaries, letters and documents that might help. Even though it was late and had been a long day, Tanya went down to the library to start work. Sitting at a table in the vast space of the library, the only light coming from the table lamp, she looked at the journals, sighed at the enormity of the task ahead, then picked up the nearest one and opened it. As luck would have it, the journal she had randomly chosen was exactly where the real story of Karam began.

Tanya 1.14

TANYA REMEMBERED HOW quickly she had become engrossed in that first journal, how it captivated her, how descriptive and detailed it was. How this led to her quickly changing her opinion about the project. She let her mind drift off, allowing the story to play like a movie, closing her eyes and having her senses and imagination take over until she could feel the dust and heat of the Punjab on her skin.

Karam 1.1

THE BLOOD VESSELS in Karam's eyes felt like they would burst. She leant against the wall, which was the only thing keeping her upright. The anger coursed through her veins, her face changed, contorting to the point that it was unrecognisable. It continued increasing, becoming a separate being that longing to break out and attack. Had Harmeet, her husband, been there within easy reach, she would have killed him. Robbed of his presence, she lashed out at the only people there, her father and his servant, Dilbagh. She pushed off the wall, attacking Dilbagh, who had delivered the devastating news that set her off. Dilbagh anticipated it, moving aside, then capturing her from behind.

It took all of his strength to hold her.

Her father was genuinely scared. She screamed. It was a sound that would haunt both men, and everybody else that heard it, for the rest of their lives. She lost her mind, kicking, spitting, pulling in every which way, then slowly she started to lose steam. She would write in her journal that is was like ice running down from her brain to the base of her spine, an eerie feeling, a realisation, an understanding. Her face changed into a wicked smile. From now on, she promised herself, things in her life would be different. Never again would she leave her destiny in the hands of others.

They were in one of the private bathing gardens of her father's house. Dilbagh removed her clothes, then with his eyes closed, gently carried her into the water. It covered her, soothing her, entering her pores and rejuvenating her, finding its way to her soul. Dilbagh left her as she floated on top of the water. Later, as she walked out naked, it was as if she was being reborn. Nothing, she promised herself once again, would ever be the same.

As she sat in her room in her father's house, she reflected how her life, up until that very day, had been nothing more than a lie. A false reality, pure fantasy, everything she had known, everything she had believed in was, in a moment, washed away, as if a great flood had rushed through, leaving nothing behind but devastation and despair.

She had spent her entire life pleasing others: her parents, then her husband. She had suppressed her natural instincts and talents; her love of business had been subdued. At seventeen she had married a man eight years her senior, a good man, she believed, experienced in business, hardworking. She had left her parent's house for a new household, a wedding gift to her husband from her parents. She smiled and made the most of it, building a good happy home. She had two boys within two years and worked tirelessly for their young family.

Then, out of nowhere, her loving husband announced he was heading off to war with the British. With no previous military experience or inclination, he had accepted a commission in the Sikh regiment. All too soon, mounted on a white horse, he rode off to war. Just like that, he was gone.

Karam was in shock, her dreams turned into nightmares so vivid, they felt real. She dared not sleep. Filled with fear, she limped through each day, putting on a brave face for her boys and the public, but she constantly broke down when she was alone. She was losing weight and spent little time in the sun. A dark cloud followed her everywhere she went, the joy disappeared from everything. The days dragged on so slowly she could feel the air move. On the brink of a total shutdown, she melted, staying in her room for three days. On the fourth day, her father arrived unannounced. The news sent Karam scurrying from her bed. The last person she wanted to see her like this was her father. Quickly she washed and dressed, her father was sitting in the parlour drinking tea. He stood when she came in, and took her hand, she sat down beside him.

'How are you, you look a little pale?'

'I'm doing well. Harmeet's absence has been hard on all of us.'

'I see, that's part of the reason that I'm here.'

Karam's interest was raised.

'I'm concerned about your brother, since Harmeet has been away, all of the responsibility has been upon him.'

'What can I do?'

'You know our business as well as anyone.'

'I haven't had any interest in commerce since I was a child.' Her father held up his hand.

'I remember how interested you were in all of my business affairs. Somebody needs to help him, I'm too old, my health is not good, you are the only option,' he said. 'Please go and see him. If you can't help then fine, at least you tried.'

'Of course, if it pleases you father.'

As she watched his carriage drive away, she felt her anxiety return, now she had the family business to worry about. Her bed was calling out to her, she had to be strong.

Karam loved her brother but had to concede that where business was concerned, he had little interest. He would rather spend his time at the cricket club or lounging around with his friends. Perhaps they had been spoilt a little too much, maybe life had been too easy for too long. They had grown up surrounded by wealth and had never wanted for anything. Her father was right about one thing, she was interested in business. When she was younger, that was the difference. Where Karam had soaked up everything with a natural curiosity, her brother had been impervious to it.

As the carriage pulled in under the portico, the head clerk, Aprajeet, appeared, to welcome her then show her inside. The offices were attached to a vast warehouse and looked out of place. There were rich leather lounges in the foyer that she had seen at the British Viceroy's residence. The offices stretched over three levels. Aprajeet showed her into her father's office and she wasted no time walking around to stand behind her father's desk, though she didn't sit down yet.

'Where is my brother? I thought he would be here greeting me.' Aprajeet looked flustered.

'He is–' he paused, unsure how to answer.

It was an important moment for him, he was choosing sides. He hedged his bets.

'If someone were to ask me where your brother was at this time of day, I might suggest they would be more successful looking for him at the cricket club.'

Karam had suspected as much. Men were just little boys lost in their games!

'And if they were to ask if he would be returning today?' Aprajeet nodded his head, bowing ashamed.

'That's alright, listen to me,' she said. He looked up and was greeted by a broad smile. 'My father has requested I assist my brother, so first things first, does he use this office or does he have his own.'

'He uses his own office on the second floor.'

'Very well, we shall conduct business in here. I shall conduct business through you with your assistance. Nobody need know I'm helping out; we will act as if it is him when he deems to bless us with his presence. You leave him to me.'

Aprajeet looked concerned.

Karam continued, 'Now order us some tea and return with your journal. We have much to do.'

When he had left, she ran her fingers along the rich wooden desk, hesitated, then sat in the thick leather chair. Karam sat deep in thought, things becoming clearer. Men always run and hide. Her brother was running from responsibility, but why? Because he was no merchant, no businessman, he had fallen into this world or rather been pushed in by Harmeet. Her father must have known this, yet he had, rather than face the problem, looked for a solution to avoid embarrassment or a loss of face. Her brother knew it too. Unable to cope with the pressure, he ran away to play games!

A darker thought occurred to her, one that gave her chills. What was Harmeet running from? Thoughts now came at a rush, clamouring for attention. Did he love her at all? Was it lust that made him say those things? Was it the joy of the marital bed? Had he experienced some sort of euphoria and wrongly, in a confused state, felt that was love? Had he been a virgin, like her, on their wedding night? She had always believed that he had been the one with experience, after all men had options not open to women. How could she have been so wrong? As the pieces fit together, she felt so naïve.

Harmeet had run a way, there was no way of ignoring it. She missed him terribly, so much that she almost started to cry. Their life had meant nothing to him. What they had, had not been enough, he had taken the first opportunity to leave. If he did not want her, if everything was so bad...? She stopped herself, there was no time for that.

She had no idea of the problems that faced her, only that they must be overcome. That strangely invigorated her, scaring her at the same time. She now had responsibilities, there were children to be provided for, mouths to feed, so many people relied on them. Wealth, she believed, carried great responsibility. She was a woman, though, and it was a man's world, the Harmeet problem could wait.

When Aprajeet returned, he was accompanied by a servant, carrying a tray with the tea she had ordered.

'Come in and close the door,' she said. 'Aprajeet, please tell me everything.'

He looked at her suspiciously; he was still unsure of her motives, did not respect the authority that she was displaying. She realised this, hated it but realised he needed further encouragement.

'Please, go ahead.'

Her smile was warm, humble. Reluctantly at first, then like the breaching of a dam, Aprajeet told her everything: the bad decisions, the erratic behaviour and rages of violence that followed. The frustrations, the losses and finally the debts. Karam was not shocked. Things, she supposed, could be worse.

It was now Aprajeet's turn to be surprised. Without any notes being taken, Karam gave instructions, giving precise details of what had to be done and in the right order. Aprajeet had a busy afternoon and evening. Karam left at 8pm and was back the next morning at 6am.

At 10am her brother arrived at the office she had commandeered with Aprajeet.

'Sister, what a surprise?'

She looked up at him from the desk. This theatre was necessary, it was part of the façade.

'Brother how nice to see you.'

He took a seat opposite her. Aprajeet, uncomfortable, continued to stand.

'Brother I can see how busy you have been. Father asked me to make sure you didn't work too hard.'

'How is Father?'

'He is well. He understands you have been doing important work at the cricket club. He suggested I could discreetly assist here, with your permission of course. You see, I have so much free time with Harmeet away, I would welcome the distraction.'

'Yes, he is right.'

'Then it's settled, you continue your good charitable work while I look after things here, in your name of course.'

Looking happier than he had in a long time, her brother left her to it and as simply as that, she had taken over the family business. He never interfered; secretly, he was relieved. He put in appearances at the office, playing his part well, while focusing his efforts elsewhere. Within a month, things started to turn around and soon prosperity returned.

People noticed; they paid her brother compliments. He enjoyed that but played it down. He was recognised as a great man of business, people sought his advice, he offered little. Karam did not care, she was happy for him to receive the plaudits. All these achievements were hollow, meaningless.

She felt numb. More than ever, she wanted to simply disappear, there was still no news of her husband. Karam had not revisited her thoughts or feelings; she had been too busy. Now things were settling, there was time to look at it afresh. The war, she heard, was going well. Late at night, she cursed it. Look what it had done. She now had the added responsibility of raising their children alone. It was now she who had to make sure they were fed and clothed, that they had a roof over their heads.

The boys went to school and would soon be men, would it be up to her to train them in business, teach them to be men. Would Karam be responsible for finding them wives, would it be her job to find a brothel for them? She allowed herself some moments of self-pity and cried. How could he leave her? Wiping her tears, she regained control. She would rise above it. She had no choice; she would do those things; she would have the difficult conversations with them. If they needed guidance, she would give it. She would step into that role no matter what it was as she waited for her husband to return. Angry, she vowed not to let him or anyone else have the satisfaction of believing she needed him or any other person ever again.

Tanya 1.15

$\mathcal{S}$ITTING IN THE armchair, Tanya could remember the emotions she experienced the first time she had closed that journal. They stirred deep within her. The journal was engrossing; she had been surprised at the way the story leapt from the pages. Her imagination on fire, she could see every detail so clearly: the opulence of the houses, the offices, all set against the dusty plains of Northern India. She felt empathy for Karam, a bond started to form across the many years, she felt her frustration, her pain.

Captivated, Tanya sat for a long time, taking it all in. It parallelled her own story. Had her aunt known this? Had she been perceptive enough to think that reading these journals would help? Looking back now, she wondered at her own state of mind as she had read it for the first time. It also brought back memories about the dream she had had about the Japanese woman Kamiko. Somehow, they were connected, though the details eluded her still. She searched her mind, but it was gone. The thought of losing Evan made her cry. This roller coast she was now forced to ride was beginning to tear her apart. Tanya had to find a way, but time was running out. The first dream haunted her still, her inability to find a way to keep Evan safe alluded her like the dream, leaving her waiting for the phone to ring. Searching for a happier memory, she went to their last week together.

Outside rain began to fall.

Tanya 1.16

Evan was given a week's embarkation leave before departing for Afghanistan. They decided to rent a small cottage near the sea, rather than travel to their house in Ibiza or spend time in the city. The cottage was only a couple of hours drive from Land's End, so they travelled there separately, alone. Evan met her at the cottage door. They embraced warmly, though immediately she felt there was something different about him, something in him had changed. Summer was gone, the weather cold, it was the beginning of the dark times, the weather reflecting the overall mood.

They woke early each morning, taking long walks before breakfast, a light misty rain accompanying them most of the time. After breakfast they went out again. In the afternoons they retreated to the cottage, where they relaxed in the warmth of a raging fire. Tanya enjoyed theses times the most, hiding from the world just as they had been in the early days. Wrapped in Evan's arms she was at her happiest. It helped fight off the growing black cloud of what was coming that hung undiscussed above them. Tanya was still not ready to accept his life as a soldier, nor was she willing to confront the change in him she had detected when she first arrived at the cottage.

The days crept slowly forward, hours passed without a word between them. There was no need to speak, their love was still becoming deeper, yet now there were also things that remained unspoken. The wonderful feeling of not needing to speak, was now tinged with the act of being unable to. The taboo subjects grew, the longer they remained ignored, gaining greater power.

Tanya, sitting alone on their second last day, became distraught as the weight of it all began to crush her. With Evan, her life had become wonderful. In him, she had found love so pure, so intense, however it came with the stress of potential loss, the fear of which was unbearable. Just when things were good in her life, it was all about to be taken away, perhaps forever. She cried and he came to her, but she couldn't share her thoughts with him. That would be unfair. Holding her, he said nothing. They kept their silence as she let it all out through tears.

Sadness hung over them as they walked along the shore later that day. She turned to Evan, looked him straight in the eye, having finally raised the courage to say something.

'Why do you have to do this?'

Her voice was strong, there was no wavering. He looked at her, staring deeply into her eyes. She saw the pain in his expression that her question caused.

As he hadn't responded, she continued, 'We could leave now this minute; not even pack We could be in our house in Ibiza tonight.'

'And I would be a criminal.'

'That can be fixed.'

He wanted to say, you knew what I was when you met me, but he couldn't bring himself to utter the words.

'Whatever I want now, it's done. If I thought that I could live with myself, I would run away. I don't care what other's think, but I have to live with myself. I made a decision in my life. I thought it over for a long time, then I made it. Now I have to live with it and do the best I can to get through it.'

He didn't lie to her, didn't tell her it would be okay. He still hid, however, his true feelings, the ones that haunted him, that he was moving towards an unknown danger, that he doubted he would survive. Run! his instincts were telling him. Forget Afghanistan, get out, declare yourself insane. But, as he said, it wasn't him.

Tanya cried; Evan joined her. They held each other tightly. He wanted something; he wanted to scratch himself, hurt himself in some way. He felt an anger building inside him. Why was he like this? He felt disgusted with himself; he couldn't run away, but why? What was drawing him to this crucible, this destiny? Why couldn't he just live out his days with the woman he loved?

Tanya suddenly realised she must push through it. She must accept him and put her faith in the universe. Would he change even more? There was a darkness about him now, something she couldn't quite place, but it was there, unable to be ignored, though she tried.

'I'm lost.' What else could she say?

That night they ate dinner at a small restaurant. It was nice, ambient. Tanya was not able to cope well on this roller coaster; she realised now why she was who she was, why she had been hardened and outwardly refused to allow such attachment, emotions. For her, she realised, deep emotions were dangerous. She smiled as they hit her. Halfway through dinner she stopped, transported to a room millions of miles away in her head, while sitting in front of him. There in the room was her father. He was sitting behind a table, the room was dark. He said one thing with no introductions, no nostalgia.

'Let go of the things you can't control, enjoy it while it lasts.' In an instant she was back in her seat staring at her fork. 'Are you okay?'

She looked up to see Evan, with a concerned looked on his face. 'I'm fine,' she smiled. 'You know what I think?'

'What?' He returned her smile.

'That in a year's time, none of this will matter and no matter what you do or who you are, I will love you forever, regardless of what happens or however much time we have, and I want to spend every minute we have, every second as precious of my life and no matter what, I would rather be here or wherever we end up, than anywhere else.'

Evan's heart soared; she had crossed the line. She had accepted him. Tanya was wondering again but no matter, she meant it. She said what she meant, lie or not, she believed it. He could be anything, she couldn't care. No matter what, he was hers and she was his and it would be forever.

The following morning when they were out walking, Evan stopped abruptly, reached into his pocket, pulled out a jewellery box and handed it to her.

'I have something for you.' His voice had a nervous edge.

Tanya loved receiving gifts from him. Her happiness spread across her face. She was filled with a warmth that radiated from the box. Excitedly, she opened it. Inside was a necklace, with half a heart pendant, not very expensive, something teenagers gave each other. She loved it, he showed her the other half already hanging around his neck. He helped her put her half on.

'I'll never take it off,' she said with deep sincerity, touching it with her left hand as she made this vow.

A heavier rain began to fall. He bent down, kissing her passionately.

Their last morning together summed up everything that had been happening. It was tragic and wonderful all at the same time. As they were to travel separately, Tanya packed her bags and placed them near the front door, ready to leave. The driver was due in an hour, there was just enough time for one more walk. They had been unable to make love on the final night, there was just too much pressure. It saddened them both but neither wanted to leave things unfinished.

They wandered along a path that wound through the woods surrounding the cottage, she could smell the sea, even though she couldn't see it. For no reason, Tanya started to run. It was a primal instinct, something ancient, long forgotten. Rain started to fall as she weaved in and out of the trees. Evan chased her, they were both laughing. She darted this way and that but he couldn't catch her.

The rain was became heavier as she entered a clearing. Evan stood at the entrance, the rain's effect lessened by the denseness of the overhanging trees. There was silence as the sound dissipated. She was wearing a thick white coat. She took it off, letting it fall onto the wet ground. She turned her head, beckoning him with her eyes and walked a few paces. She placed her thumbs into the belt holes of her jeans, pulling them down in a single movement, then leaning forward, she braced herself against a large tree. After a few anxious moments, she felt his presence behind her.

When they returned from their walk, they found both drivers waiting and the cars packed. Everything was rushing to a conclusion. Evan ran inside for towels. Tanya kissed him passionately when he returned, regardless of the driver's presence. They took their time and the last kiss was through the car window. Crying, she watched him standing there forlornly as the car pulled away.

After she had calmed down, the first half of the drive was spent trying to get dry. They stopped briefly for coffee; Tanya tried to distract herself by reflecting for the remainder of the journey. She thought about Land's End. Its age was undetermined, though it was generally agreed there had been significant buildings on the site for almost a thousand years. It had once been an abbey, although little remained of that time. The family that preceded theirs, had grand plans. The main house was started by them and was finished by Karam, who improved and added to their original plans. It seemed to Tanya that Karam had wanted to build a place that allowed her to escape from the world, a sanctuary with vast gardens, tranquil places that were there to revitalise the soul.

There were intimate spaces, private baths, surrounded by walls, with lush gardens inside.

The enormous library, the offices, the many distractions, all allowed her the luxury of not having to leave. She had an eye to the future; many of the gardens and the trees that lined the drives would only reach maturity long after she was gone. Fountains and sculptures littered the grounds, sometimes not in harmony with their surroundings, yet somehow, it all blended together. Tanya gave that some thought with what she had learned about Karam. She was used to big houses, had grown up in them. Why had she chosen this place? Perhaps she would find out.

Tanya 1.17

THE PHONE FINALLY rang. She grabbed it frantically, pushing the green button, her heart bursting. It was Evan. There were tears of joy, tears of relief and they flowed freely. It had only been forty-five days since they said goodbye, yet it seemed like a lifetime.

'I'm so happy you called.'

'It's been very hectic over here today, lots of activity.'

'I can imagine.'

'I miss you. How's your project?'

'I've been reading the journals, they are fantastic.' There was audible interference on the line. 'Sorry you're breaking up.'

'I was saying that the journals are fantastic.' More interference, call breaking up.

'That's good to hear, the call is really bad we might get cut-off.'

'I have some fantastic news to share.'

'What was that?'

'I have some fantastic news to share.'

'I'll have to call you back. They are saying we can call back later.'

'I love you.'

The line went dead.

'I love you Evan.'

She said it just to say it, knowing he would never hear it. She was shaking, determined to stay awake. She let her mind slip back to Karam's story, immersing herself in that world.

Karam 1.2

Karam kept reminding herself that it was just a dream, yet it was so real, so vivid. In it, she was in the air floating, looking down on what looked like a mountain trail. There were many large boulders and the ground itself was very rocky. She came upon a scene, where a group of men dressed in uniforms were crouching behind a large boulder, from all sides other men were shooting at them, the air was filled with smoke. At first there was no sound, then it exploded around her, battering her senses. Amidst this utter confusion, she tried to make sense of what she was seeing. The sounds of battle seemed so real, the screams, when one of the men was wounded, were terrifying. For a while, the men behind the rock seemed to be prevailing, keeping their attackers at bay, then slowly one by one they began to fall as the attackers took the upper hand.

Helpless, Karam hovered above, unable to help. One of the men looked up directly at her, his expression was desperate, pleading. Surrounded completely, he threw up his arms, then, blackness. She woke in a cold sweat, having recognised the man. It was her husband, Harmeet.

The dream haunted her all day. She could not focus on anything else. Running the business in this state was impossible, nothing could erase the memories of the dream. For the first time, she realised she had nobody to talk to, no confidante. This thought made her feel even more alone than she already was. She had too many roles to play, was too many things to too many people. Why should she have to live like this? Harmeet was meant to be her confidante; he was off playing soldiers. Karam could feel her resentment for him rising again. Harmeet! The man was now invading her dreams, her only remaining sanctuary! What was next? Her brother unable to face being an adult was off playing cricket. Was there nobody that she could turn to?

Her sadness was real, the loneliness overwhelming, being strong for the boys suddenly did not seem a reasonable enough argument to keep going. It did not seem fair to them or to her. She was frustrated by her own helplessness. Time passed slowly and Karam became obsessed with the dream. Something had happened, the anger she had been feeling toward her husband for abandoning her, turned to pity. What if he was dead?

Perhaps increasing her own charitable efforts would help, she thought. Hoping to create some good karma, she donated gold to the temple, increased her gifts to the poor. Nothing happened, her prayers remained unanswered. Every day Karam cast her eye upon the dusty road, but could see nobody. Her boys, once her only salvation, were now another reminder of what was wrong in her life. She played with them every afternoon. They were times the boys cherished, but on the inside, she remained dark, disconnected. Karam became an expert at concealing these emotions, putting on a brave face and was a good actor. She told them stories beneath a tree in the garden; they laughed while she was dying inside.

Just when she had given up hope, they brought Harmeet home on a large stretcher. It was so large it needed six men to carry it. A nurse and a physician, along with ten more attendants, made up the party. He was placed in a large room on the ground floor of the house that was quickly transformed into a makeshift infirmary. The physician and nurse were British. They had been with him since he was discovered alive and had been promised large sums of money to deliver him home, then care for him. Karam paid them. She ran to him at first, but he was cold, unaffectionate. The physician and nurse took over her home; they were rude. She didn't understand, it was confusing. So happy was she that he had returned, she forgave him. They limited her access to her husband, but it was when they started to interfere with her children that she decided it was enough, sending the boys to stay with their grandfather.

Harmeet's father brought a strange chest out of his rooms, which he took into the infirmary. She was in the dark, another mystery, it triggered a deep depression. Karam retreated into her chamber, staying there. Becoming invisible in her own home.

People came to visit; Harmeet was a hero. No story was forthcoming, so rumours started to spread. Tales of his deeds carried far and wide, there was no time for his wife. Fed up, her patience at an end, Karam decided to leave. She fled to her father's house forgoing the sanctity of her own home. She didn't even say goodbye.

As her carriage pulled away, she noticed a woman on the opposite side of the street, a woman she didn't recognise. It looked as if she was watching her house. She was hard to see, but it raised her interest. Strange, she thought.

Karam forgot about the woman on the long journey ahead, for the time being there were other things to think about. The boys ran to greet her as the she arrived. Her father had built this estate after her mother passed away; it was his domain, one into which he received few visitors. He had designed it himself and supervised the construction. Water was an important theme. There were many fountains and water features throughout the grounds. Small, well-tended walled in gardens were another important feature. Privacy was the second theme. There were two pools for bathing, one for men and another for women. These were beautiful ornate places, serene, where you could spend hours in the cool water. The whole compound was hidden behind a high wall. Everything was secret inside; the servants kept their distance; they could move around the property without being seen.

The boys' affection brought tears to her eyes. She missed them and seeing them made her realise how much.

As the servants came running out to fetch her luggage, her father, accompanied by his estate manager, Dilbagh, stepped out of the front door onto the veranda. Dilbagh looked resplendent in a black jacket with gold trim. Her father, a look of concern on his face, observed her carefully. The boys, holding onto her, walked her over to them. There were no words spoken, Dilbagh bowed, then ushered her and the boys into the parlour, Her father joined them, they were served tea. It was most welcome after the long dusty journey.

'Why have you come mother?' Karminder, her elder son asked her.

'Is it to take us home?' her younger son, Sanjeet, added.

'No, my loves. I came to see you because your father is still not well.'

'But mother, we miss our friends and school.'

As he said this, she could see the sadness on Karminder's face.

'We will organise a tutor, you can take lessons here. You will see your friends in time, run along now and play. I need to speak with papa.'

The boys ran off.

'You brought a great many trunks for a short stay. Your husband has returned you should be by his side.'

'He does not want nor need me.'

'He has told you this?'

'He,' she paused, 'not in so many words. If I can explain, since returning he has said nothing to me, he stays in his room or what has become his room. He keeps none but the counsel of his surgeon and nurse, who he has allowed to take over the household. He speaks to his father; he has cut me out of his life.'

'You have run away; a wife's place is with her husband.'

'I have retreated until I can decide what to do.'

'Your home, your children?'

'He can have the house, it's no longer a home, he does not want the children.'

'You are his wife.'

'He does not want me.'

'Do you believe that?' He has been wounded both in body and his pride.'

'He has come home, but he has not returned to us. If he wanted us, he would have embraced us, not pushed us away. He wants something else, that much I can sense.'

'You don't know what that is?'

'No.'

'Stay here as long as you like. Rest, gather your thoughts, think of your husband and how things can be returned to how they were. Think of the happy times.'

Karam smiled at her father with the full knowledge that the happy times would never return. He was right about everything. She had no rights; she could not leave unless he granted it. Everything she owned belonged to him. He was the owner of her, she hated that more than anything else. Was there somewhere she could go, something she could do to escape this? What about England? Queen Victoria led the empire, surely there she could find some freedom. Was it not even slightly possible? Something inside her told her life could be better.

The servants carried Harmeet out into the small garden that ran off his infirmary. They placed him on a lavish custom-made bed with a canopy and mosquito netting. The nurse was giving the orders. After a quick inspection, she ushered them out. A guard was placed at the door, nobody was to enter for two hours when she personally would return. Fresh air was what was needed. This would be the new daily routine, she announced.

Jasleen 1.1

JASLEEN WAS WATCHING from the street outside and through a grate in the wall. She moved closer for a better look inside. She couldn't believe her luck. There, lying on a bed, was the object of her desire, her own personal hero. She looked around and spotted a door. Not seeing anybody, she walked over and tried it but it was locked. She looked up and down. The wall was too high to climb, the hole with the grate too small to climb through. She walked around and saw another grate in the corner that was larger. Aware of how conspicuous it must look, she pushed against it. It would not move. She tried again with no luck. Trying one final time from the other side, she managed to get it to move. Using all her strength, she was able to bend it. There was just enough room to squeeze through.

She stood staring at him as he slept. She had dreamed of this day when he would return, but had started to believe it would never come. She surprised herself. She had missed him. She had lain awake at night wondering how she was missing his presence.

She moved closer to the bed, nervous, scared of being discovered. After a while, as if sensing her presence, Harmeet opened his eyes. He beckoned for her to come closer and nervously she shuffled forward. She lifted the mosquito net.

He wanted to take her into his arms but he dared not. Harmeet smiled and reached out with one hand. She took it and instantly felt the tears rising. He smiled.

'Are you badly injured?' He nodded.

'They tell me I will heal.'

'I prayed for you every day.'

'Do you remember the promises we made?'

She bowed her head. 'Yes.'

Harmeet suddenly realised something.

'My beautiful one, how did you come to be in the garden?'

'The corner, the old grate.'

He smiled.

'I will keep my promise as well.'

'Then it has all been worthwhile. I saw you on your white horse, you looked so handsome.'

'Come every day at this time, but be cautious. I will arrange for the door to be unlocked. You can come and go that way.'

'I will come.'

'Then I will recover faster.'

She put the net back in place and hurried through the door, making certain nobody saw her leave, her heart racing.

Tanya 1.18

THE PHONE HADN'T made another sound, even though he had promised to call back. It was unusual for him to say he would call if he was uncertain it would happen. She had news she wanted to share with him, news that may now have to wait a week. Her mood plummeted.

Evan emailed Tanya whenever he could, which wasn't very often, but it was easier. She did not want to share this news by email. The phone calls, although less frequent, were special, sacred. From what Tanya could understand, there were two bases that Evan's regiment operated out of. One right in the middle of the province they were assigned to and another that was relatively safer, further back. Their province was very dangerous, as were they all, only his seemed to have a higher level of enemy activity. Whenever its name came up during the evening news, her heart missed a beat.

Tanya still struggled with the change she sensed in Evan the last time they were together. It had continued growing. He was different, had a harder edge. She didn't know how to interpret it or whether it was permanent, but he was not the same as the man who she had first met. She loved him regardless.

From what he had told her, she understood the men he was

leading respected him, he described them as a good bunch. He shared so little.

She longed for him, the phone calls helped lessen her anxiety. She checked her phone constantly, even when a call wasn't scheduled, just in case, it was her lifeline. She was becoming reclusive, walking the lonely grounds of the estate on her own. She was given plenty of space by the staff. She understood from reading Karam's journals, how many of the design aspects were carried across from Karam's father's estate in India. Karam was constantly in her thoughts. Did that old estate still exist?

There were still relatives back there she could reach out to. It was a different branch of the family now; they had grown apart. She was grateful for her work; it provided a distraction. There was comfort in it as the story of Karam's own feelings of loss and abandonment were familiar to her. The phone rang, she grabbed it.

'Hello, can you hear me?' Evan's strong accent came down the line.

'Yes, it's a little faint.'

'Hold on a second.' She could hear him doing something in the background.

'Is that better?'

'Yes, I can hear you clearly now.'

'Sorry about earlier something to do with the satellite?'

'I'm just happy that you could call back,' she paused, 'I miss you.'

'I miss you too. The other day, while on patrol, I saw this little girl and boy, they were standing near the side of the road. The little girl was holding some flowers, it made me think of you. I wonder how many children we will have.'

Tanya started crying. She hid this by muting the microphone, with her finger. Taking her finger away, Tanya spoke quickly in an attempt to continue hiding her emotions, 'How many would you like?'

'Three, a boy, a girl and one for luck.'

'Three it is, I love you.'

'I love you too.' There was a pause as each felt the pull of various emotions, clinging to the phone, the tenuous link, each gripping this connection more tightly. Evan spoke next steering in a less emotional direction.

'It's very hot over here.'

'It's freezing here,' she replied, with little interest, not wanting to be drawn into a discussion of the mundane. She then took a deep breath.

'I have some news that I need to share. Some fantastic news,' Tanya said excitedly.

'Oh, damn, I'm going to have to go again.' Tanya could sense the frustration in Evan's voice as he said this. Her heart sank, realising he had not heard her. 'I'm really sorry.' She was touched by his concern, then in a voice tinged with frustration of her own, she tried to share again.

'Please wait, I have to tell you something.'

'Okay, what is it?

His annoyance at her persistence, raised an almost childish anger in her. In an instant she decided not to tell him.

'It's okay, I'll save it for next time.' This came out more coldly than she had intended. 'Take care of yourself,' she added feeling remorseful, in an attempt to soften the blow.

'Are you certain, I can try and call again?'

'Don't worry, Evan. I'll tell you next time.'

He was gone, and she wasn't certain that he had heard her. She cried; this could not go on.

After calming down and feeling fed up, Tanya decided to go and soak in one of the heated baths located in a special walled garden, an addition to the estate that had been installed during Karam's reign. It had been renovated by her aunt into what was now known as a wellbeing centre incorporating a yoga studio and gym.

As she walked along the path through the garden that led to it, a light misty rain began falling through the cold night air. It reminded her of the last time they were together. She wondered when the season would start to change.

In the bath she replayed the call in her head. Even though they had expressed some emotion, it was largely impersonal, she decided. Maybe there were others nearby and he was unable to talk freely.

Back in the house, her phone rang. There was a rule against bringing phones into the wellness centre. Although she was loathe to do so, she left her phone in her room. The call went through to voice mail. It was Evan. He had managed to call back. He left her a long message. She slipped naked into the warm water and closing her eyes, she dreamed of a house filled with children, a house with love where they could hide from the rest of the world. Her hand drifted down to her stomach and warmth spread through her body. Forgiving herself for her earlier behaviour, she managed a rare, contented smile.

Evan 1.1

*T*HE TALIBAN HAD taken their time, watching from the shadows. They hid behind rocks, filming them, learning. After gathering all this information then analysing it, they carefully planned the ambush. Evan's regiment maintained an outpost that was at the furthest point of their sector, right at their vehicles' operational limit. It was a small outpost with only fifty personnel. There was a hospital that acted as a clinic, where villagers could visit for treatment. To reach the outpost by road, vehicles were forced to climb a narrow dusty trail that then wound through a ravine and down to a valley below. This was a known danger point. Whenever a patrol passed through, it would be supported by attack helicopters whose presence alone was a suitable deterrent to keep any would-be attackers at bay.

The helicopters were the problem. If they could be removed, the convoy could be attacked while it travelled through the ravine. The Taliban's first move was to slowly build up their forces into the area, surrounding the outpost. Then over a two-week period, they slowly increased activity, in the hope this would attract a patrol. They then increased their numbers, placing them into the ravine and surrounding area and waited.

When the patrol convoy was spotted, they moved into position.

At the same time, they launched an attack on the outpost, just as the helicopters were moving into position to escort them through the ravine. They didn't stand a chance. The armoured personnel carriers entered the ravine. The helicopters, having spotted no enemy combatants, broke away to assist the outpost.

Evan was distracted. He was thinking about the call to Tanya. He would blame himself for everything that happened later, though at this point, he was simply a pawn in the game. His vehicle was third in the line of six. The first explosive went off beneath the lead vehicle, instantly disabling it, blocking any movement forward. Then the rear vehicle was targeted, blocking any retreat backward, trapping them in the ravine. After that it was easy. Trapped, the soldiers remained in the vehicles as bullets thudded into the metal and ricocheted off the bullet proof glass. Inside, frantic radio calls were made for immediate support. Safe from bullets, but not from rockets or explosives, they prayed. A man staggered from the lead vehicle, badly wounded. Evan and another man instinctively leapt from their vehicle to help, the air exploding around them. They crawled beneath another vehicle to gain cover. Evan heard the whirr and thud of a helicopter blade somewhere above them. They're prayers were answered. One of the helicopters had heard their call. It began strafing the rocks nearby with machine gun fire.

His thoughts turned to the injured man they had come to assist. Evan signalled to the man with him but as soon as they exposed themselves, he was hit. Evan looked up as a rocket went whizzing into the air toward the hovering helicopter. It missed. Evan, desperately searching for the wounded man, was unable to see him. He tried to return to his vehicle, then all hell broke loose. As they spotted him, his sergeant appeared out of nowhere. Together, they fought their way towards the edge of the ravine. Evan became someone else, fighting with great determination. Fear was present but his bravado was bigger. It was intense, barbaric and primal.

Narrow paths led them away from the vehicles. A Taliban fighter appeared, fired two bursts from a machine gun, then disappeared amongst the rocks. His sergeant fell forward as if he had tripped. His body hit the ground with a thud, causing a cloud of dust. It was a brutal and unforgiving place they now found themselves in.

Evan dived under a ledge waiting for death, his bravado disappeared. Scared, he closed his eyes thinking of Tanya as gun fire erupted above him filling the air with lead. He cowered beneath the ledge, bullets ricocheting off the rocks, evoking an evil wicked sound. This pushed his anxiety level into the red, intensifying his fear as he sought desperately to clear his mind and remain calm.

When death didn't come and the fire died down, he emerged from under the ledge, convincing himself that it was safe, only to have another fighter pop up almost immediately. Bang! He was thrown back to the ground with incredible force.

I'm hit, he thought. He went numb, blood was flowing out of him, his senses were dulled. Then came a dark time where he moved in and out of consciousness. He crawled amongst the rocks, blood continued flowing from his wounds. Desperate, frantically he hugged the ground dragging himself along. He saw a narrow opening in the rock and somehow, he managed to squeeze through it. It opened up into a small cavern. Unable to keep on going, he collapsed as he hit the dark dusty floor. He called her name, 'Tanya', then everything went dark.

He lost all concept of time. Strange dreams made him believe he was in purgatory. In one, he was swimming across a river, trying to reach Tanya who was holding a small child. No matter how he tried, he couldn't reach them. It was vivid. Covered in sweat, delirious, he drifted in and out of consciousness. In time, he realised he was in a bed, there was light, but he couldn't focus. There were voices, but he couldn't understand, he fell back to sleep as the fever returned.

Slowly, things started to make sense. He could feel something in his arm as it was sore. Feeling it with his hand, he realised that it was a drip. The voices returned; this time they were beginning to make sense. He could make out colours and shapes began forming, although slowly. In this vast slow-moving expanse something began to appear, the tiniest glimmer of hope, then the realisation. I'm alive, he thought.

He was thankful, very thankful. He became elated. From this point, he was becoming aware, no longer grasping at reality. Hope coursed through his body like a drug, a warm fabulous sensation. He was alive, he shouldn't be, but he was. His fears subsided and he slept soundly, now dreaming of Tanya. Visions of her sustained him, the memories coming in bursts, sometimes confusing, a mixture of fantasy and reality. A distorted view. His view and how he wanted to remember things; the primal urges that fed the fevered love-making, the private, tender moments they had shared, whispered thoughts that were secret, dream- like moments between two lovers swept up in their own world.

He revelled in feelings of how lucky he was to be chosen to find his soulmate, to be with someone that evoked such feelings. This gave him a new determination to do anything necessary to get back to her. That was his one purpose, to get well, to get out of this place, to live and go on living, to never again be separated from her, not by anything or anyone. As the clouds of confusion slowly lifted, Evan began to wonder where he was. Somebody bathed him, changed his dressings, he could make out shapes in the haze. Perhaps he must be in a hospital. These thoughts were comforting, it would soon all be over. He woke to a woman busying herself around him. A nurse. He tried to understand what was happening as she spoke English. Her voice was soft, soothing.

In the confusion he focused on that and it relieved his anxiety. 'Remain calm, everything is going to be alright. You are safe here; your wounds are healing and you are in good hands. Just relax.'

She took a small towel, moistened it in a bowl, folded it and placed it on his forehead.

'Thank you,' he said, his first conscious words since becoming wounded, then went back into a deep sleep. When he woke again, she was there.

'Stay relaxed,' she said.

A small boy entered the room and went and stood behind her, hiding and peeking out. *That's strange,* he thought, *that didn't add up.* His world began crashing down around him. The woman spoke.

'This is Farrah, my son. Say hello, Farrah.'

But the boy was shy. He would not venture out from his position of safety. Shocked, not knowing what to think, he spoke to the boy.

'Hello,' Evan managed. The boy peeked out, smiled, then retreated again behind his mother.

The realisation hit Evan hard. Instantly, he became fearful, his body tensed with every fibre springing to high alert. This was no hospital. Frantically he looked around the room, trying to process what he was seeing. The room was clean; it was a mixture of concrete and natural rock, a cave of some sort. His blood pressure was rising, as he became frantic, survival instincts began to take over.

'Where are we?' Evan demanded.

His anxiousness apparent, the woman sought to calm him down. 'You are not a prisoner, please remain calm. You are safe here, very safe. You are a very lucky man, lucky that we found you, that you found us. This cave was built to hide someone important. It's very well built, very hard to find.'

Evan was still on guard, his mind still grappling, trying to make sense of it all.

'How did I come to be here?'

'I was near the cave entrance. I heard a noise, opened the door, and there you were, a true blessing. I brought you inside, locked the door and offered a prayer of thanks. You have been here ever since.'

'How long have I been here?' He was beginning to calm down.

She shrugged. 'Seven days.'

'Seven days?' The number rang in his head, that ached. Questions flooded in his mind. He realised he was far from well.

'I understand that you are scared, but you must trust me for now,' the woman said, as she tried to calm him. 'Think, I have been caring for you for a week, why would I hurt you now? God has blessed me with the opportunity to care for you. This cave is well stocked with everything we need. It is secure and we are safe, for now, until you are stronger. You must take a leap of faith, pray to your god, trust in me to deliver your wellbeing. No harm will come to you. You must rest and in time you will see, we are only here to help.'

Evan didn't acknowledge her words, but he did find some comfort in them. There was something, a definite sincerity. His gut, or was it instinct? Telling him she was not just placating him, but she was being truthful about rescuing him. That she would, as she proclaimed, do everything within her power to care for him while he remained vulnerable. He gave over to her wishes by drifting off once again. Against the training he had received and all logic, he did pray, placing himself in her hands, retreating into his fevered memories.

Farrah left his mother alone with the strange man. He was a quiet boy, wise beyond his years. He had seen too much, grown up too fast, in a world surrounded by death. There were few happy memories. His sleep was filled with nightmares, that he attempted to hide. His mother was his world. They had run away together and it was a shared dream they had chased together, to get to Pakistan, or perhaps England. One of their most precious possessions was an old magazine that had a real estate section for houses in London.

One of their favourite things was to look at the pages and dream of the places where they would live. The cave was their sanctuary and hunted he feared ever leaving it, though he knew that the day would come. His own family was hunting them. He didn't understand it, only that they wanted his mother to marry one of his father's brothers after he had been killed. So they had run and God had smiled upon them. They had met a man who knew about the caves. It was this man who introduced them to a doctor who was also in hiding. The doctor shared their dream of escaping to a new life. Few people knew about the caves, that had been built for a now dead former war lord. The doctor had been the man's personal physician.

They were reinforced with concrete, turning them into bunkers. There was food, many years' worth of freeze dried ration packs, water, power, sanitation. The caves had been built for people who wanted to stay hidden, for a long time. The doctor's cave was connected to theirs by a steel door and they trusted him. He had helped them care for the foreign man. Farrah liked the foreign man and he was already fantasising about him taking the place of his late father, helping them to leave. Previously, the doctor had held this place in his mind.

He preferred the foreigner. He sometimes heard his mother and the doctor talking, and he realised that he may one day be his father. He was a good man, yet he liked the idea of the foreigner more, even though they had never spoken. In the dark world they occupied, everyone retreated into their own fantasies. In the place where there was no sun, no moon and time stood still, all they had were their thoughts and dreams. Dreams that manifested into desires, bringing feelings of deep longing. Longing for a life away from caves, from fear of detection, fuelled by images of tree lined streets, large houses with many rooms, lived in by smiling happy people who knew nothing of death and had never seen the bullet riddled body of their father carried lifeless before them.

Tanya 1.19

WHEN SHE CHECKED her phone, she became angry at herself. By respecting the rules, she had missed Evan's call. When she listened to his message, the tears flowed. After replaying it several times, she fell into a restless sleep.

The sound of the phone ringing woke her. She grabbed it, thinking it might be him. A new nightmare, one she had feared the most, was about to begin.

'Missing! What does "missing" mean?' she cried out in the dark after putting the phone down.

Emotions were running high as she battled to calm herself. What could she do? Do *something!* she screamed at herself.

'Do something!' She was completely lost. *Was there somebody there with her?* the person who called had asked. She lied, saying, 'Yes.'

No sooner had she put the phone down, it started ringing again. *It's a mistake,* she thought, *they had gotten it was wrong.* Then she saw who was calling. It was her mother. Tanya was hysterical, she answered but was incoherent. The general came on the line.

'Tanya,' he barked, realising from bitter experience what was happening, 'Tanya, listen to me. Stop, breathe deeply, in out, in out.'

It worked. Tanya felt herself beginning to calm down. On the other end of the phone, the general was relieved, her mother was bawling. He ignored her, focusing on Tanya.

'Now, I understand how difficult this is.' There was a knock at her door and he heard it.

'Answer the door, Tanya.'

She complied. A servant was waiting with a tray that held a mug of tea and a glass of brandy. Her aunt's housekeeper arrived at the same time, looking flustered. Tanya allowed them into the room. Mrs Giles, the housekeeper, took her by the arm, leading her to an armchair.

'Tanya are you there?'

She was still holding her phone. His voice was clear, authoritative and she placed the phone back to her ear, responding in a weak, barely audible voice.

'Yes.'

'Tanya, you have undergone a severe shock, drink the brandy.' The servant offered the tray. Gingerly, Tanya took the glass and drank it in two gulps.

'I'm finished.'

'Concentrate on the warmth as it flows through your body, now drink the tea. We are packing already; we will be there as soon as we can. What I want you to do is follow my instructions. Mrs Giles will sit with you while you finish your tea, you need to stay warm, she will help you get ready into bed. She will care for you until we arrive. Rest now. By the time you wake up, we will be there.'

'I will.'

'Good everything will be alright; we will be with you soon.' He hung up the phone.

Mrs Giles spoke in a low voice, helping her into the bed. She covered her with extra blankets, turned up the heat, then switched out the light before taking up a position in the armchair. Mrs Giles wouldn't sleep a wink as she watched over Tanya, who tossed and turned for some time, before starting to calm.

Feeling completely lost, Tanya cried out in the darkness for help. It startled Mrs Giles. Her request floated off into the night where somewhere it was heard, then answered. Tanya was carried off in her dreams into the past, back to when the second world war was raging. Mrs Giles felt a change in the room. There was something happening, an energy, the presence of something. She stood up and approached the bed where she saw Tanya's expression go from being tormented, to becoming peaceful and serene. She would remember it always.

Stella 1.1

$\mathcal{S}$TELLA TURNED OFF the empty road without indicating. The gravel at the edge of the road crunched beneath the tyres as she parked the big yellow convertible against a wooden fence, facing the unseen ocean. Stella picked up her towel from the backseat, then climbed out of the car. The air was fresh, salty and wasting no time, she quickly walked down a narrow path that wound its way through a series of sand dunes, before emerging onto the beach. She paused, admiring the view, then, remembering why she was there, removed her shoes, pausing again for a moment to feel the sand under her feet, then started, almost marching, towards the water's edge. Finding a spot just outside of the water's reach, she dropped her towel. Unbuckling her skirt, she let it fall onto the sand, then very purposefully strode towards the water.

A strong breeze helped fuel the waves that pounded rhythmically onto the shore. Stella waded in and the dance quickly began. She retreated a couple of times, but kept pressing forward, until she was beyond where the waves were breaking. As rough as it was, she now gently bobbed up and down as they passed by, breaking behind her. Stella was a confident swimmer, however, she respected the ocean and would venture no further out while alone.

The cold water turned darker in the fading light, Stella stood rising and falling with the ebb and flow. Daydreaming, for the thousandth time that day, she wondered where her husband was, praying he was safe. A deep sadness, mixed with anger, overtook her. Abruptly she turned, walking out of the sea, stumbling, falling, she was thrown about as she passed through the breakers. She spread out the towel on the sand, then sat down shivering; she stared at the ocean, trying hard to keep the bad thoughts at bay. They emerged, ever stronger, from the back of her mind, quickly taking over.

Eight months, it had been eight months since the U-boat had struck somewhere in the middle of the Atlantic. The same ocean she had just been swimming in. The enemy could be out there now, perhaps waiting just beyond the waves. She shivered again, this time from the thought, rather than the breeze. Alone on the beach, the only light from the still rising moon, she felt very alone. Darkness enveloped her as the moon moved behind some clouds. Let them come, let them march up the beach right now! She was disappointed when nobody came.

His survival was impossible, yet she still clung to the slightest hope. There had been survivors but he was not amongst them. Was he really going to just turn up? the logical part of her brain asked. Where could you hide in the middle of the ocean? Maybe he was rescued by another vessel, maybe he was now in a prisoner of war camp.

Hope existed because her heart was not yet ready to accept the logical ending and let him go. Chance. People were quick to remind her there was a chance. A chance for what? Had he been taken prisoner she would have heard by now, everyone else had. If he had been rescued, a nice telegram would have been delivered. She could have hugged the delivery boy. Neither of those things had occurred.

Stella's friend Jean had been lucky. Her husband had also been on a ship that was attacked, his left leg had been lost at the knee. He was rescued and recuperating in a nice comfortable hospital. Jean missed her husband, but she knew that one day soon he would come home, even if it was without a limb. She envied Jean who had the comfort of children to keep her company, two girls and two boys.

Stella had never been blessed with a child. She had fallen pregnant once, but that had ended in disaster and they had buried an unnamed baby boy. Skippy, her husband, had promised that one day they would adopt when they were told another pregnancy was not possible. Thirteen years later, they had never so much as had a meeting with an adoption agency. The boy lived in her dreams. At thirteen, he was preparing to enter high school; he was an athlete who liked to play football, went fishing and hunting with his father on weekends, the two were inseparable. His school reports were good; he never tired of her cooking. On Saturday nights they all went out together to the movies, then dinner at a restaurant where everybody knew them. He made them laugh, riding upfront with them in the car. Every now and then, when he was little, Skippy sat him on his lap and let him steer.

It worked. Her fantasy son pushed the bad thoughts away. She continued staring, the waves were reduced to sound only in the growing darkness, willing Skippy to be alive, offering all prayers, all arguments for the preservation of his life. She did this fully knowing that somewhere, a German woman was making the same request to the same God. What did the war have to do with them?

Keith, "Skippy", had joined the navy between high school and university. He had joined for free tuition; over the years he had stayed in the reserves becoming an officer. When war broke out, he was given six weeks of advanced training and his first command. He was thirty-six years old and the ship was considerably older. He was proud of his new career direction as he felt as if he was doing something worthwhile.

Escorting convoys was a risky business. The odds for survival were against them. With crossing, the odds moved further in their opponent's favour. A year was a long time and finally, the figures no longer added up, you could only be lucky for so long. The navy told the survivors' families nothing; they kept whatever they knew, tightly guarded. The ship was attacked, he was reported missing, that was all. What was filed away? Facts were dangerous, they could affect public morale. They were never told the destroyer had stayed afloat, burning for nearly fourteen hours, and they never would be.

Her husband had been seen by witnesses in a lifeboat. A day later, when rescue finally arrived, a survivor reported that he had given up his place in the lifeboat to another. He was last seen clinging to the side. At some point, one that nobody could agree upon, he was simply gone. Why was he even there? He should have left the reserves years before. There were too many "what ifs" and "whys".

She sat on the sand; her feet were now dry. An hour passed, then another, she brushed the sand off. Time had no meaning to her anymore, she no longer cared. The breeze was picking up. It was time to go so, reluctantly, she dressed, picked up her things and headed for the path. As soon as the car came into view, she was in trouble. Her heart sank, the headlights were on and they were very dim. She reached inside, switching them off, knowing that there would not be enough life left in the battery to start the car. This had happened before, especially when she was rushing.

Stella knew what she had to do. She would have to push start the car, all she needed was a nice flat piece of road. She could do this; she released the handbrake, then put the car in neutral and began pushing it in the direction of the road. The car built up some speed, but at the edge of the road was a hump. It started to go over it, but ran out of momentum. The car rolled back. She pushed with all her might to no avail, it was no use.

She sat down on the running board and cried.

Stella 1.2

THE BOY APPEARED out of nowhere, right when she was at her lowest. She didn't see him arrive, simply looked up and there he was, standing with his dog, a fishing bag over one shoulder and what looked like a BB gun over the other and a fishing rod in his hand. The dog was a golden retriever, a breed she knew well. Right away, there was something familiar about the boy: a facial expression, the curve of his mouth, the nose that seemed a little small. He was dressed only in shorts and a t-shirt, wearing no shoes. The breeze picked up, it became cooler, she was concerned that he was underdressed. The dog reminded her of one her family had when she was a child. It had been a nice dog; she had spent many happy years playing with it.

The boy was distant. He gave the feeling he was a thousand miles away. He stood, not staring, but looking straight at her sitting on the running board of her car. I must look a mess, she thought to herself. In the dark, the remnants of the tears that had been streaming down her cheeks, were not immediately noticeable, but Stella was self-conscious and sensitive, her emotions on high alert. There was something odd about the boy suddenly appearing as he had, well many things, all making her wonder. It was a strange place hear by the ocean, yet in the context of strange, on this night at this time, it felt strangely normal.

Stella made the first move, as the boy seemed happy to stand there silently, forever if necessary.

'Catch any?' she said. He shook his head, then took a step closer. She called to the dog.

'Hey.'

The dog ran to her, she scratched its head and patted it. 'What's his name?'

'Billy.'

For a moment she went cold.

'I once had a dog with the same name,' she said. Then she shrugged it off and continued to pat him.

'Hungry boy?' she said to the dog. She leaned over into the back seat and retrieved a picnic basket.

She unwrapped a sandwich, removed the roast beef and fed it to the dog.

She noticed the boy's eyes following the sandwiches and offered him one.

'I have ham and cheese, peanut butter, more roast beef and I even think there may be some with just cheese.'

She offered the basket and he helped himself. 'What did you say your name was?'

The boy shrugged, busy eating. She decided not to push him, placing the basket on the front of the car, out of reach of the dog.

'Help yourself to as many as you want.' He nodded.

'Do you live far from here?' she asked.

He nodded again as he devoured his second sandwich. 'My name is Stella,' she told him.

Between bites, he smiled.

'My car has broken down. Maybe when you finish your sandwiches, you could give me a hand. I want to try to push start it.'

He nodded. 'I will if you come down to the beach and fish with me and Billy first.'

It was a strange request she thought, at this late hour. 'I thought you might be finished for the day.'

'No Ma'am, we haven't anything for supper or tomorrow morning's breakfast yet.'

'Alright, won't your mother worry?'

'No, Ma'am.'

'Please call me Stella. We don't have to be so formal when there are just the three of us.'

His smile was constant now.

'No, Stella, she knows we are okay, besides Billy and me take good care of each other,' he said patting the dog.

Stella wondered if she should bring her towel and the basket of sandwiches and decided it was a good idea. In the back seat she also found a cardigan and a jumper. She picked up both, closed the door of the car and picked up the basket. She headed towards the path, but he motioned to her to follow him.

'Let us go through the dunes, we might find a rabbit I can hunt with my rifle.'

She thought that was cute, the little hunter. Stella had never hunted, but she had brothers and a father who liked to hunt deer; her husband had also enjoyed the odd trip. She knew enough to know that BB guns were best used for bottles and tin cans. You needed to be very close and very accurate to bring down even a small rabbit.

Stella followed the boy and Billy. They knew their way well, weaving this way and that in the light of the moon that was now shining more brightly above them. They came across no rabbits and emerged a long way from where she had been earlier.

'This looks like a lucky spot,' he said.

He strode toward the water. They set up camp not far from where the tide was reaching. The boy waded in until the water was up to his knees, Billy at his side. He then baited his hook, casting his line into the small area, between where the waves were breaking and the shore. Stella sat watching him. Every now and then, he would wind in his line and Billy would get excited, but each time it was only seaweed and not a fish that he had caught.

There was some driftwood nearby that was dry and it gave Stella an idea. She gathered it together and then dug a small pit with her hands. She placed the wood in the pit and from the bottom of the basket under the sandwiches, she took a newspaper and a box of matches. Using the paper as kindling, she wrapped it around the driftwood, leaning into the pit to stop the breeze from blowing out the matches. She struck one and the paper caught and soon the driftwood followed. Within no time, she had a nice little fire going. The boy and Billy stayed fishing for a long time, but the fire was a good draw and soon they both came with a lingering drawn out walk, back up to join her.

'Come and get dry,' she called out.

Billy needed no invitation. After shaking the water from his fur, he lay down as close as he dared to the fire. The boy was more cautious; he sat in the shadows just out of focus and slowly moved in closer. Too many things did not add up, so Stella decided to be bold.

'Will you tell me your name now?' No response. He just shook his head.

'There's nothing to be frightened of. I told you mine.'

'Do you have children of your own Stella?'

She had not expected this and decided to be honest.

'No. My husband and I are yet to be blessed. We were going to once, but the poor baby passed away.'

'Do you believe in heaven?'

The boy's face came into view, an orange red glow from the flames enhancing his features. She was not sure what to say. She decided to deflect as, in a way, they were sparring.

'How old are you?'

He became silent again, a few moments passed. 'Time doesn't move in the same way here.'

Stella thought about his question. It was something she suddenly wondered herself. The conversation was moving in a strange direction, but he was talking at least. Was he a runaway, living out here amongst the dunes?

'What does your father do?'

'He is missing. Me and Billy are waiting for him.'

'How long have you been waiting?'

Then she remembered what he had said before and changed the subject.

'Does your mother know? I bet she would be worried about you.'

'She knows.'

'Well, it's getting late, maybe we should head back.'

He looked around, peering off into the distance. The moon and fire cast a little light, but not much could be made out beyond the reach of the fire. She decided to answer his earlier question.

'I believe in something beyond death, I believe your soul lives on and that you are happy and contented.'

The boy looked happy again.

'I should get back to fishing.' He stood up, before she had time to protest and was gone.

Billy stayed by the fire; Stella decided to look for more wood. She started to wander in the direction of her earlier swim location but changed her mind. She could not remember seeing any wood there. She had only gone a short way when she found some she must have missed earlier, carried it back and stoked the fire.

Billy was asleep. Looking at him, she felt the weight of the day upon her. It would not hurt to lie down for a moment and shut her eyes. Within moments, she was fast asleep. The boy returned to join them, soon all three were sound asleep and dreaming.

Stella 1.3

IN STELLA'S DREAM, she was walking to the park with her grandmother on a warm sunny day. It was nice, strolling along without a care in the world, holding her grandmother's warm, soft-skinned hand. They headed to the play area where Stella climbed onto a swing, her grandmother pushed her.

'Higher, higher,' she called out. The next minute, she was lying on the ground and her grandmother, amongst others, was looking down at her.

She woke with a start. The fire had burned down, but was still alight, the boy was fast asleep. Billy stirred but did not wake. Stella placed some more wood onto the fire. Soon it was burning brightly again. The sky was pitch black now. She wondered about U-boats and if they were they doing the wrong thing with the fire, placing themselves, possibly others, in danger. She dismissed the thought.

She looked at the boy, asleep next to his dog. He looked so peaceful. It was a lonely place at this time of night. As soon as they woke, she would ask him again to help her get the car started. She suddenly felt cold. Clutching her cardigan around her tightly, the fire was inviting, she almost lay down again. She considered waking them up, but could not bring herself to do it. They were too peaceful.

She let her mind drift back to happier times, when they had decided to start a family. Skippy was so excited; they built a new house to prepare. Hours were spent drawing up plans. It was fun, bringing them closer together. Employing an architect, they had their rudimentary drawings, turned into plans. Skippy had always wanted a swimming pool like the movie star houses in Hollywood. Stella enjoyed tennis, so they indulged, including both a pool and tennis court. They found a builder and a lot, big enough to build everything on.

Every night after dinner, they drove out to the work site to check on the progress. Those were exciting times, they were both absorbed, united in the same goal. Everything was new, the smells were intoxicating. It took every cent of their savings and a mortgage to realise their dream. When it was finished, the house was so big they needed to employ a housekeeper and a gardener to help look after it. Stella kept working well into her pregnancy. One goal was achieved, another had seemed within reach until the baby died. After a brief convalescence, she simply went back to work. The years passed, they paid off the mortgage, the nursery remained the only unpainted room in the house.

Stella wanted to sell the house and move back into an apartment, perhaps in a new city. Their money sat in the bank, growing without purpose. She wondered if that is what her life would forever now be.

She reflected on her relationship with her husband, wondering why she married him. Why him? What was so special about him? The thought made her smile, which was an answer itself. They had been introduced to each other by a friend. She had accepted an invitation from him to the theatre after talking to him for half an hour on the phone. He picked her up at her apartment, they went to dinner first and later they had enjoyed coffee before he dropped her off at her door. They kissed goodnight; it was not overly romantic, but it was nice.

On the second date, he started to talk about his childhood. Both of his parents had passed away. His father had been a businessman who was killed in an auto accident; his mother never recovered from the loss and soon joined him. He was passed around relatives until he was old enough to join the navy. After three years he qualified for study assistance and went to university, grateful he remained a naval reservist after he graduated.

He held a good job as an engineer with a power company. With no family, he had no issue about travelling, so the company he worked for sent him far and wide. Stella liked him enough to go on a third date, after which he didn't call for a week. She put him out of her mind and was on another date with someone else when she saw him with another woman. Seeing him with someone else sparked jealousy within her. All the next day, she found herself thinking about him. *Was that it?* she wondered. Was her entire life built upon that, or was she selling herself short. She searched her feelings for answers but none came.

She engineered their next meeting, phoning him with the excuse of needing help with a new sofa. He came over on a Saturday afternoon to help her. Afterwards, she made them both lunch, enjoying each other's company they went for a walk. Stella turned on the charm and, feeling brash, she invited him out to dinner, after which they went for a drive. From then on, they started to date more seriously.

A year later, they were married back in her hometown, with a honeymoon in Cuba. Stella continued working in the city library. Skippy, as she had started to call him, was working as an engineer at a power company. Sitting in front of the fire, she recalled the little things, like watching him work in the garage of their home or watching him coach Little League baseball. Seeing him work with the boys, warmed her heart.

Stella had trained as a schoolteacher, teaching third graders, until she found the job in the city library. This job allowed her to combine teaching with her love of books.

When she fell pregnant, they were already ensconced in their new house. Friends visited, they barbequed, they swam in the pool, they were so close to being complete, sharing it with the people they would spend the rest of their lives with. When the baby died, people rallied around. It was good to have so many people care about them.

As time passed and Stella did not become pregnant again, one by one, the friends drifted away. They were all establishing families of their own and they now began to move in different circles. Keith stopped coaching the Little League boys; he started working longer hours and Stella did the same, often leaving the library long after it had closed. They rarely ate dinner together during the week, both now worked Saturdays. On Saturday nights, they went through the motions of going out, normally to the movies and for Chinese food.

Jean remained a friend. They had known each other the longest, but even Jean was more distant than she had been before and they never discussed anything relating to the death of the baby. She would drop by and catch up on the gossip or Jean would visit her for lunch. Jean would profess to be envious, but it was Stella who was envious of Jean, as their friends' children became teenagers, the gap between them became larger. Stella lost all hope of a family of her own.

She wondered if he was unfaithful but had never seen or heard anything. Stella had been guilty of thought crime but had never acted on it. There was a man who worked in the library, the deputy director, who she occasionally had lunch with. She thought to herself that he would make an ideal candidate.

Her assessment was, she had married Keith because they were a good match. She had feelings for him but, as the years went by, their intimate moments were less and less frequent and less intense. She had perhaps pushed him into it, trapping him when he became disinterested. Now they were financially independent, shared similar views and values and for a long time held similar goals, but their lives had no purpose. She had let them down, she felt, by losing the child. Not entirely, but by not being able to fall pregnant again, then by not pushing hard enough to adopt. But should she take all the blame? He had never gone beyond saying things like, we can adopt, to calm her when she was upset. He had never done a single thing to bring it about.

After Pearl Harbour, when his papers had arrived to report for active duty, he was the happiest she had seen him in years. He had faced opposition because the work he performed was designated essential. Initially, the navy agreed, but they needed trained men like him. A deal was struck. The navy would keep using him initially and then send him back when they had increased numbers, or if he was urgently needed. When she dropped him off at the train station, he was excited. Under those conditions, he was meant to remain based stateside, but things could be changed and, before Stella or anybody else had time to react, he was at sea and in action.

Apart from some teenage infatuation, she had never experienced anything like the feelings she had seen on the silver screen in the movies that she loved. When she was younger, she had wondered when she would meet someone and fall madly in love. She had never met her Prince Charming. Would she have married Keith or even have gone out with him if he had, for example, been an unemployed motor mechanic? The answer was 'No'. Unlike the women in the movies, who fell head over heels for a man, even if he turned out to be a murderer or worse, she had never been so enamoured with anyone. Had Keith decided to rob banks or gamble all their money at the racetrack, she could not have run far enough away.

There had been a boy in her high school, Tommy Parker, she had melted the first time she saw him. Captain of the football team with his own car, she had caught his eye and they dated briefly, but it didn't last. Although he was the first boy she ever kissed, she soon tired of him and was happy when he caught the eye of another girl. Her friends were more upset than she was; Stella never cried a single tear.

She wondered what the future held for her now. The prospect of continuing a life without Keith was more than she could bear. It had been bad enough living a pointless existence with him. Her mind fell silent as she considered this, a life in that big house with just the housekeeper and gardener, until she retired. Plenty of money in the bank, but nothing to spend it on. If she sold the house, she would have even more money than she knew what to do with. Should she move back to her hometown? Maybe travel the world on cruise ships? What if he did return one day? What then? Would he just go straight back to work? Would they simply carry on as before until they retired? He could then spend his days on the golf course, she could volunteer somewhere, and they could keep out of each other's way.

Had he left her when she had taken him to the train station, or had they left each other years earlier? Stella wondered why they had never fought to keep their marriage alive, but it only depressed her further. That was a simple one to answer, there had been many opportunities to discuss things, to sort all those issues out, but they had never taken up on any opportunities to do so. It was that further proof of the lack of love. Had their relationship been meaningless or was that the only way to cope with the loss she felt? The irrational notion of leaving the one you loved to go to war.

How had Skippy felt about things? Were their weekly encounters meaningless? Had he felt the same or was he confused? Even with no male role models of his own, he had been a very good husband. Had she suffered such a deep depression that he simply could not pull her out of it? There had been good times, fun times, she recalled the time when he took her to dinner and asked her to marry him, down on one knee in the crowded restaurant. Later, they had made love in her apartment, they were very intimate moments. What about the times he had sent flowers to her work or dropped by without warning? He had never strayed, never abandoned her.

He had been patient. Maybe adoption was just too hard for him after living like an orphan himself, maybe she should have pushed him. There were so many what ifs, too many regrets.

In their house somewhere there was a list, a list neither had tried to find since that day. On one side of the page were girls names, on the other, boys. Next to each, there was an initial placed by the person who entered it, next to any they both liked was an asterisk. That list was their last happy memory. It had disappeared by the time Stella returned from hospital. Maybe Keith, maybe the housekeeper, had removed it. Perhaps they had planned to return to it one day.

The boy slept on, a peaceful expression on his face. She wondered what he was dreaming about. Worn out, she laid back down joining him.

Stella 1.4

WHEN SHE AWOKE again, the sun was sneaking over the horizon. She looked for the boy and saw him paddling at the water's edge. When she called him, he came running.

'What do you say, can you help me with my car? I'll buy you breakfast, pancakes, bacon anything you like?'

The boy considered the proposal.

'I think the fish might be biting now. Let's wait.'

'I can't wait any longer, it's time I was leaving. If we can't start the car, I need to walk back to town.' The disappointment she felt at his refusal, infiltrated her voice. He looked troubled as if that was not acceptable.

'I'm going now.'

She picked up her things and started towards her car. He waited for a moment, then ran after her, with Billy following close behind. She was determined now, walking with great purpose. *One way or another,* she thought, *it was time to leave.*

The car was heavy and proved difficult to move. Looking around in vain, she wondered when, or if, someone would come along. Finally, by rocking the car back and forth, they managed to get it onto the asphalt. She sighed with relief and took a moment to rest before straightening it and getting ready for the jump start.

'Okay, you push from the rear; I'll push from here at the door. When we get up some speed, I'll jump in and pop the clutch.'

He seemed to be in a darker mood. She had given up trying to learn his name, hoping he might finally open up to her and talk to her over breakfast. She liked the boy; he had continued to grow on her. If he did have nowhere to stay, maybe he could come and stay with her. There was plenty of room with Keith away.

They pushed with all their might. When they had built up some speed, she jumped in, put the car in gear and popped the clutch. Sure enough, it fired into life. A broad smile opened on Stella's face. Triumphant, she performed a three-point turn, then returned to where the boy and Billy waited. She pulled over, already tasting the pancakes and fresh coffee.

'Jump in,' she called.

Just as the boy was about to climb aboard, the car sputtered and went dead. *Darn,* she thought, *it must be cold.* She turned the key and it burst back into life, then sputtered and died. She looked at the fuel gauge. Empty. That was odd, she had filled up just a few miles back, this was frustrating. In an instant, she had figured it out.

'I bet, while we were asleep on the beach, someone came along, found the car and took the gas. Oh well, we'll just have to walk back to town.'

The boy seemed almost happy at this.

'We can wait. In an hour or so the fishermen will start to arrive, one of them will have a fuel can or will drive us. Here, we should push your car back off the road.'

Stella was reluctant, but felt it might be the best option and took her position near the door. They manoeuvred the car back into roughly the same place they had started from. She felt deflated.

'Let's head back to the beach,' said the boy who seemed to have woken up and was now almost cheerful.

'No, let's wait here. We may still have to walk and get it ourselves.' She sat in the driver's seat, legs facing out through the door, dawn breaking. They waited and, sure enough, a pickup truck appeared, a

Ford. It parked just across from them. Stella stood up and waved. A man and a girl, about eleven or twelve, climbed out. The man eyed the car suspiciously, Stella called out.

'Hello.' No response. 'Hello sir, I hate to bother you.'

The man circled the car ignoring her. She went close to him, the girl looked scared.

'Sir, can you hear me, sir?'

Then suddenly the boy was by her side. 'It's no use, they can't hear you.'

'What do you mean? He's standing in front of me, I could touch him.' She reached out and for the first time, she noticed there was something attached to the tailpipe. She went over, bent down and looked closely. It was a hose. She followed it and saw it went into the passenger side window.

The man was looking at the hose as well. He looked at the girl and was concerned. He could see nobody around. Maybe he should get back into his truck and go get the sheriff.

'They see what they want to see and hear what they want to hear. We do the same,' said the boy.

This triggered something inside her. Suddenly, it came flooding back: memories, fragments at first, then solid. She had received a letter from a man on the same ship as her husband. He had survived and written, saying that Keith had given up his place in the lifeboat for another, how he had clung to the side, how he had been gone when someone checked on him, how they had searched after they had been rescued, to no avail.

Another memory came to her, even more horrible. Preparing the basket with her favourite sandwiches, driving to the beach, filling the gas tank all the way to the top, flirting with the pump attendant, removing and attaching the hose, the darkness, the coughing, staggering out of the car. All on instinct. She must reach the water, must reach her beloved Skippy.

Running, she headed for the path to the beach. The boy called out, ran and tried to stop her.

'Wait, no.'

Billy was barking excitedly. She ran onto the sand in anguish. Everything was a blur and there it was, the answer lying on the sand. Stella fell onto her knees.

Stella 1.5

$\mathcal{S}$TELLA SAT ON the sand with the boy and Billy. She had watched the man run back up the path, shielding the girl from the gruesome sight. She watched as first a policeman, then an ambulance and finally an undertaker, arrived.

The events came flooding back to her now, replaying slowly through her fragile mind. She had been feeling unwell and decided to phone in sick at work. She noticed the mailman arrive from a downstairs window. Not wanting to interact with anyone, she waited until he had finished before going out to check the box. There was a big pile of mail. She flicked through it and stopped at a small nondescript envelope. She did not recognise the sender. She carried the mail over to her porch. Sitting down on the step, she opened the letter and started to read. It was from a man who had been with her husband after his ship was sunk. She read and re-read the letter.

Taking it with her, she went back into the house in a daze. She had made the sandwiches and taken a shower, before leaving the house. After packing, she took one last look around. Noticing the garden hose, an evil idea formed; she stood perfectly still while in a struggle.

Shaking, she picked it up, packing it into the car. On her way to the beach, she had stopped twice to re-read the letter. Each time it said the same thing, there was no mistake. The cool water of the Atlantic had attracted her, she felt that it brought them closer. Stoically, she stared, memories overwhelming her. A stop at a diner to eat pancakes, toast and bacon, filling up the car, arriving and sitting, waiting, a final reading of the letter, tears. Attaching the hose to the car exhaust, sealing it with a scarf, a final prayer, the engine running, smoke filling the interior, feeling overcome, changing her mind, a glimpse of hope, clutching, scratching for the door, trying to suck in fresh air, realising it was too late, staggering down to the beach. They carried her body away; the scene was once again empty, as if she had never been there.

Looking up for the first time, she noticed them. There were people walking out of the ocean, a steady stream of them. Stella wondered why she hadn't noticed them before. She looked at the boy. *We see what we want to see,* he had said. Now she understood what he meant.

'Do you see them, Stella?'

'Yes, where do they come from?' Stella asked.

'I don't know, but lately there have been more and more of them.'

Somebody walked past, very close to them, a man wearing a life preserver. He did not glance at them, just continued straight up the path. Stella did not weep; she had chosen her fate. The boy was watching the people emerging from the ocean closely.

'Who taught you how to fish?' she asked.

'Nobody, one day the idea just appeared in my mind. I came to the beach where I found this rod and tackle bag.'

'What about the BB Gun?'

'I had a dream a nice man took me hunting, showed me how to use it. When I woke up, this gun was here in a box, wrapped up with a bow on it and a card.'

A memory came to Stella. She had purchased a BB gun as a gift. Stella had developed a habit of buying gifts for the child who never was, later giving them away. But this was preposterous.

'How long have you been here in the dunes.'

'Always.'

'Why? Do you have any idea why?'

'I'm waiting.'

'Waiting for what?'

There was no response just a long pause, then he said, 'In this place, we see what we want to see, hear what we want to hear. Time passes differently. One thing doesn't necessarily follow the other, everything may seem confusing and mixed up but in the end it all makes sense.'

They sat in silence for a long time. People continued emerging from the water. As the day wore on, others came to the beach, none of them seemed to notice them. The boy never grew restless or wandered off, Billy stayed by his side the entire time. They felt no hunger nor thirst. Stella realised these things she had experienced because she had wanted to, in effect she had been lying to herself. The boy did not catch fish because he did not need to, however, had he wanted to, he could have caught as many as he liked. A man walked out of the waves and strode up the beach; he was barefooted. Unlike the others, he was looking straight at them, his clothes were soaked but she recognised the uniform. A yellow life preserver hung around his neck. He removed it, throwing it onto the sand.

'You said the gun was wrapped with a card attached.' 'Yes.'

'What did the card say.?'

They repeated the words together.

'For our special boy on his birthday, with love, PS be careful.'

The man had stopped in front of them. Stella looked up and was greeted by a familiar smile!

Stella 1.6

S KIPPY STOOD BEFORE her again as she had dreamed he one day would. Although it was far from the reunion she had envisaged, they were together and nothing else mattered. Turning to the boy she looked at him with different eyes.

'Can you tell me your name now?' He shook his head.

'I was never given one.'

Skippy unbuttoned his shirt pocket, took out a folded piece of paper and handed it to Stella. She unfolded the missing list of names they had made while awaiting the birth of their child. She quickly scanned it, noticing for the first time that although several of the girl's names were joint favourites, only one of the boy's names was. Smiling as all the pieces fell into place, she read the name.

'Charlie.'

He smiled, joined hands with them, then, as a bright light appeared, led them into the dunes.

Tanya 1.20

*T*ANYA WOKE UP with a condition akin to a hangover, The dream was so clear, as if it were real, burned into her brain as if she was there, the events happening to her. It was an unforgettable, incredible story. Just the thought of Stella brought tears to her eyes, yet there was happiness. She could feel it. Stella was reunited with her family, though tragic as that was, it was something. There was hope.

Mrs Giles was seated in the armchair, reading, a small light attached to her book the only illumination in the room. 'How are you feeling?'

Tanya thought carefully before responding. 'Much the same.'

'You slept peacefully eventually. It took some time, but then you were as quiet as a church mouse.'

'I dreamed.'

Mrs Giles nodded.

'I sensed that. Are you hungry, would you like some breakfast?'

'Yes, please. Some muffins with jam and some tea.'

Mrs Giles phoned the kitchen to place the order.

'Tanya, will you be alright if I leave you for a short time? Your mother should be here any minute and some maids will bring the breakfast up shortly.'

'Yes, thank you, Mrs Giles. Thank you for sitting with me last night.' It felt unusual to suddenly be alone again, even after days of solitude.

Breakfast arrived and she climbed out of bed. She took her time realising she was on the precipice mentally. She could go either way.

There was a knock at the door. She had no time to answer it as her mother and the general swept into the room. Her mother hugged her, but the biggest hug and outpouring of affection, surprisingly, for her came from the general, who practically promised to travel to Afghanistan and find Evan himself. They insisted Tanya begin eating while they placed their own orders for breakfast. The kitchen staff were fast and soon all three were enjoying their meals.

'Now listen Tanya,' the general spoke, adopting his more formal tone, 'you have received a great shock. The only thing for it is rest. Now, I have been in contact with all the right people and I can assure you that everything that can be done is being done for our poor boy out in the field. You leave all that business to your mother and me to worry about, you continue to rest.'

Tanya was overcome by the emotion that their generosity evoked from in her. As tears ran down her cheeks she spoke, 'Thank you both for coming, thank you for caring.'

It was all she could manage without completely breaking down. They chatted, though conversation was difficult. A doctor arrived and the general and her mother gave her some privacy. Just a precaution, they assured her. The doctor, a nice young lady roughly Tanya's age, took her blood pressure. She told her that her name was Monica, she would be available twenty-four hours a day for as long as she was required. She was friendly. It gave Tanya a level of comfort knowing someone who might understand her better was involved in her care. She trusted her, even though they had just met.

'Tanya, would you consent to a mild sedative, just something to take the edge off, give you a bit of a break from things, say four hours max?'

Tanya liked this approach, there wasn't much to consider. 'Yes.'

'Then you just head off to the bathroom, jump into bed and I'll administer it there.'

The sedative worked quickly. Within minutes, Tanya's eyes were fluttering and before too long she entered a deep sleep and, once again, her mind opened. She fell headfirst into another powerful dream.

Helga 1.1

THE THREE BOYS stood on the muddy soccer field with their mother. Each of them feeling slightly embarrassed, even though there was nobody else around. The boys were wearing football uniforms and boots as they took soccer practice very seriously. The jerseys were bright green, for the colours of the club they supported, rather than the club they played for. It was an impromptu session called by their mother, because, based on recent efforts, they needed it.

Soccer was a skill that could be learned, she told herself. She was dressed in a track suit and looked the part, was also wearing a pair of soccer boots. A pair that had once belonged to the boys' father. He had played soccer, or football, all his life. This she had told them repeatedly. People at their club remembered him and they were proud of this.

Their father had gone missing on the Eastern Front while serving in the German Army, sometime in 1944. Hans, the eldest, now sixteen, was only five back then. He had no memories of his father. It was on his list of things that embarrassed him. Jonah was a year younger, born in 1940 and Christian, the youngest, was the happy outcome of a visit home his father made when wounded in 1942. That wound was very severe. It should have seen him discharged from the army. They were surprised when he received his orders to return to his unit. Helga had encouraged him to find a way to escape to Switzerland. He had a sister there they could stay with. It proved impossible.

Helga held a football instruction book in her left hand, the boys all wanted to leave.

'Okay,' she said taking control, 'Chris, you go into the goal. Jonah your place is just outside the box ready to strike, Hans, come.'

They walked over to where the corner post would be, from his position on the right wing. Hans was expected to take the corner kicks for his team.

'Now, place the ball.'

'It's no use,' Hans said, 'somebody else should take them. I can't do it.'

Helga understood her son's frustrations, but she could not let him give up on himself so easily.

'I'll tell you what,' she said, 'if I can bend one, anyone can. How about I take the first shot? Remember, our target is Jonah, not the goal.'

Hans looked around, worried they were being watched. 'Okay,' he said nervously, taking another quick look around.

Helga lined up the ball with her right foot, walked back a few paces, ran and kicked it straight up the field towards the halfway line.

They both laughed.

'Best two out of three,' she said.

Jonah kicked the ball back to them and she lined up again. This time, she closed her eyes and tried to remember a corner kick. She had seen hundreds in her life, surely it could not be that hard. The image came to her, she visualised it. She had competed in athletics as a sprinter when she was a teenager and a coach had taught her to do this. When the vision was clear, she ran up, this time on a slight angle. When she kicked the ball, she twisted her foot and to their combined amazement, it sailed through the air, curved, landing not far from Jonah, who captured it and fired it at the goal. It was not perfect, but it was a million times better than the first one and Hans could see the possibilities.

'How did you do that?' he said.

Helga smiled. If Hans was embarrassed, or had any doubts, they had disappeared. She patiently explained it all, talking him through the visualisation method and how to time his kick. After a dozen attempts, he could land them almost at Jonah's feet. Most importantly, he was smiling. Each of the boys had their turn, working on a skill. Then they had a quick two on two game, before they cycled back home for some lunch.

When the war was over, they were amongst the lucky ones, because they were alive. The Americans, who occupied their sector, treated them well while remaining aloof. Every able-bodied person was expected to help clean up the rubble and that was all they did. The children came with them and played as the adults slowly worked. There was nothing else to do. Food was in abundance for the first time in years, there was no threat of arrest or death. People were happier, Helga thought, happier than they had been for a long time. Her house was damaged, as were most of the buildings in the town. Slowly, as materials became available, working at their own pace, little by little, they put it all back together.

One day in 1948 a small postcard arrived from the Red Cross. Written on it was a message that read, 'Alfred Zimmerman, Prisoner USSR.' followed by a reference number.

He was alive, but they had heard nothing more.

He had been a carpenter while Helga worked in the town bookstore. Her parents had owned the bakery. Her brother had taken it over when they had retired to a small villa in the Alps. They were all gone now: her parents caught in crossfire at war's end, her brother and his entire family killed when a bomb broke through the roof and concrete floor, then exploding in the basement of the bakery where they were hiding. She now owned the abandoned burnt-out villa of her parents and the site where the bakery had once stood.

Those thoughts led to only one place and the tears came freely; the loneliness was crippling and she longed for adult company. Alfred's sister was only a short trip away, but they had never been close. Now he was missing, there was no connection. The days were long, although she put on a brave face. When the boys were not there, she would sit alone in a darkened room in a near catatonic state. He was alive, that was comforting in one way, but haunting in another. Horrible stories of the prisoners' treatment were rife. Surviving would be another thing. She hated to think of him suffering. She had no idea where he was. When she had travelled to Berlin to visit the Soviet Embassy, they laughed at her. A woman, dressed in a uniform covered with medals, told her she would never see him again. Heartbroken, she returned home. Loneliness brought reflection, like many Germans she had many regrets about the war. For the years wasted, for the damage they had done, the endless guilt. What had she ever done to deserve him back?

When the owners of the bookstore, where she worked, disappeared, she knew, as much as anyone, what had happened to them. They were nice people, had given her a job, encouraged her, got her out of the boring old bakery. Estelle was like a second mother. She took Helga shopping, helped her choose clothes, treated her like a daughter, giggled with her at the Hollywood gossip magazines like a sister. Frank was a father figure, patient, wise. He taught her everything about the business. She was the surrogate for the childless couple.

Then the shop had all the windows broken. Her real parents had told her to stay at home, to not become involved. There was fear in their eyes as they told her this. She defied them but became scared. She looked for them, but they were gone, disappeared, and the shop was closed. She hoped they had fled, gone to Britain or America, but deep down she knew the truth, everyone did. They were in a forced labour camp somewhere, their assets confiscated and nobody had better say anything. Nobody did, including her. This depressed her.

Helga went back to the bakery, back to her real parents. She loved them, but she missed Frank and Estelle. Just after she turned eighteen, she met her husband and moved into the house he had built Those were happy times. Her twenty-first birthday was spent alone after he joined the army. He went to the front for the first time the year Hans was born. The other two were conceived on brief trips home. She spent her days wondering a thousand times, how he was. How many innocent lives had he taken? That was a dark thought. She tried to avoid it, but it persisted. Even darker was the thought of how many, through her own inactivity, she had caused.

Helga pondered other things, like why Alfred had joined the army in the first place. He was a carpenter and could have done things to remain at home, pulled strings, done essential war work. Tradesmen like him were in short supply. They could have taken more extreme measures, run away, hidden up in the mountains. What was this need to be a part of it all? What business did they have as a nation invading those countries, forcing their will on others? Alfred was her husband, but he left her alone to go off and be a part of this foolishness. Should she divorce him, claim he had abandoned her or that he was dead? The Russians certainly didn't seem to care. Her mind was racing, she could not focus.

At the end of the war, she had tried to find out who had killed her friends, Frank and Estelle Weinstein. Somebody must know, she thought. She was wrong. The mayor was not aware of any such arrests. In fact, out of everyone who lived in their town, she was the only one who knew anything and she knew little. It was ridiculous. Her friend, Hannah, made a breakthrough. She found a man who, for a price, would tell all, a man who claimed to have been there when they disappeared. She decided that even if the story would haunt her always, she had to hear it. Hannah had arranged for the man meet them in the park in the middle of the town. They found him sitting on a bench alone. There were no introductions, they sat either side of him.

'I know what happened to your friends as I was there,' he claimed, restating what Hannah had learned.

He did not speak again until Helga opened her bag and handed him an envelope containing the money they had promised. He accepted it without counting it. As he did this, Helga noticed, for the first time, that he only had one arm. There was no small talk.

'They were the only Jews left in our town, the only Jews anywhere nearby.' He said this in a matter-of-fact manner, completely devoid of emotion. 'I was new to the party, eager to prove myself.'

Hannah and Helga looked at each other. Helga was going numb, she could feel her blood temperature dropping, every part of her body ached. She twisted in her seat.

He continued, 'Our job was to cause disruption for all Jewish houses of business. We smashed windows, painted a star of David on the door and placed a guard outside to prevent people coming in. There was nobody else left in this town. We were also unsure of whether people would join us or would they become angry. We wanted a riot, to drag them off in front of everyone, to make a spectacle. But somebody must have tipped them off, because they ran and hid in the church.'

The women were horrified.

'From there it became complicated. At first, we negotiated with the clergy, then an SS officer arrived. This man was more experienced than us; he simply threatened to burn down the church with everyone inside Of course, after the priest realised he was serious, they were handed over.'

He laughed at the memory. They felt dirty, he sensed this and laughed harder, savouring the moment.

Helga spoke, 'You took them to a camp?'

'No, we had other plans for them. You must understand, we were embarrassed by them. We loaded them onto a truck and drove them out to the forest.'

He hesitated, starting to realise he was about to admit something evil, something he had done, a crime and in front of a witness. *Would there be consequences?* he wondered.

Regaining his courage, he continued, 'We ordered them off the truck and then, well, if you look hard enough, you will find them, or rather what's left of them. I'll let your imagination fill in the details.'

Helga almost fainted. This man was truly evil. That he, and those like him, walked free, was wrong.

The next few days passed in a blur, as she struggled to come to terms with everything. Hans' team played well the following Saturday. A goal was scored from one of his corner kicks, but they lost 3-2. Jonah's team was lucky, Chris' lost, but the boys were more confident. On Sunday they went fishing.

Helga 1.2

$\mathcal{H}$ELGA HAD HELPED the boys learn an incredible number of things. Anything that caught their interest, through careful research, then trial and error, she learned herself, then in turn taught them. From kicking a soccer ball, to catching a fish, or solving mathematical problems, Helga found a way. Emotionally, she taught them to deal with their feelings, develop relationships and cope with the problems of life. Her boys were resilient and strong, their minds open, they were emotionally and spiritually aware. She noticed they were different to many of their peers. Helga could see it different in a good way, a better way. They had great empathy for all people, all things.

A young couple came to the town looking for a location to build a supermarket. The mayor, an enthusiastic supporter of the project, took them to see Helga. She had deliberately not done anything with the old bakery site, avoiding the place. The subject, along with its horrors, was taboo, its ghosts pushed out of her mind. Now, confronted with an opportunity to bring about closure to that episode in her life, she surprised herself with how quickly she made her decision. Within the time it took to drink one cup of coffee, before they had even finished their initial discussion, she had decided to sell. Just like that, the business and home that had been purchased by her great grandfather, that held so many of her family's memories, was gone. Those memories, that history, it would all die with her.

Helga wanted to move house, she wanted to live outside the town, a bigger house with a few acres of land, possibly close to the forest near their favourite swimming spot. The boys could cycle to school, they were old enough to be able to. She had never been overly fond of the house her husband had built. There were plans for additions that were never completed, Helga and the boys had to make do with a house that was built with three people in mind. She remained there with the knowledge that he was alive, yet may never return.

She would leave the house, but she would maintain it. Then one day, if he returned, he could decide its fate, or if not, then one of the boys could live in it. She started to look around for somewhere to live. With her penchant for avoiding things painful, she stayed away from the house owned by the Weinsteins. That home was one of the finest. The main building set in beautiful walled gardens on two acres, twenty minutes from the centre of town. It was confiscated and a party official had taken it and lived there until the end of the war. Then the American commanding officer had lived there, but the Americans had now departed and it sat empty.

The year 1955 was a landmark one for Germany. The occupation ended in May. One day, a large brown envelope arrived that changed everything, a new chapter in Helga's story was about to be told. The envelope sat on the kitchen table, a phone call was placed to Hannah, who came straight over. Helga brewed coffee, now they both sat staring at the envelope silently while they drank. Helga could not imagine what the envelope contained, but she could not face it alone. She was grateful Hannah was there.

'It is time, open it,' Hannah said. 'I can't, it can only be bad news.'

'Bad or good, we will deal with it.'

'Please Hannah, you open it for me?'

Hannah picked up the thick, heavy envelope and opened it. There was a letter with a cheque pinned to the back and three thick documents. Hannah read them, then a smile appeared on her face, growing brighter the further she read.

'Well?' said Helga.

'There's a lot to take in.'

'Okay give me a moment.'

Helga drank her coffee, her anxiety growing.

'You're the sole heir of the Weinstein's estate.' Helga was confused. 'Here read this.'

Hannah handed Helga an official looking letter. Pinned to it was an explanatory note. Shaking, Helga began to read:

When the US military moved out of their home, it had triggered an investigation into who the owners of the Weinstein villa were. A search of official records uncovered that ownership was transferred to the state. This transfer was found to be illegal; it was ordered to be transferred back to the original owners or their heirs, along with all other property and assets. The owners being deceased, a search was conducted.

No living relatives were located, however, a search of records at three local solicitors uncovered a will dated 15th June 1936. This document confirms you as the sole heir. In the absence of an executor, the State Solicitor General has acted as executor and the will probated. You will also find attached a cheque, which is assessed compensation for the missing items of the estate, including stock and fittings from the bookstore, and missing furniture and paintings from the villa, the whereabouts of which are unknown.

The amount of 8,000 deutschmarks, taken from their bank account, details of two bank accounts, both located in Switzerland, are detailed in the last will and testament and must be privately followed up by you. Any state taxes or levies payable are waived by the state.

Helga was dumbfounded. She went through the documents locating the will. As she read it, the Weinsteins seemed to reach out to her from beyond the grave. Touched, she wept as she read. They were leaving the business to her in the hope she would carry on their work, making books available, promoting literature and preserving their legacy. She wondered at the wealth they had amassed. She realised then that she did not know much about their earlier life.

There were documents to fill out and forms that required signatures. In the bottom they found keys. Helga cycled to the house alone. Hannah had some things to do but promised to be available the following day to help with anything she needed. The gate was padlocked so she searched the keys for a match. She opened the gate just wide enough to go inside and locked it behind her, then walked up the drive pushing her bicycle. The gardens were already showing the need for some work, it would keep them busy she thought. Helga hesitated at the front door. Ghosts were waiting inside. She had promised herself there would be no tears, but that proved too hard. Memories flooded to the surface; it was with great strength that she opened the door. She wandered through the empty rooms. Here and there was a piece of furniture, some wallpaper, echoes from the past. There was not much. The paintings that once hung from the walls were gone, the outlines of which could be seen where they had been. The home she had known was gone. Maybe that was a good thing, the memories were strong and she was fragile.

She sat on the stairs, soaking it all in. Why try to make sense of the world? *I will only go insane,* she thought. Her benefactors took on a new life within her mind. She would fulfill their wishes; their dreams would live on in her. She would rebuild their book shop, books would return to the town, the place that had betrayed then ultimately killed them.

Their legacy would live on, perhaps an annual literary prize, or something, anything. But it must live on. Those senseless deaths must remain in their minds to help prevent it from ever happening again. If this angered people, she would deal with it. She wanted to start straight away. She would gather the boys and bring them here; they would move immediately. Helga had money now, she could employ people to help. The house would be given a new lease of life; it would become their home. She would share it with her boys, but not at the monument. It was time to move forward, to climb out of the grave they were trapped in.

With a vigour that bred excitement to all around her, Helga led the boys, along with Hannah, to the new home. She hired plumbers, gardeners, electricians, painters and carpenters, infecting them with the same enthusiasm. The boys pitched in to help, while she directed everyone. In just a few short weeks of hard work, they had a new home. Max Steiner was not a person Helga would seek out, a short man with a limp. During the war he had worn a long black leather coat and he had exuded evil. A high- ranking party member who was excused from active service, he was rumoured to have met Hitler once. Helga loathed him. The boys had left for school and Helga was pottering around the garden. She was on her knees, pulling up some weeds, when she looked up and there he was. The allies had arrested him after the war, yet no charges had ever been laid. He escaped the hangman's noose or a long jail term and had stayed in the town. Many, including Helga, had hoped he would leave. He was a dark reminder of a past they longed to leave behind.

When he smiled, a chill went down her spine. 'Frau Zimmerman,' he said, looking down at her. She was curt with him.

'Herr Steiner, how can I help you?'

'I will come right to the point,' he said. 'I have a somewhat a delicate matter to discuss with you, is there somewhere we could go?'

Helga got up off her knees and was now looking down on him, it gave her more courage.

'No, I think here will do.'

He suddenly looked sheepish for a brief moment. She thought he was going to run away.

'Well?' she said being outwardly rude to him. He cleared his throat.

'There is a rumour, that you will re-open the "Jew" bookstore?'

'No that is incorrect, Herr Steiner. I am re-opening The Bookstore, the bookstore that had been in our town for years, until you and your friends closed it.'

'Come Frau Zimmerman, we were all in it together, all on the one side.'

'Don't throw me in with you and your kind, there's no blood on my hands.'

'Frau Zimmerman,' he began.

She cut him off, 'Are you serious? You come here and threaten me because I'm opening a bookstore. Does it hurt that much? Did you never go to the bookstore? Have you ever read a book?'

'It was a symbol.'

'The Weinsteins never harmed anyone; tell me one thing they ever did.'

'They owned the bookstore.' This made Helga laugh.

'You imbecile, I can barely believe my ears. When your father was alive, did he believe that or did your mother, when she was teaching at the school? How is it that two intelligent people gave birth to such an ignorant moron? Well, you had better get used to it, because the "Bookstore" will re-open and it will bear their name and if you, or any of your idiot friends interfere in any way, I'll call in the police.'

'That's very noble Frau Zimmerman, but you and your boys have to live in this town. You may find you have less friends than you imagine.'

'No Herr Steiner, I think it is you who will be surprised and don't threaten my boys. If my husband were here, he would beat you, for what you have said.'

'Are you sure? Besides, he is not here. Good day, Frau Zimmerman.' She should not have said that. Why involve her husband? Her argument lost weight. The exchange unnerved her, she returned to the house and made herself a cup of tea. Were people still like this? Had nothing changed? She dwelt on it; it made her angry. Helga felt even lonelier than normal. Where was he, her husband? Why was he not here? She scolded herself. Why did she always run to him to solve her problems, run to him for protection? Consumed with anger, she hurled the teacup at the wall and placed her head in her hands on the table.

Someone cleared their throat. 'Excuse me.'

She looked up and a man was standing in the kitchen.

'Sorry to bother you, the door was open. I was knocking, you might not have heard me.'

Helga was struck immediately by his good looks. There was instantly something about him that attracted her. She blushed. What was she thinking?

'Sorry I didn't hear you.'

'I'm very sorry, I hate to bother you, hate to impose, but I was cycling past when I got a puncture. I can't seem to find my repair kit. I noticed your bicycle and wondered if you might have a spare one I could borrow to repair it?'

He spoke fluent German, but his English accent was very profound. 'Yes of course. I'm sure we can find what you're looking for out in the shed.'

Whereas Steiner had made her nervous, this man made her feel at ease. *How could a stranger have that effect?* she thought. They walked across the lawn to the shed. Helga opened the door for him. He went in and looked around and quickly found what he was after.

'Ah this will do nicely.' He held up the puncture repair kit. 'You speak German very well, Herr.'

'Do forgive me, Colin, Colin Maxwell.'

'My name is Helga.'

She smiled demurely. What was she doing?

He walked over to where he had left his bicycle and started to work.

Helga followed him, it was sunny and pleasant outside. 'Lovely home you have here,' he said.

'Thank you, we have only recently moved in,' she said. 'How did you come to be in our part of the world, Herr Maxwell?'

'Please call me Colin.'

She smiled again. *This was becoming ridiculous,* she thought.

'During the war, I passed through here. I remember thinking it would be a great place to travel through one day in peace time. I had some time on my hands, so I thought, why not. All these towns, I only remember them as rubble. It's interesting to see them ten years later.'

'What did you do during the war?'

'I was an interpreter. I also wrote official records, took statements, wrote accounts, that sort of thing. I'm a journalist, I also studied French and German at university which helped with my war service.'

He was charming. The mundane details of an ordinary life sounded interesting when they came from him. He continued working on his bike.

'Do you have a bucket of water I can use, to check the tube?'

'Yes of course.'

Helga went back into the house and returned with a bucket of water. He pumped up the inner tube and held it in the bucket, took note of where the bubbles were coming out and marked it with a piece of chalk from the kit. Helga watched him work. She had seen a thousand punctures repaired from a lifetime of bicycle ownership, but what Colin was doing was suddenly fascinating. He roughed up the rubber, then applied the glue and the patch.

'Would you care to stay for lunch? I could make us some sandwiches, we could sit under the trees,' she asked him, pointing to a clump of trees in the garden.

He looked at her.

'That's awfully nice of you but won't your husband mind?'

'No,' she responded, 'I haven't see him for a long time.'

Colin nodded, bowing slightly. 'A picnic would be perfect.' He smiled as he said this.

Helga returned to the house to make the sandwiches. She had beer and lemonade in the refrigerator and placed them both into the picnic basket. By the time she came back out, he had the bike back together. She led him through the garden, past the flower beds to where there was a large pond. A small bridge led to an island and the trees. Helga laid out the blanket on the ground and brought out the sandwiches and drinks. Why did she feel so comfortable with this strange man?

'When I came in you seemed upset, very upset actually. Is there anything I could help with?'

'Before you arrived there was man here, a man who used to have–' She paused and looked around. The flowers were blooming and she decided it was too beautiful to discuss those things in such gorgeous surroundings. She wanted to choose her words carefully.

'A man who used to have some influence over things around here. He had heard a rumour and came to threaten me. He wants to exert his influence again, but I told him to go away or I would report him to the police. That, along with many other things, all built up into what you witnessed.'

Helga suddenly felt embarrassed. Throwing the cup at the wall now seemed very childish.

Colin took her hand in his and for a glorious, few seconds she could have fallen into his arms as she seemed to melt. She looked up, snapping out of it and gently let his hand go. It was beautiful here. She had been blessed. Words, what could either of them say after such a tender moment? They sat for a while enjoying the silence and the outdoors.

'I really should be going,' Colin finally said. 'Must you?'

Helga was again surprised by her response. It was unusual for her to think of herself, it seemed her subconscious was not willing to allow this opportunity to pass. She noticed his look of confusion. Was she misreading the signals? Or was he having doubts? *No,* she thought, *he had agreed to this intimate lunch picnic, hadn't he?*

'What happened to your husband?' he asked her.

'He's a prisoner of war in Russia. He went missing in 1944. We received a postcard a few years ago. I travelled to the Russian Embassy, but they laughed at me, they say that prisoners may be released now the occupation is over, but well, he may already be dead. I lie awake at night wondering where he is, I've been waiting for him for so long but I'm not sure that he is still alive.'

Only after she had made that last statement, she realised it was true and that she had been aware of it for some time.

'We were young when we married, it was a different world back then, the party, Hitler. My husband was a carpenter. He could have stayed home doing essential work, but he wanted to be a soldier, now when I think about it, I do not understand why he married me. He joined up, was promoted to corporal, he left for the front the year we had our first child, my eldest son Hans. I fell pregnant each time he came home on leave. I wrote every week until the end of the war. I waited for him, but he never returned, I knew he was on the Eastern Front, but I didn't know where. There are few records, fewer survivors, but as his death was never reported I held out hope. It is possible he is still alive somewhere in Russia held as a prisoner. We hear stories of camps, men have returned, are still returning, but who would he be now? I can't help but thinking that.'

He was struck by her honesty, fighting the urge to take her into his arms. Did true love really exist? Was it true that somewhere out there was the person you would meet and instantly fall in love with, a person you would immediately do anything for and who would do anything for you forever until your dying days? He was fascinated to see where this would lead. Would the day end with him riding off into the sunset or would it end somewhat differently?

Helga stood up. Framed in the sunlight, she looked even more beautiful.

'Will you stay to dinner?' she asked. 'Meet the boys?'

'Yes, yes of course, I'd love to. Do you think I'll be able to find a room in the town?'

'Let us worry about that later,' she said. 'Come, let us go back to the house.'

Colin spent the afternoon sitting in the study, writing in his diary for distraction and reading. Helga went back out to the garden until the boys arrived, then prepared dinner. Colin came out of the study to help her, The boys were shy at first, but soon warmed to him. They ate outside in the small courtyard garden. They played football on the lawn after dinner then a lively game of tag. Helga won, as she wove around them easily, staying a step or two in front of them and avoided capture until purposefully allowing Chris to tag her. It grew dark and they retreated into the house. Several times Colin stopped himself and asked if this was really happening.

'You will have to stay here with us tonight, Colin.' He looked at her, able to judge the meaning of the invitation by her expression. 'It's too late to find a room now. I'll make you up a bed in the study. You will be comfortable.'

'Most decent of you, I never expected to receive this much hospitality.'

They stayed up late, drinking schnapps; the boys went to bed leaving them alone.

They sat close together in the parlour but were wary of the proximity of the boys, so were careful.

'Sometimes I dream of a life away from here,' she confided, 'There are too many ghosts in this town. Perhaps in Berlin or Munich, in those places attitudes are changing, but here, they are sometimes still, well though I hate to say it, backward.'

'I know what you mean. Back home, things are also complicated. Everybody was touched, somehow, by the war. There is a lot of resentment, it is easing, yet I fear, that some of the people who have lived through it will never change their opinion. It may take fifty years or longer.'

Colin saw no point in sugar coating things. It was only fair to be honest, things were changing. Although the world was coming back to itself, things would, in his opinion never be the same.

'I've lived here my entire life, I have a purpose, but I will travel, in a few years, maybe five. I want to see the world, I have a few things to do first,' she told him.

'Where would you go?'

'Africa. I want to see where we have come from. Africa by way of Italy and Egypt, I remember that from the bookstore.'

'Bookstore?'

'Yes, the people who left me this house owned a bookstore in the town. I worked there before the war. I used to love to look at the books from Africa and Egypt, travel books, atlases, that sort of thing. Have you ever been to Africa?' she asked.

'No, I have been to Italy and most of Western Europe. I visited Spain as a child, but I don't remember it. I have travelled to America, the eastern states and the Caribbean Islands for the newspaper I work for. This current trip is meant to be a holiday, but an article or two might emerge.'

The hall clock had struck midnight when Helga went up the stairs to bed, she lay there fighting the urge to return downstairs. Helga also pondered the questions around true love. Did it really exist? Was this it or was it simply the primal urge of a woman who had been alone for so many years? Was the attraction simply nothing more than infatuation? If they did sleep together, would these feelings disappear moments after they finished? Her mind was racing. Did it really matter? If she went to him who need ever know? Then if this was something more, something truly wonderful, then let it happen, why die never knowing? Alfred was gone. She had a loyal faithful partner, was it fair to expect that she would wait for him forever? Helga's heart ached. Just being separated by only a few metres of stairs hurt. How would it feel when he left? There were too many questions, each one only made things worse.

Downstairs, Colin lay awake, his mind was also jumping all over the place. His feelings were tormenting him in the same way.

Helga was a married woman, though she gave the impression her marriage was over. Colin respected it, making it a difficult line for him to cross. *Live in the moment,* his inner voice told him. Images of watching her walk upstairs, returned. How she had looked back over her shoulder when she reached the top and smiled. Was that an invitation to join her? He had never been good at reading the signals. *Ask your heart,* he thought, *be honest with yourself.*

Upstairs, Helga's own heart continued to ache. She was torn. She had kissed others, as a teenager, but had entered her marital bed a virgin. She had never been with another man. Their sex life had always been satisfying. It had maintained its intensity, had become even more so during the years when they thought each encounter might be their last. Even if her husband were alive, would it be such a crime to have one encounter with a stranger? She was certain her husband would have found solace in the brothels that she heard followed the soldiers around. Was this any worse? She was trying to talk herself into it, there was guilt though because there was emotion. She already had feelings towards this British stranger. Helga realised she was again waiting for someone who may be a ghost. If so, he was reaching out from the grave to control her behaviour. She hated the guilt, but there seemed no way to dismiss it.

Conflicted, she was angry now that Alfred was gone. She was also angry that he might return and now the guilty feelings returned in earnest. Had she made vows to a dead man, a man who had willingly sacrificed himself for a stupid cause, a cause that had brought down the wrath of the world upon them? Searching for solace, she tried to imagine her husband here with her, but it was all a blur as she tried to recall him in bed with her.

Just when she thought she would burst, there was a soft knock at the door. The tempestuous storm of thoughts and emotions subsided, followed by a wonderful feeling of calm. Nervously she called out to him, a moment later, he joined her.

Helga 1.3

COLIN CHANGED HER life. Her heartbeat increased whenever she saw him, food tasted better, wine was sweeter, she was full of energy, all the clichés it seemed were true. The boys did not like sharing her at first, even if they liked him. This quickly passed and they soon became a family. Helga and Colin decided to move. She would find somebody to run the bookstore, then lease the house. New York, London, Berlin, the world was theirs to choose from. She had had enough of small-town German life; it was time to go. Colin was still working for the newspaper; he was now a special correspondent writing features. There was nothing tying them down. At times, she felt sorry for poor Alfred, but she had waited long enough. *Even if he returned,* she thought, well, they would cross that bridge if he ever did, though she knew there was no going back.

Colin had changed also. He no longer wanted the fast-paced life he had been living at the newspaper; he preferred taking his time. He wanted to keep writing, only he wanted to do something different. One of his ideas was to write an historical account of the war, using first hand stories and experiences. He also had been making notes on story ideas and considered writing some fiction.

The town was a bit small and stifling for his tastes. He could wait though, there was no rush to leave, everything would work itself out. He stayed in the study making it his new home. His London house was kept for the time being. There was a small apartment above the bookshop. They had furnished it and it provided a good place to get away from everyone, yet remain close by. They had only spent more than twenty-four hours apart twice since that first night. The first time when he had returned to London to arrange his affairs, then once more when he had travelled to Zurich for a story.

The winter was wet and cold, the harsh winds blew in from the east, traveling over the Alps. They picked up speed, arriving full of malice. Inside the bookstore it was warm, almost too warm. One almost needed to go out into the cold for five minutes to acclimatise.

Helga noticed him straight away as she looked out of the window. He was on the other side of the street, coat collar pulled up over the sides of his face, wearing a cap with earflaps. He walked quickly, waiting until the last second to glance around, their eyes met. Helga ran through the front door as if she were pursuing a book thief. Colin, drinking coffee, stopped what he was doing and ran to the window. She raced across the empty street. He watched as she caught a man by the arm, swung him around and fell into his arms. In an instant, he knew what had happened. Herr Zimmerman was home.

Helga returned arm in arm with her husband, she was crying. He understood straight away that they were tears of joy, not for herself, but for Alfred.

'Colin, this is Alfred my husband,' she said. 'Alfred this is Colin, my fiancé.'

Then she started to laugh hysterically. They each took an arm, leading her to the small section they had built, that had armchairs and a lounge where people could enjoy a coffee and read. They sat her down. The store was empty except for Rita a clerk who Helga had hired. Colin sent her home, put the closed sign up and locked the door. He then went for tea. When he returned, he handed mugs to Alfred and Helga who were seated opposite each other. He took a seat in an armchair.

'I apologise for this intrusion,' Alfred said.

'Quite alright, completely understandable under the current circumstances.'

Realising he was babbling, Colin stopped speaking, there was silence, Helga was in shock. There was a blanket draped over the back of the lounge. She wrapped herself in it and laid down. Colin tried to keep the conversation going.

'When were you released?'

'Three months ago, it has taken that long to travel here. I was in Siberia, the trains are slow, especially at this time of year. Many delays.'

'Welcome home.'

He raised his mug in way of a toast and he immediately felt foolish. Alfred took out a pack of cigarettes, Colin, although he felt like one, declined when offered. Helga was coming apart on the lounge. He felt unable to go to her, even though his heart longed to. *Idiot,* he told himself, *she's the love of your life, get up sit next to her, put your arm around her.* Hesitantly, he put his mug down, stood up then went to her, putting his arm around her. She looked at him with her beautiful eyes and he knew what she was thinking. Even if she had run to Alfred, even if now, less than six feet apart her emotions were raging, Colin was the man for her. He had just proved it. He was the one, the love of her life, the one promised in the fairy tales.

Alfred looked on, impassive. Whatever had once been there, whatever he felt when she ran to him on the street, was gone. He had been replaced, with someone that she loved more than she had ever loved him. It hurt, but it was undeniable. He smiled; she was happy. He had worried about that for years, worried he had betrayed her. The pain was enormous, yet he understood, this was fair, he felt a like a criminal no more.

'How are the boys?' he asked.

They returned to earth and Helga let Colin do the talking.

'They are well. Hans is almost a man, Chris and Jonah are growing all the time, you will be proud of them.'

I am proud, Alfred thought, *but I do not know them at all.* How old had Hans been the last time he had seen him? He must be sixteen now, a lifetime had passed. This man may be more of a father to them. He played his part, now was not the time for depression, there was plenty of time for that.

'Your house is still intact. We maintain it, you can move in any time.' Helga regretted saying this as soon as the words left her mouth.

'My house? I thought it was our house?'

'I inherited the–' Here she faltered. 'We don't live there anymore. We will go and see the boys; I will take you. It is important, better to come now than let them hear from others. Let me just take a few minutes.'

Helga was flustered, she must do this, must look after him. Guilt flooded her body, sinking into every pore, a look of anguish appeared. It shocked Alfred and worried Colin. She took hold of him tighter, she was shivering. They sat silently at times. Helga caught herself looking at Alfred with great longing.

They were so wrapped up in what was happening that they did not notice him, the small man standing at the window. Having heard the news, Herr Steiner had come to see for himself. There, sitting on the lounge opposite his wife was one of their heroes, a genuine bona-fide legend. The scene disgusted him, but he would make it right. He would do what he should have done months ago. Others might forget, but his memory was sound.

Three hours passed quickly; Helga's senses were almost fully restored.

'Why don't you two go to meet the boys as they arrive from school, have dinner and spend the evening together?' said Colin, 'I'll stay here, tidy up and have an early night upstairs, then tomorrow we can see about getting Alfred settled into his house.'

'I have a room for tonight,' Alfred said. 'Perfect, what do you say?'

Helga nodded, although she would have preferred Colin to join them. She understood that maybe it was for the best. They said goodbye.

Alfred turned and went to open the door. She clutched Colin tight like lovers do, a mad almost panicked embrace. She kissed him deeply, passionately. Reluctantly, she let him go, neither wanting to be the first to break free. He followed her to the door and out into the street. In the shadows, Steiner counted three leaving, then turned and walked away.

Colin watched Alfred and Helga walk away. He had a strange feeling. The wind suddenly blew harder, almost knocking him from his feet. He retreated into the store, switched off the lights and headed upstairs, determined to find a bottle and crawl into the bottom of it.

The joy Alfred felt on seeing his boys, overcame him and he shed his tears. What could be more important than this? They ran to him crying, 'Pappa.'

He had longed to hear that word from Hans' lips, had it not been just a dream. He loved Helga for this moment, one of the greatest of his life. She was a wonderful woman, how could he blame her for moving on with her life? He understood without asking. He had seen the way Colin and Helga looked at each other and he understood. The pain was something he would have to deal with. Rejection, hurt, he must acknowledge that. All three boys hugging him at the same time was therapy enough.

They ate too much as he listened intently to everything they had to say. He owed them this and he would pay. Helga had raised them alone and it was up to him to do his share. He would find work to help provide for them and the rest of the time would be dedicated to them so long as he lived. So long as Helga allowed and he was certain she would. He must be careful, he understood he was and would be a stranger.

What did he know about raising children? But he would learn, he would learn from Helga. She would teach him even if she didn't realise it. He would be kind, patient, things he had already seen her be. Oh, how he loved them. Proud, that was an understatement, but if she wished him gone he would go without a backward glance, such was his love for her and the respect to which he held her for everything she had done.

As the hour grew late, Helga suggested he sleep in the house, assuring him Colin would not mind. There was much to talk about but that was for another day. He was just turning in when they heard sirens, a fire engine. They thought nothing of it, a long and emotional day had ended. Helga fell asleep thinking of Colin and a future that seemed closer than ever. Alfred dreamed of his boys, of times spent together, watching them grow. Colin drunk and dead to the world, dreamed only of her beautiful eyes and her smile.

Helga 1.4

EVERYTHING FELT WRONG, everything was distant, detached. After she returned from the funeral, Helga became withdrawn, she did not leave the house, not for anything or anyone. The shutters were closed, the gate locked, the boys the only ones allowed in. Colin's mother had personally asked her to come to the funeral, otherwise she may have stayed away. Her son had confided in her about Helga; she understood how important she had been to him, even though their relationship was brief.

His mother was so nice to her, as were his friends and relations. She accompanied the body and watched as they put him into the ground. His wake was filled with kind speeches and fond reminiscences. There was great warmth and love, a feeling of such value and gratitude for a life well lived. She returned home to the news that Herr Steiner had been arrested. He had, she was told, confessed to the fire but claimed he had waited until he saw all of them leave. None of this interested her; she wasn't interested in excuses, nor was she interested in revenge.

'This is the world in which we live, nothing evil, ever truly goes away.' That was her statement to the press. A national fundraising campaign across Germany and Great Britain raised 20,000 pounds. What should we do with it? Colin's mother had asked in a letter Helga had yet to answer. A package arrived containing a diamond engagement ring. It only made her fall into a deeper depression; the promised new life was now forever to remain just a dream. Letters arrived from Colin's solicitors. Those also remained unanswered. There was life insurance, a pension from the newspaper, his assets, all left in part or full to her. She left them on the desk in the study. In her darkest hours, she imagined the supporters of Herr Steiner coming to burn down the house in the middle of the night. The police must have shared those views because, more often than not, especially at night, a police car would park near the locked front gate.

Even with those precautions, she asked the boys to sleep at Alfred's. Poor Alfred, how cruel life had been to him. He was now mixed up in this tragedy, another shock to the system for him. He had stepped in and helped keep people away, cared for the boys while Helga grieved, spoken to them, tried to explain things, helping them to heal. He had been flung into this while still wrestling with his own demons.

In her own world she had not recognised the signs. The doctor confirmed it. Within her dark world, the smallest flicker of light began to appear. It grew in her, literally, emotionally. In her mind she could liken it to being at the bottom of a well, when slowly a rope begins to pull you out. She was not too old technically at thirty-five. A new joy started to form, even on the darkest days she found something to be hopeful for. She invited the boys and Alfred to a picnic, in the same place she had shared that wonderful meal with Colin, and broke the news. Alfred was excited for her; the boys were ecstatic. They hugged her before running off to find a football. It gave Alfred and her a chance to talk.

'What will you do?' asked Alfred with a tinge of the serious and the unknown in his voice.

'Have this baby, raise it, love it, try to keep going,' she replied, 'We have suffered enough, all of us. As someone who is used to suffering, I have to say it's easier suffering together.' Alfred was shaking as she said this.

Helga looked at him carefully for a moment, she felt an anger rising in her.

'Why were you so accepting of Colin, Alfred? Why did you not protest, scream do something?' she asked. Helga was surprising herself again. Was she really that angry at him for not fighting for her, even if the fight wase pointless.

'What good would that have done? You looked at him like you had never looked at me. We had something between us, something wonderful, something I will never forget, but you never looked at me the way you looked at him. Whatever we had was dead a long time ago. It sat dying while you huddled with three babies at the end of the war, while you stood alone raising our children. It died in the remote frozen wilderness of Siberia where I tried to remember what you looked like, when I couldn't see your face anymore in my mind.'

This stopped her.

'You couldn't remember me?'

Alfred's face took on a blank look. He had not meant to say that. 'At first, I remembered you or rather my memories were clearer, especially when the bombs were falling. When I was close to death, there you were in your blue dress, the sun behind you and your hair down. Then in time, it became blurred. I could not see your face clearly anymore, Then I was not sure I was seeing your face; maybe it was the face of an actress, or pictures of a stranger on the street. The children I could not remember at all. They were completely lost to me. I had lost the photographs I had carried in my pocket. When they were no longer there, it was as if I could no longer understand what was real or fantasy. I had given up on everything; I expected to die there in the frozen wasteland. I never allowed myself to dream of freedom, of ever seeing you again. Every morning, I was reborn, my lifespan was the length of the day. Every night, I went to sleep not expecting to wake up. I thought that I would die, that they would throw my body into the old mine. They had stopped digging graves, nobody could be bothered. They would just carry you into the mine then throw you down the shaft, maybe two hundred metres deep. There you lay for eternity in the cold darkness.'

'I can't live with you Alfred, not like we were, not like that. I can't turn back time. If you came–' she stopped, not wanting to say it, not wanting to damn him to a time to rob him further. 'The year with Colin was–' She did not need to finish the sentence, they both knew. 'You will always have a place in my heart.'

Alfred smiled. 'I could not ask for more.'

Now, for the first time, he looked broken. Had he really seen a way back to their former life? Thought that perhaps she would fall back into his arms?

'It's time to move on with things Alfred. I will speak to my solicitors, if you agree, and we can dissolve the marriage.' This came out harsher than she had intended.

Once again, Helga felt a pang of regret and a feeling of disappointment. No, she did not wish to remain married to Alfred, however, he had just sat there, passive, nodding, and this she also found offended her. Had the world so beaten him down? Just moments before, he had found the courage to ask for her back. Now he sat resigned to the fact that she was gone forever.

It was a beautiful afternoon. Helga, strong and resilient as ever, had risen from the depths to find new meaning in life. Poor Alfred. She worried about him. Maybe he would find happiness; he had found some in the boys. They had enriched his life in the short time since his return, as they had hers. She could feel her life with them shifting slightly; she was okay with that.

Helga named the baby Eleanor. Even as a newborn she reminded her of Colin. Little things, like her facial expressions, how she sighed, she had the same eyes. The family were smitten. Colin's mother came to visit. For the first year Helga enjoyed raising Eleanor and helping the boys adjust to the divorce and life with two parents. She had wished to stay away from the murder trial, but had been forced to give evidence, as had Alfred. She hoped that when she saw Herr Steiner in the dock it would be the last time. After a year and putting all of that behind her, she was able to focus on her next project, one she hoped would make a difference for years to come.

Helga 1.5

THE MEMORIAL WAS built in the middle of the forest to honour all the victims of the former regime. Due to the lack of records, exact locations of bodies and the exact date of death were impossible to ascertain. They took oral history from anyone willing to speak, however, few took up the offer. People would only talk at all under the strictest anonymity. Piece by piece they were able to record the morbid details of many of the victims. Remains were found, identification, though, was almost impossible. Some information matched, but there was always uncertainty. Helga hoped it would help people, especially the young to learn, that things like this could never be allowed to occur again, that the memorial was stark, the silence in the middle of the forest was eerie.

The town was divided, the desire to forget was still very strong. Films from the camps were shown, high school students arrived by bus. The remote location, the stillness of the forest, the gruesome exhibits and the names of the victims, all contributed to the surreal atmosphere. Helga still felt detached most of the time, unable to find any real and lasting connection to anything. Time passed differently now; she just existed.

When Eleanor turned five, Helga moved them to London. It was like the removal of a great weight as she left her past behind. They began their new lives in a city that held memories of him; Helga felt a closeness to him there. Colin's mother, who had seemed to be nearing the end of her life when they first met, had become rejuvenated. She took great joy in spending time with Eleanor, collecting her from school in the afternoons, spoiling her. Left alone, afternoons became times of deep reflection for Helga, though without Eleanor to distract her, she, at times, became morose. Without realising it, she was mourning for both the important men in her life, unable to completely move on. She had fallen into a prison of her own making, trapped inside.

Hannah had fallen in love with Alfred. It had happened gradually. Hannah ran the reconstructed bookstore and sat on the board of the foundation Helga had established to manage the Victims Memorial. Alfred, who also was on the board, had slowly worked his way into her heart. They planned to marry. Helga was torn but wished them all happiness. Hannah had been her closest friend but somehow things were no longer the same between them and she feared they never would be again. *Time passes,* she thought.

Hans changed his university courses three times before settling on Law. He would also complete a degree in Psychology; his goal was to become a human rights lawyer. Helga supported him financially. Happily, he had shocked them all by marrying a lovely girl from Czechoslovakia, Alena, a fellow student who wanted to be a journalist. They lived in a small apartment in Berlin. On the weekends they shared her big house with Jonah and his wife.

Jonah, a builder, had just left to construct houses in Africa. He enjoyed the work, it gave his life purpose and meaning. He would spend six months working at home, saving money, and four months in Africa building for free, followed by two months traveling the world. His wife was a kindergarten teacher who followed him, teaching in Germany and Africa.

Christian was living in Rome, studying to be an architect. He worked hard and was showing great promise. Helga had many regrets about her later motherhood. She felt, in some way, she had not been there enough for them. It was only after she had visited Christian, that she realised how independent he was, how independent they all were, how rich the lives they were building were. After that, she made peace with herself. Those things made her happy. Still, conflicting emotions would surface. In many ways she was jealous, jealous of the ease with which people were able to move on with their lives, jealous of everything. Life went on, Helga felt it went on largely without her.

He approached her while she sat reading in the library. Smartly dressed in a grey suit, he reminded her of a businessman, a banker perhaps. He offered her a card and she held it as he spoke. A well-crafted voice hiding an accent she could not place.

'You must forgive me Frau Zimmerman, or is it Mrs?'

'Please call me Helga.'

He nodded and smiled; he preferred informality.

'I recognised you from the newspaper reports, the unfortunate circumstances surrounding your fiancé.'

'That was many years ago now.'

'Yes, I'm a great admirer of your work, the work you have done. You have many admirers, in fact, if you were not aware.'

He intrigued her. There was something about him; he was suave, confident.

'You're not being very clear, Max,' she said, reading his name off his card.

'My apologies, I have always appreciated the way you got on with life, how you have not just waited for things to happen, your courage. My business is a lot like yours, yet very different.'

'I'm sorry Max, you are speaking in riddles. My life may look as you describe, but I assure you, it is very different from that.'

'Let me explain. Where you look to uncover the secrets of the past and find the dead, searching for answers, I also search for answers amongst the living and I seek justice for the dead.'

Helga processed this information still not fully grasping his meaning. 'My colleagues and I search for the criminals of our past and, when we find them, we bring them to justice. We wondered if, in some small way, you would perhaps be interested in joining us.'

Helga felt a twinge from inside as an idea began to form. Life, she reflected, always had a way of surprising!

Tanya 1.21

TANYA AWOKE WITH the same feelings she had had after dreaming about Stella, and just like hers, Helga's story was now burned into her mind. Once again, she felt great sadness, yet there was also joy. Helga had experienced true love, just like Tanya, then it was tragically taken away from her, leaving her in despair. Somehow though, she had managed to overcome it and then slowly rebuild her life.

Sitting up in bed, she noticed a bottle of water had been placed on the bedside table, her phone was gone. She opened the water; after taking a drink, she sat in silence thinking. Finally she decided she had to know. She picked up the landline and asked for Mrs Giles. They all came at a rush, her mother, her aunt, the general and the doctor, the room suddenly felt very full. Her mother was about to speak when Tanya interrupted her.

'Is there news?' She looked from one to the other, desperate for news. They exchanged glances but the general answered the question.

'The rescue team couldn't locate him. There is hope, though.' He paused, his eyes locked on the floor. A few moments passed then he looked up.

'They haven't found his body. That means, well it means, he must still be alive, or at least he was. They recovered the body of his sergeant.

The last time he was seen, they were together. So, there it is, there is hope.'

Tanya reached for the water and took a large drink while the others looked on with concern.

'Thank you everyone. I think I need some rest.'

'Would you like another sedative?' the doctor asked.

'Not now. Maybe just give me a few hours?'

Her phone, or anything else for that matter, wasn't important. She just needed to be alone. She took a shower, put on fresh clothes. It was cold, but she wanted some fresh air. She planned her exit, slipping outside without anybody noticing, staying away from the windows and making her way into the nearest walled garden. She sat on a bench, processing everything. *Think,* she told herself, *what can you do? Is there anything you can do or is it a hopeless situation where I have to wait?*

She was losing control of the situation. Her recent dreams came to her. She remembered the women, the strength they showed, how they fought through, showing great resilience. What to do? There was hope, the general had said that, but what else could he say? If Evan was a prisoner, what was the likelihood he was still alive? There were no prisoner of war camps, if they had him, the clock was ticking. The thought chilled her to the bone. More horrible thoughts followed, such as, they would torture, mutilate and murder him, probably online for the world to see.

The tears came. Be strong, she told herself. It did little good. Back in her room, she decided to try and face things. She called for the doctor as it was time to learn some home truths. The doctor took some tests, promising to send them immediately to pathology. Her aunt, mother and the general came in to see her. There was an awkward silence. Then the General began, 'I have more news. I spoke with Evan's commander on the ground and his regimental head back here; the news is not encouraging. Further patrols have been unsuccessful in the location or whereabouts of Evan. They have activated operatives, friendlies who work for us. They, also, have been unable to locate or discover anything about his disappearance. Evan was last seen in the company of his sergeant, who was not as lucky. Near where his body was found, they discovered blood trails. They lead nowhere, it's almost as if he disappeared into thin air.'

'Can we travel there? Can I be on the ground? Is there anything I can do?'

'Darling,' her mother spoke, 'we are following all the channels. The general has, perhaps, even moved beyond that. His men, the entire regiment, is doing everything within their power to find him. I cannot imagine what having you over there would possibly do to help.'

'I feel so helpless.'

'That's understandable,' they all said in unison.

'You are welcome here always. If you would prefer to return to London, though,' her aunt said.

'No thanks, Aunty, I just need,' she started to cry, 'I don't know what I need.'

Nobody moved, then her aunt approached the bed and put an arm around her. In that moment, she understood something of the pain her niece was suffering. She wanted nothing more than to remove it, to help her in any way possible. The general and her mother also closed ranks around her. Feeling their warmth and protection, she cried rivers of tears.

<h1 style="text-align:center">Evan 1.2</h1>

A MAN, THAT WAS the woman's name, who was caring for him, made him change into clothing that matched the local population, hiding his uniform. She told him it was just a precaution. He still had his weapons and spent hours cleaning them. It was boring in the cave, hours of nothing. She dared not let him out. His wounds were healing quickly and the doctor was happy with his progress. He felt that ten more days rest, then they could move him, get him back to his unit, base, whatever, return him to his people, the doctor had said.

He had been in the cave for fifteen days, but it seemed like a lot longer. Tanya, he worried endlessly about. Tanya, how was she? What must she be thinking? He had to wait; it would not be much longer, he promised himself. He was determined to survive this and get back to her. Aman was kind, she cared for him. He wanted to repay the favour somehow. People were looking out for him, there was an unseen community around him all working together, all trying to survive. Everybody committed to finding their way out of this nightmare.

The little boy, Farrah, brightened his days. His name meant happiness. They spent hours playing in the dim lighting of the cave, games Evan invented. In a way, they became a little family; they entered a bizarre domesticity while the world around them raged.

$\mathscr{A}$man 1.1

$\mathscr{A}$MAN CONSIDERED HERSELF lucky that she had been at the entrance to her hideout when she heard Evan. Had she not been there, perhaps he would have died or been found by somebody else less friendly. With the help of her friend the doctor, who was also close by, they carried him into her cave. The doctor then collected his things and went to work with her assistance.

Evan was a strong man and was recovering quickly. She had made a promise to see him safely back to his people and would fulfil this vow, regardless of the consequences. Once he was well enough, or even if the opportunity came earlier, she would do so.

She had to be careful, her own predicament was vicarious. She was hiding from her dead husband's family, who would kill her if they found her. Her husband had gone out to meet a friend and been killed. Without a thought to her loss, they demanded she marry one of his brothers. Aman now dreamed of a new life, a life where she could live in a place without war, without needless death and hardship, a place with houses, tree lined streets and parks where her little boy could play. Where she could find a job and take care of him, watching him grow.

Early on, she had fantasised that this man had been brought to her by divine providence. Once she learned that he was married, she immediately stopped these thoughts. Still, she loved the way he played with her son, she found purpose in caring for him. The doctor had told her ten more days and he was becoming increasingly worried about their being discovered. He was keeping an eye out for any nearby patrols so they could hand Evan over earlier, then perhaps gain some assistance for themselves. Both wanted to reach Pakistan, perhaps they could find a way.

Aman had never known peace. All her life there had been war, fighting was just a way of life. So many of her relatives had been killed: brothers, uncles, cousins, the innocent. Her own sister was killed, along with a cousin, while riding in her uncle's car. So many friends, neighbours, the list was endless. She had seen pictures in a magazine of houses in England. That was the dream. Aman was still a young woman who looked older than she was. She believed in fate, believed in destiny, but this was another woman's man. Her job was to return him to her.

Tanya 1.22

THE DAYS WERE agonisingly long. There had been no news and it would soon be a month since Evan went missing. Tanya was in a strange, listless state, existing in a world somewhere in between fantasy and reality. Desperate for distraction, she decided to return to her work. Her aunt, mother and the general, all of whom remained in residence, agreed with her decision. The doctor had confirmed her intuition and had been sworn to secrecy. Tanya would reveal things at the appropriate time. They would all stay with her until Evan was found. She drew comfort from this, but knew it would not last forever.

She abandoned working in the library and moved up to the small cottage on the cliff where the stone bench and vine covered gazebo were the place dubbed the waiting room. After settling in, she picked up her research where she had left off, learning more of Karam's journey. She found that now, with all that had happened, she had a far greater understanding of her ancestor than before.

Karam 1.3

DILBAGH WATCHED KARAM carefully for three days, after she had arrived. Her father had asked him to speak to her, to see if she would confide in him what was happening at her home. Her father worried about her. Dilbagh, as his confidante, knew everything: his worries, his dealings, his secrets. He doted on his grandchildren, spoiled and worried about them. He was concerned for their safety. He had heard of life in London and Paris, the many good schools and universities, opportunities they could only imagine. The family had connections. Their teas and spices were exported to England and they had a partnership with an English company, there were options, possibilities.

Then there was America. He had heard great things about that country.

Perhaps they should seek their fortunes there.

Each day, Dilbagh watched as Karam entered one of the baths. She remained inside most of the day, taking her meals, resting there; she spent most of this time alone. In the late afternoon, she spent time with her boys. When he was certain that she was alone, he entered the bath through a door at the rear of the garden. She was lounging in the pool on her back, naked. He almost retreated, before gathering his courage.

'Please, don't be alarmed.' He spoke softly, not wishing to cause any alarm.

Karam stopped floating and stood up with a start, her hands crossing her body. Dilbagh walked to the end of the pool, turned, facing the stone wall and sat down.

'Don't be afraid, I mean you no harm. We are alone and even if someone came in, they would say nothing, only I needed to speak with you privately.'

'I'm naked!'

'I can't see anything. We must speak. I promise I will not look, relax, remain in the water.'

Karam found this behaviour strange, only she was now intrigued, wanting to hear what he had to say. She had known Dilbagh since childhood. They had played together just the same as if he were her own brother. She approached the end, where he was sitting, just a few feet away. Sensing her, he kept his word, looking at the wall.

'I was surprised to see you here and I wondered if there was anything I could do?'

'Why would my father's servant be surprised, or take interest in anything that I do?'

'Please, there's no reason to be impersonal, we have known each other all our lives. Your concerns are my concerns, as they are the concerns of your father. He shares everything with me.'

'Are you here for him, here for yourself or here for me?' It was difficult to answer honestly.

'A bit of each,' he replied.

'Answer me this, why does my father entrust so much to you?'

'Have you never wondered about me?' Dilbagh said remaining calm.

Karam froze. She had expected an answer of convenience, not honesty.

'Do we share the same father?' Karam asked, as she had often suspected this.

'All I know is that he gifted my mother an estate, then when she passed away, he brought me here to live, ensured that I received a good education, and all the benefits of my mother's estate when I became of age. He may be my father; he may just have been my mother's lover. Many men courted my mother at one time, they tell me. Your father has treated me well, even if he has not acknowledged me. Perhaps he does not know for sure, I do not resemble him.'

Karam took this in. It was true, Dilbagh had never been a servant. Karam considered his final remark. She could see elements of her father in him even if he couldn't. True, he did not resemble him, but nor did her own brother. There were times, mannerisms, a facial expression, things that could not be learnt, that were natural. Sometimes it was the way he walked, spoke.

She could build a good case for his paternity in her mind. In an instant, she decided to share a little, see where it would lead her, after all, she was in desperate need of allies.

'Things are not the same in my house, war has changed everything. Relations with my husband and my father-in-law have become strained. I no longer feel comfortable, nor welcome, in my own home. He has installed a new mistress, his nurse. He has shown little interest in his family, less in me. He has not requested my company once since his return. I feel the same rejection from my father-in-law. The new mistress told me I needed to give him time to recover, so I decided in the best interest of all to leave until things change.'

Dilbagh listened thoughtfully, stroking his beard. Her father had shared his concerns, his assessment looked accurate. Karam was certain in what she had said, so he did not insult her by asking any questions to confirm.

'These things happen, the lives of men and women are complicated. What suits us today, may no longer suit us tomorrow,' Dilbagh said.

Karam smiled.

'Time will reveal it's answers. Our world is changing but it changes slowly. You are still his wife; he is still your husband. Society, our society, has strict rules. But for people with means there are alternatives. You are a person of means, let me consider what you have told me. Time is with us for now. I will consider things and visit you tomorrow. I may not have answers, but they will, as I say, reveal themselves.' He stood and without a further word or backward glance, left the baths in the same way he had entered.

What Dilbagh had heard, saddened him. He believed in the sanctity of Karam's relationship; he had believed it to be genuine. He learned a lot about people, watching from the shadows. He had learned that things were not always as they seemed. He tried to see into their souls. *There was more to this,* he thought, *things, they could not see now, would become clearer. What was to happen, only time would tell.*

He trusted her, but he needed to have all the information. He dispatched four of the younger servants to gather information, three boys and a girl. His instructions were simple. The boys were to blend into the busy street life around Karam's house. They were to observe it, day and night, watching everyone who came and went, looking for anything out of the ordinary. They were to mix with delivery boys and anyone else of interest and pick up any gossip or rumours. They were to follow any visitors who were out of the ordinary and learn what they could, without raising suspicion.

The girl was to visit the house on the mission to collect more of Karam's things. She was to find a way to delay her return, then stay at the house for a few days to listen to the servants for any gossip and observe things from inside the house. The girl was known to Karam's servants, so it would be easy for her to visit undetected. After three or four days they were to return. Dilbagh's mind was racing. Normally, he was able to calm it through meditation. Not today! Sleep was difficult that night. He rose early, pacing around the grounds. When Karam returned to the baths, he was waiting for her, his back to the bath, facing the wall. She disrobed and entered the water. She took her time, while Dilbagh meditated. Sensing her presence he spoke.

'Good morning. Did you sleep well?'

'No,' she responded.

There was no point in lying, she thought, *these were difficult times.* Dilbagh kept his own lack of sleep to himself.

'I need to ask certain things. If you do not desire to answer anything, then don't, but I need to understand everything before I can help.'

'I understand.' Karam moved away from the wall, swimming on her back.

'Why did your husband go away with the British?'

'Pride, patriotism. I do not understand his decision, it remains a mystery, something completely out of character for him. He was a successful man; he had a family. All my answers are just speculation, it eludes me. He was never an adventurer, even when he was young. He would avoid violence and was very conservative.'

Dilbagh was satisfied, he believed Karam, but there was something that they didn't know.

'Was he truly happy?'

Karam paused, giving the question great consideration.

'I felt that he was, now I'm not sure. What do I know of the ways of men? Like most, his heart remained hidden, his true desires were, it seems, a mystery to me. I am now of the opinion that he was trapped into a life he did not want.'

'Why do you think this?'

'Because when he went away, I realised my brother had certain deficiencies. Our father, I believe, realised this, then found a solution by marrying me to a man who would make up for my brother's inadequacies, allowing him to leave our family's business affairs in safe hands. This allowed him to come here and live a more peaceful life.'

Dilbagh fidgeted and played with his beard. He remembered when Karam's father had arrived all those years ago, just after her marriage to Harmeet. He was overweight, in poor health, suffering great stress. His health had improved over the years, free from the worry, from the responsibility. Had he just transferred that to Karam's husband?

'I believed in our marriage, believed he loved me. He told me as much, but in reflection there was never a spark of love there. The marriage on his side, was a transaction, a contract, one he now wishes to terminate. Before you ask, I don't understand why, not fully, but he has left us. I have been waiting for someone to return who simply no longer exists. Whoever Harmeet was, or really is, he is unknown to me. I only know the character who played the role of my husband in the first act.' It was difficult for Karam to be this honest. Dilbagh was again saddened to hear her speak that way. There must be a reason for Harmeet's actions and they must find it. Only then they would know what needed to be done.

He tried to ease her mind. 'Leave everything with me. You relax, let me see to things, in a few days we will know.'

'Thank you.'

He stood and once again, without a backward glance, left.

Karam 1.4

HARMEET **FELT ENTITLED** to things: a new life, a fresh beginning. He felt that life had cheated him; he had been seduced by his father-in-law who had promised riches, happiness. They had money, they had large houses, but there was no happiness, there was only the illusion of happiness. Life with a woman who was smarter than him, even if that was unspoken, in his mind, it made things worse. At first, he had not understood her interest in the business, her suggestions, then he came to realise that his life was nothing more than implementing her plans, building her dream. She secretly despised him and he could feel it. The children, he saw how much they took after their mother and he grew to feel the same about them, though no man can ever really despise or hate his own children. Even if your child became a devil, there would still be love there.

A natural actor, there was no outward evidence to support anything being wrong, nor his true feelings betrayed. Then Jasleen had come along.

They had encountered each other by accident while she had been shopping for cloth. Her beauty captivated him, causing an immediate infatuation. He chased after her for weeks, learning everything he could about her. She was always escorted by a chaperone, making direct contact difficult. She lived with her father, a merchant. Harmeet found it difficult to learn much about them.

He lay in bed at night, tormented by images of her beauty, but it was dangerous. Men were killed for less. Then one day, he encountered her at the market. She looked straight at him and smiled. His heart soared. That night, a small boy approached him on the street, with a message from the chaperone. Would he care to meet her? *How could this be?* he wondered. It was so unusual. he didn't know how to react. Yes, of course he would. He worried that it must be a trap, but his desire overcame his worry. The boy asked for money as he explained, arranging these things was expensive. Harmeet willingly handed the sum over. *How do I know the message is from her?*

The boy handed him a small piece of paper. On it was written a small poem. As he read it, the emotion rose within him. He would treasure it forever. This was the moment his life changed, the moment the long desired happy part began. With tears in his eyes, he began counting down the hours until meeting her.

The meeting was arranged in, what he was told was, the garden of a friend's house where they were promised privacy without fear of discovery. The truth was indeed very different. Jasleen was the daughter of a failed businessman and gambler, who had lost his own family's fortune and half of his wife's before she died. He subsisted on an allowance from his wife's family, which was not nearly enough to cover his vices, and whatever money he could steal from others. His own family had disowned them. His brother was desperately trying to rebuild their fortunes and had threatened to kill him, but that was some time ago. Jasleen and her father had spent many of the following years in the house of his courtesan, where she had been trained in how to attract and maintain the attention of men, of how to manipulate them and control them. She was amazed at how easily some could be manipulated. She came to worship money like her father and began chasing wealth. Her trips through the town and markets were calculated, designed to draw attention to her.

After establishing her presence for several weeks, she had smiled at four different men, then followed this up with an invitation to secretly meet with her. Of these invitations, the only one to immediately accept had been Harmeet. The boy who made the offer to him was the son of the chaperone. They together were a formidable team.

Within a very short space of time, they had gathered a great amount of information about Harmeet. They knew about his marriage, his wealth, It provided for them, endless possibilities. His actions, though not revealing everything, gave indications of his intentions. He was, potentially, a great source of income for them.

The memory of that first meeting with her was burnt into his mind forever. As he rode in the carriage afterwards, he could recall every moment. The house had in its centre, a courtyard with the most beautiful tranquil garden. Beneath a tree was a small bench where he found her waiting. She wore a green sari that mirrored her beautiful green eyes. She was sitting on the bench beneath a tree with no shoes on, a gold anklet was visible on her left leg. She blushed as he approached, turning her face away. Nervously, he sat next to her and she covered her face with a veil.

'Hello,' he spoke softly, 'my name is Harmeet, thank you for inviting me to meet with you.'

She glanced quickly in his direction, nodding. It was over before it began, but his pulse quickened, his heart fluttered. Slowly and very deliberately she reached over, picking up a water jug that was placed on a table next to the bench. Carefully, she poured a cup, then with great ceremony turned to him and holding it in both hands held it up, offering it to him. When he took it, she smiled, this time staring directly at him. His lips trembled and his hands shook as he lifted the cup and drank from it.

It was the sweetest drink he had ever had: cool, rich, his taste buds alive, feeling every drop as it passed on down his throat. She then picked up a small tray with sliced melon and stood, then kneeling in front of him offered some of the sweet fruit. Still holding the cup, he reached out, taking a piece. The refreshing sweetness burst in his mouth with each bite. When he took no more, she stood, placing the tray next to him, then waited. It took him a few moments to figure out what was happening.

'Please sit back down.'

Smiling, she resumed her place next to him on the bench. She was the complete opposite of Karam. She waited for him to speak to her; she listened, rarely saying anything. She was innocent in his eyes as she looked at the ground. After an hour, it was time for him to leave. As he stood to go, she reached out, taking his hand in hers. Very gently, she drew a circle in his palm with her finger. While doing this, she lifted her eyes to his.

'Please,' she almost whispered, 'say that you will visit me again.'

As soon as she said it, she dropped her eyes again, continuing to draw the circle in his palm. He reached out with his other hand, lifting her chin until their eyes met again.

'Nothing on this earth could keep me away.'

She smiled, letting go of his hand. As he was leaving the house, the chaperone stopped him.

'Did you enjoy yourself.'

The way he looked at her, no response was required.

'Very good, are you able to assist with some more money? All of this is very expensive.'

Harmeet didn't want to seem stingy.

'Yes of course, as much as you need. Send the boy to my warehouse tomorrow, here is some more for today.'

He reached into his pocket, removing a bag and handed it to her. 'Come again in three days.'

He felt no guilt afterwards, only elation. He had met the woman of his dreams. Now he only needed to do one thing and that was to find a way they could be together. If he was to think with his head, the simplest of inquiries would have uncovered some of the truth, but he was thinking with his heart, confusing lust with love.

Jasleen, her father and the chaperone met in the parlour room of the house that Harmeet believed belonged to a friend of Jasleen's. The chaperone spoke first.

'You did very well, dear. He gave me more money and asked me to send someone for more. He will return in three days.'

'Good work, Jasleen,' her father added, eyeing the money bag the chaperone was holding. 'Do you think there is a way we could get a larger sum from him?'

'I've been considering it,' Jasleen said.

Both the father and the chaperone's eyes settled on her, eager to hear her plans.

'If I slept with him and became his mistress, he would have to take care of me, but we would be at his mercy. We would receive small amounts, gifts, but we would have to remain discreet and if he tired of me, then it would end. However, if we could make things more permanent, get him committed, then perhaps we could get a large sum from him, something that would last us.'

They agreed it was a good plan. Just then, an idea occurred to her father.

'What if you were to convince him to undertake a great adventure. I have heard the British are seeking suitable gentlemen to join their army as officers in a Sikh regiment. What if you convinced him to do this. He would then have to give you a large amount to last during his absence. Then if you were to tell him you might be pregnant when he was leaving, it would plant the seed in his mind that when he returned, he would live a double life with you, instead of returning to his wife.'

Jasleen's view of sex was as a tool to be used for gain and felt no embarrassment in discussing the topic with her co-conspirators.

'Why would he do that, leave his family, go off to war? I can lure him into my bed, trap him that way, but make him change his entire life.'

'You can do it my child, just let the idea grow on you. Meet with him a few times, then we will be back where we once were.'

Jasleen did as she was asked. Over the following weeks Harmeet continued to visit, already head over heels for her. His obsession grew in intensity with every moment he spent with her.

One day, she asked him to buy her a necklace, one that would be made to reflect her unique beauty. Harmeet visited a man he had dealt with before, a Persian who was a master jeweller, who had made many pieces for him. They designed it together. Harmeet decided it would have three layers with woven gold links encrusted with precious stones that reflected her beauty: emeralds for her shimmering eyes and rubies for her luscious lips.

As it would take some time to make, so he brought her some other pieces, including another necklace with a blue diamond that opened in the back, revealing a small gold locket where a keepsake could be held. Jasleen was excited to receive the gifts. She blushed as he presented each one and decided to allow him to kiss her as their time was coming to a close. He left her reluctantly at the end of that visit, happier than ever.

Keeping all these expenses from Karam was proving difficult, she had an eagle eye and could spot anything unusual in the ledger. He, therefore, had to take money from his father to cover the ever-increasing costs of maintaining the relationship. It was a week after he had given her the jewellery that Jasleen made her boldest move.

'Harry, my love, I have been thinking.'

'Yes, my precious one, what is it?'

She bowed her head. 'How can we be together all of the time? My heart aches for you when you are not here.'

'I know, I feel the same way but at the moment, it is not possible.'

She timed it brilliantly and in her most petulant voice said, 'Why can't you be brave, like those men who have joined the British in their fight against the Afghanis? If I were in love with a brave man like that, nothing would stop us being together.'

Harmeet was surprised at the tantrum.

'But my love, if I were to fight with the British that would only keep us apart.'

'At first, but when you returned, we could be together.'

'My wife would still be here!'

'But you would be a man of your own. You could send her off to live in the country, and well–' Jasleen paused.

'Go on.'

'If you were going off to war and you had made provision to look after me while you were gone, I would, well I would have to show you how much I appreciated you before you left.'

That did it, his deepest darkest desire was his, but join the army? 'Let me think it over.'

She smiled and a moment later, released one of her breasts from her sari. He pounced on it. Feeling brave, he touched the other one. Lost in this bliss, his mind was made up, he would seek an audience with the British Viceroy.

Becoming an officer took less time than he imagined and in just four short months he was ready to leave. Karam was beside herself with worry, baffled to understand his decision. Jasleen had welcomed him into her bed for the first time on the day he handed over a huge endowment to last her while he was away.

She had conspired with the chaperone, telling Harmeet that her father was ill and would not learn of his generosity on the eve of his departure. She confided in him the news that she was pregnant. He was overjoyed. On the day he departed, he looked up to see Jasleen and Karam separately in the crowd, both of whom considered him a fool, but only one of which loved him. Instead of focusing on her, he focused on the one who was robbing him. Seated upon his white horse, his thoughts of her were of love, love in all its purity.

When he thought of Karam, he thought of deception and greed, there was no comparison. He was correct in his assumptions; he had just mixed up the two women in his mind. True to his beliefs, lurking in his character was a fierce and formidable warrior, a man who quickly won the respect of others, including the British. Then he was wounded and the bitterness that came, made him more hateful towards his old life. As they transported him back home in the ambulance, all he could think about was the return to the drudgery and passionless existence he had been escaping. The British respected money, they were not enslaved by it, but they respected it. There was something in their society he did not understand, something similar to their own system, that separated people. Money, however, did not.

He paid the surgeon and the nurse, using them as conspirators and forced Karam from the house. He missed his children. One day he would make that right; now was the time for him. His own father was unhappy, yet he joined the conspiracy, the missing piece was Jasleen. Had he known then what he would learn later: that she was not a part of his game, but he a part of hers. One day she was there, then when he had healed, she made good her promise; she climbed into the day bed. They shared it together and now he was hers.

Though he did not learn all of this, Dilbagh listened to the reports of the servants when they had returned, then made his conclusions. He took Karam's father with him when he went to report, and it was at this point that she lost her temper and had her outburst. Later, after she had been given time to calm down, he sought her out again. This time, her father was nowhere to be found. They sat opposite each other in the garden.

'What news?' she asked him, getting straight to the point, not wishing to dwell on what had happened earlier.

Dilbagh looked pained.

'Your life as you knew it, is at an end.' Although almost expected, it hit home hard.

'He is gone. He wants you to be his past. He misses the boys and that may become a problem.'

Rejection, it hurt. She knew this already, but it hurt. 'There is another woman, she visits him.'

'Another woman? That explains things.'

'Were you suspicious?'

She shrugged, there were many things in the end that made no sense.

'One day, shortly after he had left, a jeweller arrived at the house. He was seeking payment for a custom necklace; he showed it to me and explained that the elements were meant to reflect me. He was excited to do this, telling me how they had gone to great pains designing it. That was okay until he said the green rubies were to reflect my eyes, but my eyes are brown. I told him, "See." He said that it was possible he was mistaken. I paid him for it, after all it was a gift and very beautiful. Tell me, does this woman have green eyes?'

'I don't know, I will find out.'

'It's not important.' Dilbagh made a note to find out.

That explained things. Oh yes, that explained a lot. In her mind she could not believe it, though she knew it was true. This wounded her, her skin was only so thick.

'I think it's time for you to leave. To remain here could be dangerous. If you leave, take the boys to England, one of the modern cities.'

'How could we do that?'

'I have written to one of our business associates. You may remember he visited us, Albert Symes, our business partner from England. I'm sure he will help, then you can start afresh.'

'What of our interests, my brother, my father?'

'Aprajeet will look after our interests here, manage the farms, the plantations, your brother can supervise. I will be here also; you can see this as an opportunity to secure our interests there in England.'

'You should come with us Dilbagh, find a wife, help me build things, have a fresh start.'

The idea appealed to him.

'Let me think, I will have to speak to your father, perhaps I could.' Karam felt light-headed, absorbing all this was too much.

'Do you want to see him?' She looked confused.

'Before leaving, or will you just one day go?' She thought about this for a long time.

'Yes, let us settle things. His business and ours are intersected. Send for Aprajeet, we need to make plans, his father will look after their interests. We need to–' here she hesitated, 'we need to make sure our position is clear, that they understand. He needs to be certain we know of his treachery and use it to our advantage. They can have what is their due.'

'I agree.'

'Then make the arrangements, visit my brother, he needs to prepare also.'

Dilbagh set the wheels in motion. On the day she visited Harmeet, he accompanied her. After this, everything would happen quickly. She had already decided to give up their home, there were no happy memories there anymore, but they would be more ruthless with their interests. His family would only keep that with which they came, a share of the profits that was all. What belonged to her family, the majority of their empire, would be retained.

Dilbagh opened the door for her, he stood guard while she went inside alone.

Harmeet looked shocked. He felt the anger in him rising. Karam almost laughed. She dismissed him with a wave.

'Don't worry I won't keep you long, your lover will be here soon.' This disarmed him.

'What?' He was lost for words.

'Come husband, let us speak the truth between us.'

'Karam, I'm not well, I need rest.'

'Can you not be truthful?' He looked confused.

'Suit yourself, you can have what you want, all that you desire. Dilbagh is waiting, he will see your father. You can have this house. The children and I will stay with my father, your business interests are yours as you came to us, fully restored, along with profits. Consider us finished, your dream come true.'

'Karam, I–'

'Be quiet, now it's almost over, do you agree? If your answer is "yes", we are finished. Nobody need know, you can do whatever you want. I will not interfere. Tell people I'm dead, for all I care.'

He was not expecting this, it humbled him in a way. 'The boys?'

'They stay with me. You don't want your past holding back your future.'

He considered what she had said. His pride was wounded as he should be dictating the terms, not her.

'I need money, more than what we came with.'

Karam let her intuition guide her. She had won, it was now just down to sort out the details.

'Work it out with Dilbagh, but leave us in peace. Unlike you, I do not worship money, I can always make more.'

He remained silent.

'Say no and I'll move straight back in, your friends can move out. I can care for you; we can continue our life. Of course, the back door here will remain closed forever.'

That did it.

'I tell you, in time I will simply disappear. I will travel to another city and at that time I will send the boys to you, to raise if it is your wish. From that time, consider me dead.'

'I agree,' he said.

'Goodbye Harmeet. I will not bother you again. Oh, a man delivered a necklace you ordered. I have thrown it down a well. Your whore will have to wait until you have another made for her. Dilbagh has some things to discuss. Summon your father, you men will sort the rest.'

And just like that she was gone within moments, disappearing through the door Dilbagh entered. She waited in the carriage. There was much for Dilbagh to do. She loved him for this, a wonderful gift he was giving her; she smiled at him when he emerged.

Harmeet was also happy; he had been given what he wanted, now he could live the life he thought he was owed. As Dilbagh climbed into the carriage, there was no need for anything to be said as they rode away. Karam had never felt so free.

Karam 1.5

THEY LEFT SECRETLY after midnight. The party was fifty strong and included servants, bearers, guards and an official from the British Consulate. They moved quickly and quietly, a sense of fear pervading. At midday they stopped. The heat was stifling inside the carriage that carried Karam and her boys, they welcomed the break. There was little time to relax as everyone was tense, on edge. This would last for the entire trip with constant looks back over their shoulders. She had said farewell to her father over dinner. They had spoken about future meetings, yet both of them knew they would probably never see each other again. He promised to visit her, yet they knew it was a lie. The thought of it made her sad, so she concentrated on controlling her thoughts and emotions for the sake of everyone.

She hoped Harmeet would forgive her, her own lie about the boys. Perhaps, after hearing of their departure he would still believe they would come to him.

If she stayed, honour would mean her death before Harmeet could remarry. Running away was the same as if she had died. He could, after a respectable time, marry Jasleen with no bloodshed, no loss of face. Nobody, knowing she had gone, would also help, no tearful send offs. The British representative and the guards ensured her safe passage to a degree only. Harmeet could still come after them, hence the trepidation felt by all. Dilbagh, the great man that he was, had negotiated everything. All parties would be satisfied, except the issue with the boys, for a lot of gold.

They rode on throughout the rest of the day and into the night, not stopping until several hours after the sun went down. The following days passed much the same, travelling with one eye always cast on the road behind them.

Most things happen at the beginning or the end of a journey, this one was no exception. One day out from their destination, Karminder, Karam's eldest son, feeling restless, went for a walk while everyone rested after a meal break. He was wandering along daydreaming, when he almost stepped on a snake. Panic ensued. He tripped over his own feet, trying to get away. The snake struck three times. He was bitten on his hands and arm. He was screaming as he ran back to the camp. Karam almost fainted. Dilbagh, along with the British diplomat, sprang into action as the entire camp woke from their post lunch slumber.

Everyone had an opinion of what should be done as the two men worked feverishly, shutting out the noise around them as they tried to remove the poison. A tent was quickly erected and Dilbagh held the boy down as the diplomat worked on him. Karminder was screaming. When they had done all they could and the boy lay covered in sweat, Dilbagh told Karam it was in the gods hands. All they could do now was pray. Every member of the party petitioned their gods that night. Nobody slept.

Karam stayed by her son's bed all night and her thoughts drifted. In one moment he was a baby held in her arms, in the next, a small boy playing in the garden, then the young man he had become. Her heart ached. She wiped the sweat off his brow as he murmured incoherently. Dilbagh stayed with her. They sat waiting together, waiting for mercy. Hours passed with no change, others in the party sat outside the tent wanting to contribute, hoping that through their presence alone, they could swing the decision.

Exhausted, Karam passed out. She woke up in a strange place, her son was gone. When she went outside, there was another large tent, this one made from black silk. She entered; it was cold inside. A strange creature, approached, eyeing her carefully. It spoke in a low, threatening tone.

'Karam, I'm surprised to see you. Why have you come?'

Karam looked carefully into the eyes of the creature. They were fiery red, like a hot poker, and exuded evil. Summoning all her strength, Karam found the courage to speak, 'You have me at a disadvantage. You know my name, but I don't know yours.'

'My name is not important. Why have you come?' the creature said.

'I don't know, I don't know where this is or who you are?' Karam continued politely.

'I thought that perhaps you had come to barter for your son's life?' Suddenly, Karam understood what this was.

'Come see.' A mirror appeared and the demon pointed towards it. Karam looked into it and could see her son lying on a bed. He seemed to be getting weaker.

'See, his life force has nearly run out.'

'Save my baby, what do you want? Ask, I will pay it,' she said, pleading, her voice filled with desperation.

'Karam, you ask for something. Offer anything. Are you certain you understand your own words? He is already with us, the chapter is closed, anything we would take would be–'

Karam interrupted, 'Take anything, I beg you.'

'Very well, but we must take like for like, you understand this?'

'Yes, please help.'

The demon waited, thinking, then with an evil smile it spoke, bowing, 'Very well.'

The scene faded and Karam was returned to the tent with her son. 'Mamma.'

Karminder was awake. Karam cried out and a cheer went up as the news spread. Everybody in the party was relieved. Karminder's recovery was remarkable.

By the middle of the afternoon, they were underway again, continuing their journey. When they arrived in Calcutta, a ship was waiting. The ship's captain gave them a trunk full of clothes, chosen for them in London. It was strange dressing in them and took some getting used to. New beginnings, Karam continued to remind them all.

Newly attired, they attended a photographic studio. Each had a portrait taken, then a group portrait of Karam, the boys and Dilbagh. Those were the first photographs ever taken, of anyone in the family to her knowledge.

That afternoon, Karam found little Sanjeet, her youngest, alone in their hotel suite staring out the window. The look on his face pained her. His face reflected a deep sadness and he looked extremely distressed. He started to sob as she approached him. She kneeled down as the little boy attempted to hide his tears.

'What's wrong little one?' she asked him with a loving voice.

He looked up with tears in his eyes, the weight of the world on his shoulders. He shook his head from side to side. She leaned forward and hugged him and could feel his tears as they ran down his cheek. Karam just held him. What else could she do? She understood his sadness, a sadness so deep he could not put it into words. He was leaving his home, his father, his grandfather, everything that was dear to him, but he would survive it. They all would. Happiness would return one day. Somethings only time could heal. She held him until he stopped crying, then she took him by the hand and they went for a walk. They didn't say anything, but they didn't have to.

Two days later, they were on the high seas destined for a new life, the future uncertain. It was thrilling. Everything had to be re-learned: how they dressed, ate, acted, how they spoke, not just the words. They could all speak some English, courtesy of the British presence in their homeland. Karam was determined they would improve. The captain was a good and enthusiastic teacher and every day he gave them instruction. Ten personal servants, along with two guards, accompanied them. They also endured the lessons, though with less enthusiasm.

Karam drew the boys closer. The snake episode had scared her. Just like that, she could have lost her beautiful son. Putting this out of her mind was not easy, the memory clung to her. The dream had not completely disappeared but the meaning was gone, sitting just out of reach and it worried her.

They were the only passengers on the large steamship that was filled with cargo, mostly her family's. It had been chartered just for them. Madras was the first stop and they spent a day touring the city in Colombo. They shopped in the markets, trying different types of tea. The supply port of Aden was next stop and by now they were seasoned travellers.

Excitement levels reached their height for the boys and Dilbagh as they travelled through the Suez Canal in Egypt. The exotic ancient land, with its mysteries and monuments, seduced them. Karam found it interesting but was untouched. Port Said was the final stop before London, they enjoyed their final days in the East.

The sea was rough as they sailed close to the shore on the last leg of their journey. The captain had asked them to remain indoors. The boys were excited, so they walked along the deck to get a closer look. The ship pitched from side to side and Karam suddenly became concerned, calling to them to come back inside. Sanjeet's last words to her, standing close to the rail, were, 'Look Mamma our new home,' as he pointed towards the cliffs.

Just then, the ship dipped sharply. A wave broke across the deck and the little boy was gone. Dilbagh, never one to hesitate, tore off his jacket, diving over the side. Crew men yelled, springing into action. Karam reached the rail in time to see Dilbagh struggling through the waves as her beautiful boy disappeared. Hands grabbed for her as she collapsed. Ropes and a lifebuoy were thrown over the side, a small boat lowered into the treacherous sea.

Karam found herself once again in the black silk tent. 'Our business is concluded.'

'No, you cannot do this, take me instead.'

'Not possible. He is already with us, you asked for this.'

'I did not understand the terms.'

'Come we were plain; you made your choice.'

'Dilbagh,' she hesitated, 'my brother?'

'No, he is not yours to give, his life belongs to another. Karam, don't play games, you asked for one son and we explained we would take same.'

Suddenly the dream she had while sitting with Karminder, when he lay dying, made sense. She had bargained one son for the other. How could she be so foolish?

'I know what you are thinking Karam, your soul is open to me, Sanjeet is with us. You cannot join him. Your story, that of your son, that of your brother, has yet a long way to journey. Sanjeet's is over. You are correct, the victims of war are not always the combatants. Now rest, you will need to be stronger than ever.'

Karam remained in bed for the remainder of the journey. Dilbagh, accompanied by Karminder, visited her daily. When the ship docked, Albert Syme, their business partner, took over where Dilbagh left off, organising everything. An ambulance arrived, conveying her directly to the Westminster Palace Hotel, where they took up residency. The trunks containing gold and precious stones, were taken directly to the bank. Karam remained distant. She accepted visitors, but there was a difference in her, a notable one.

She sought to quickly learn all she could about business in her new country. She read newspapers daily, researched through books and paid for council to advise. Dilbagh's main job was to find people who were willing and able to guide her. It was while reading The Times, her favourite newspaper, that she came across an article about Queen Victoria. After reading this and thinking upon it, she decided to end her mourning.

She asked for a carriage and, accompanied by Dilbagh, went to Albert Syme's offices. At first, he was reluctant to meet with her, to discuss business, as that was a man's game. He quickly put aside these prejudices when he heard some of what she was proposing. He guided them to move from the foyer, where he had welcomed them, and into his boardroom. Karam had planned everything during the short journey. As the fog of regret had slowly lifted over the previous weeks, her brain returned to life, stronger and faster than ever. Karam wasted little time.

'With your permission, Mr Syme, I propose we form a new business, Albert Syme and Partners. This business will be separate to both your current enterprises and ours. You will contribute no capital, but we ask for use of your facilities, your staff and your knowledge at no cost. In return, you will receive twenty-five percent of the new business. My brother, Dilbagh, will own twenty-four percent and my son, Karminder, fifty-one percent. Dilbagh will be our representative. I will work in the background, but this will only be known to us three and we will only meet in private.

'The new business' funds will be provided by some of the funds we brought with us. Initially, we will place at its disposal, the sum of 25,000 pounds. My father and other brother, Harry's company, will enter into a contract to sell all goods, tea, spices, linen and soon, tobacco from our plantations and farms in India and also now, Ceylon, for exclusive sale through our new company. Albert, we will rely on you to transport the goods in your vessels and then distribute and sell them. If you agree, then your solicitor can draft the documents and register the business entities.'

There was a fortune to be made here, Albert thought. They would buy the goods directly, transport and sell at perhaps six to seven hundred percent profit, with markets secured and supply guaranteed. Syme readily agreed. How could he not? There was little risk for him.

Two weeks later, in the same office, they toasted the new enterprise with champagne. Karam sat watching without picking up a glass.

Karam found a large house that she purchased in Belgravia. Karminder would live there with Dilbagh, who needed to be close to the business in London. Karminder missed his younger brother as the death had aged him. He was obedient and complied with his mother's requests, even though he would miss his mother. He was to be tutored by Mr Syme and Dilbagh.

Her second purchase was Land's End, a manor house on the coast. It was an emotional purchase, the home of a former barrister turned politician. It had been built by a religious order hundreds of years before. It was built a short walk from cliffs that overlooked the channel. The house was made up of a magnificent collection of stone buildings that interconnected. It would be her home, a place where she could retreat from the world.

Karam built a path from the house to the cliffs, where it wound its way along. At the end of it, she built an elevated stone pergola. Over the coming years, vines grew over it and sprouted flowers at different times of the year. She would sit and watch the waves breaking below from there. Karam rarely left and when she did, it was to visit the London house where she would meet people or conduct business. She transformed Land's End into her sanctuary and the servants and guards, they had brought with them from India, stayed with her. As the years went by, she built a small bungalow near the pergola, spending most of her time living there.

By the time Karminder was fully grown and left for New York with his new wife, she was only receiving visitors in the bungalow. Dilbagh, accompanied by Albert Syme, visited her often. Dilbagh had met a beautiful woman named Emma; his own story was finally beginning.

Tanya 1.23

TANYA, AWASH WITH emotion, put the volume of Karam's diary down. She had never believed much in the supernatural, yet there were too many things in the world that could not be explained. *It was strange,* she thought, *that Karam would document it.* Perhaps it was her way of coming to terms with what had happened to her children. Karam was a strong woman, practical, intelligent. Tanya had to give respect to what she was saying. There would have been feelings of blame and guilt after what had happened.

The pain Karam had endured, reached out across time, touching Tanya. Imagine losing a child like that. Your baby gone within reach of your destination, within reach of your dreams. Tanya couldn't get this thought out of her mind. Finding the strength to go on, being rejected by everyone, the incredible loneliness she must've felt. There were so many whys. Why did she disconnect herself from her other son?

Tanya tried to understand, why did this not bring them closer? Then the answer came. Karam blamed herself for her son's death, there was no other reason. She took the dream, where she bargained for her son, as real. *Could it be?* Tanya wondered.

What of her own dreams? The powerful dreams that she had been having about women like her. How much was Karam like her? She felt

Karam's presence now, coming to understand that she had built the bungalow she was working in. She had given up so many things, yet had found the strength, the resilience to carry on.

It emboldened Tanya. It was time to face up to things, to deal with everything that hung precariously above her head. And the necklace she now possessed, was something that had been made for Jasleen, the adulterous woman who had so hurt her family. *History,* she thought. The necklace was still beautiful, but it took on a new meaning now.

She felt her stomach. It was a nice feeling, her arm cupped it. Evan. Whatever had happened to him, should never have, but it did, that must be dealt with. Karam was there in the bungalow, or at least a part of her. She had searched the estate for her relative, only to find the only notable trace, here in this small bungalow.

Tanya only worked in the main room, looking out of the large floor to ceiling window with a view all the way to the boiling seas below. The cottage was painted white, nondescript. The same vines, that covered the gazebo next to it, covered the bungalow in the same plague-like proportions that kept the gardeners busy. The grey entrance door opened onto a room, that although smaller than the majority of those in the main house, was still large. The desk sat against the window. Apart from that, the only other furniture was a lounge chair in front of the fire on the other side of the room and a small table with two chairs, where you could take tea or dine.

The floors, along with the cabinetry inside, was all rich dark timber. Tanya, like Karam, only spent time in this front room. The kitchen, bathroom and bedroom out the rear of the house, had all been updated through the years. Only the lighting had been graded in the front room.

Tanya called everyone together and they met in the drawing room of the big house. It was mid-afternoon, teatime. The servants outdid themselves, preparing enough refreshments to feed an army. When they had all gathered, Tanya sat in the green leather armchair. It was a chair likely to be found in one of the better gentleman's clubs in London.

Tanya always felt comfortable sitting in it. She stayed seated, looking at them, as they gathered.

'I wanted to tell you all at the same time, perhaps you have guessed, still there's no putting it off any longer, I'm, that is Evan and myself, are having a baby.'

There was silence, then as one they rose, surrounding her. Tanya was pulled to her feet and embraced by everyone, in an outpouring of love and affection.

'It's the best news, we had no idea.'

Her mother was ecstatic, they all were. Tanya had underestimated their reaction, the love and affection she had always felt was missing, was now outwardly displayed. The tea turned into a party as they celebrated.

Their celebrations spilled over into dinner. Sober as they were, when Tanya finally made it back to her room, she felt exhausted. She was almost happy. She checked her phone and email, there was no news. Her brother had sent his best wishes by text message, and was as anxious as any of them for good news.

Evan, where was her true love? Tanya had convinced herself he was still alive, that she would know if he were not. She looked out at the moon and wondered if he was looking at it.

'Where are you Evan?' she said, the tears starting to form. Then she remembered what she had said earlier about resilience. She wiped away the tears.

Karam's story was taking shape in her mind. Soon she would be able to begin writing. There were other records she needed to analyse. There were diaries from Dilbagh and his wife, Emma and Karam's elder son. Albert Syme left journals as well as others. There were also official documents, but the essence of the story was being told in Karam's own words.

The little boy lost in the ocean, perhaps just off the coast here, explained her purchase of the house. Her need to remain there, slowly retreating from the world. She had lost so much: her life, her father, her husband, then one of her children. Under her supervision, the family's wealth had grown exponentially, but everything that she loved was gone. Tanya showered, then got ready for bed. She did a final check of her phone, said a prayer, then closed her curtains, climbed into bed, and switched off the light. Soon she was fast asleep and dreaming.

Marta 1.1

THE MACEDONIAN VILLAGE was known for the long-abandoned monastery that sat high on top of the mountain above it. The priests only visited it now during religious holidays: Easter, Christmas, New Year and Saints days, preferring to stay further down the mountain. Marta's grandparents were the last to live in the old house full time. Her father had left the village to become an architect, ending perhaps a two or even three hundred year residency. He lived in Rome now. He had not been seen by her for many years as they had never been close. Her mother died when she was young.

Marta grew up in Skopje, the Macedonian capital, where she trained as a primary school teacher. When she turned twenty-five, she met, fell in love with, then married a man from the nearby city of Bitola, named Branko. He had once aspired to become an actor, but that time had passed. Disappointed, he had opened a restaurant. As a listless drunk headed towards alcoholism, becoming the host of a restaurant seemed a natural progression. A natural host, he made up stories that entertained his customers and, in return, they shared their wine with him. People liked him and he prospered. These were happy days.

Then the war began.

When he told her he was joining the partisans, she laughed. He could not be serious.

'Stop believing your own lies,' she told him. 'Who will drink with the customers?'

He was soft, had never fired a gun, knew nothing of that world. The thought of him fighting the Germans, or anybody, was hilarious to her. When he explained it was his patriotic duty, he sounded like a moron. She told him how she felt and he took offence.

Wounded, he walked away from their happy life to join the war. As she watched him leave, she realised how much she loved him. Marta ran after him and he held her in a tight embrace. He promised to return home in one piece, to come back to her. He told her to leave Bitola, to stay at her grandparents' house in the village, it would be safer there. He may even be able to visit from time to time. She held him tighter, begging him not to go, he broke free, leaving her alone.

That afternoon, she packed her things, taking some food, wine and two suitcases. She lied to one of the men who worked in the restaurant, telling him she needed to care for her ailing grandmother, who had been dead for twenty-five years. Leaving that man in charge, she gave no forwarding address, just a vague promise to write. Another lie. He promised to take care of everything and she wanted to believe him.

Two days on the bus took her close to the old village. A donkey and cart took her the rest of the way, slowly winding its way up a thin dusty road. The small house was exactly as she remembered it. Some of her cousins lived in the house next door, more in the house opposite and they helped her move in.

There was a small school in the village that had not had a teacher for many years and they reopened it for her. There was no money to pay her, however, the villagers made sure she always had plenty of supplies of wine, cheese and bread. All arrived daily, along with yoghurt, fresh milk and everything she needed. All Marta had to do was mention something she wanted and soon after, it would appear.

At night, the loneliness crushed her. She would read or visit someone she could drink with, her cousins, anyone. But each night ended in the same way, alone in her bed. She lay beneath the covers scared of what might happen, scared of what she didn't know, scared of everything.

Hearing news of the partisans activities, Marta feared persecution for her husband's deeds. Six months passed with no word, then a year. German soldiers with their Albanian counterparts, came to the village, but they left her alone. She breathed a sigh of relief. One morning, she awoke to find a note pushed under the door. It was unaddressed and simply read:

Safe and well. She burned it.

She put on a brave face, but she felt dead inside. Life had no meaning anymore. The villagers all adored her, but it was of little comfort. Every night she battled, scared to wake up in the morning for fear of receiving another note, the one that read:

Dead.

She lay, curled up in bed, paralysed by fear.

Climbing the steep path to the monastery became a weekly crusade. Rising before dawn, with only a cup of water to sustain her, she would head off. She took a candle with her that she lit in the chapel, before sitting quietly as it burned. Marta had never been a regular church attendee, but these vigils had taken on a very solemn and sacred meaning for her. She prayed, waited, tried to keep going. No news was good news, but no news was a torture so cruel she could not have imagined the pain it generated within her. It was after one of these pilgrimages to the monastery that things changed. As she came into view of her house, she saw the black uniforms waiting for her.

Branko was an idiot, but he was her idiot. A tear escaped, running down her cheek.

Marta 1.2

WHEN A HEAD rolled out of the bag onto the ground, she was horrified, yet dared not look away. A guard picked it up by the hair. He held it where she could not avoid seeing it.

'This is your husband?'

'No.' It was almost a whisper. 'Do you know this man?'

The Germans had returned. They had come looking for her. She shook her head, although there was something familiar about him. There was the possibility she had met the head's owner but she could not identify it. The very thought scared her. How many of the men she had known, were now just a head in a bag?

The officer made a gesture and several soldiers entered her yard carrying bags. The first head was placed on a table, then a never-ending stream of heads were paraded then held up for her inspection. Marta's skin crawled and her body ached all over. She was desperate, the pain, emotionally torn one way then the other, while standing as still as possible.

As Marta dismissed each head, it was placed on the table forming a gruesome pile. With her life hanging by a thread, she wondered how they had tracked her to the village. How could they possibly have known about her? She managed to maintain a passive reaction while inside she was dying. Would anything be left? When they showed her the head of Branko's cousin, Milcho, she screamed. Her hands flew to her face in a futile attempt to cover the horror, but it could not become unseen.

The officer stepped forward. 'This man is your husband, yes?' She shook her head frantically. 'Who is this man?'

His hand went to the holster. The man holding the head moved it closer. Marta sank to her knees but the head followed her. She shied away. The officer drew his pistol and the crowd of villagers, who had gathered, let out a collective gasp. The pistol was now hovering above her head, there was no choice.

'My husband's cousin.'

He returned the pistol to his side and the questions continued. 'What is his name?'

'Milcho.'

'Last name and age?' Marta had to think.

'Vukovic, he was thirty-four, I think.'

'And when was the last time you saw him?'

The tears wouldn't stop. The head was back now that the pistol was gone. She was staring into Milcho's cold dead eyes. Her mind filled with memories. There he was in the restaurant dancing, a bottle in one hand, a cigarette in the other. The absurd thought of what would happen if you poured wine down his throat, now occurred to Marta. It elicited a scream and a maniacal laugh that would haunt anyone who heard it.

'Answer the question!'

The pistol returned, more threatening this time. She did not think he would ask again, but she was paralysed. The old priest, Draskovic, intervened. He stepped forward from the crowd.

'Please,' he said, holding up a calming hand, 'she is in shock. Give her just a moment to compose herself.'

The officer, non-committal, took a step back. Draskovic spoke softly, 'Come child, you must answer, find the strength.'

He called for water then offered it to Marta. 'Drink a little, then answer.'

'A long time ago, in our restaurant in Bitola.'

'You have not seen him since?'

'No.'

He looked directly into her eyes and showed her another head. 'Was this man with your husband?'

'No, my husband abandoned me, then disappeared. I have not seen him since.'

This statement was true. Another officer appeared, summoning her interrogator. They moved away from the crowd for privacy.

'Leave her here. If she is in contact with her husband, she might lead us to him. Have her watched; we have friends here.'

He nodded. 'She is as good as dead anyway; we can collect her whenever we like.'

Marta remained on the ground; the priest put his arm around her. She flinched when the officer returned, burying her head in the priest's side for protection.

'We know you aren't telling us everything. When we return, hopefully your memory will have improved. You can go for now.'

The priest helped her to stand, then took her inside her house. The soldiers put the heads back into bags, except that of Milcho. They placed it on a stake in the middle of the yard while the crowd disbanded. 'You must be careful child. Danger is everywhere these days; it can fall upon you in an instant.' The priest was earnest, she could feel the genuine concern in his words. He sat her in an armchair then, wrapping a blanket around her, he searched the kitchen for brandy, pouring her a glass.

'Drink.'

Marta didn't argue.

A soft knock on the door preceded the entrance of her cousin, Vlatko and his wife. They were tentative, nervous. The priest turned toward them.

'Come help her, she needs you.'

He moved aside and they cautiously took over. Vlatko went for more brandy and returned with both the bottle and a glass for himself. The priest joined him for a glass, it had been a hard afternoon. The priest finished his quickly, requested one more, then a final one for the road.

'I leave her in your hands. After a good night's sleep, she will feel better. Tomorrow will be a new day. I'll keep you in my prayers.'

The priest motioned for Vlatko to follow him out. 'Is there anywhere you can send her?'

Vlatko gave it some thought. While he did this, the priest took the bottle he was still holding and drinking straight from it.

'Nothing comes to mind.'

'She won't be safe here now. They will return. She should be dead but they must think they can get something from her, or she would be.' He pointed to the stake.

'Where can I send her? They are everywhere,' said Vlatko.

'If they return here, they may take others with her. Everyone is in danger.'

Vlatko was turning white. It suddenly dawned on him that, as a cousin, he was a potential target. The priest handed him the now empty bottle.

'Be strong my boy. Now is not the time for falling apart. If you have relations, friends, somewhere remote she could disappear to, give it some thought but tell nobody. When darkness finds you, it is not easy to escape.'

Satisfied, Draskovic headed out of the gate, his work complete. He could go home and enjoy a few glasses, free from guilt. He had performed a miracle. The girl was alive, they would have to settle for that. He basked in his own glory.

Vlatko watched him leave. For a man who had drunk so much, in such a short space of time, he was remarkably steady on his feet. He then stared at the head as the priest disappeared from view. He was not the man for situations like this; he was not the man for any situation. He had hidden away in the village his whole life, but now the world had found him. If she left, he would have to go too.

A neighbour approached, carrying a pot. It was Lydia, one of their friends.

'Soup?' she asked.

He followed her into the house.

Marta 1.3

LOSING MY MIND, I am losing my mind. She stopped. It was an overwhelming spiral with no end. I live in a house with the head of a cousin on a post outside, this is either hell or I am losing my mind! She was wearing a red shirt that belonged to her husband. Run! Every fibre in her body was screaming to run, just go, get as far from there as possible. The Germans were on to her. Regardless of the facts, they would eventually kill her. She was terrified. How could people be this cruel? She had heard somewhere in history there were women who were just as evil, but the men as far as she could tell, had a monopoly.

The story will roll on, her father had once told her. We are simply players, observers. You may think you have control, but you are only fooling yourself, people are stupid. She did not doubt that he believed this, but she was not so sure. If she reflected on events though, she would have to agree with him.

Marta could never have imagined that one day she would live six feet away from her husband's cousin's severed head. There would be more heads, perhaps next time hers. She started to weep uncontrollably. Once more, her inner voice shouted, 'Run', then she thought of her father. What was the point? It would happen.

The priest, what of him. He had saved her life. She cursed him, better she had fallen right there and then. Bitterness formed in her mouth, a foul taste, testing her resilience. Some grappa, that was what she needed. Just one glass, but there was none. Another relative came to her, this time her grandmother. She could see and hear her clearly.

'You can sit dying of thirst or get up off your ass, then go drink your fill.'

Marta said this out loud, stood and left the house. She found Lydia, her friend who had brought the soup.

'Did you enjoy the soup?'

'No, it was awful.'

They drank a bottle and started on a second, they were small bottles. Lydia smoked a cigarette; Marta was undecided as to whether she wanted one or not.

'I thought maybe you would have left us?'

'I have nowhere to go.'

Lydia shrugged; Marta was being realistic. 'What about your father?'

'He could be in Rome, I have no contact with him, no idea of his whereabouts.'

'He is still your father, blood is blood.'

Marta was tiring of the same questions, the same line of thought. She had sought out Lydia to get drunk, not to discuss her circumstances or philosophy. It crossed her mind that the Germans would set a trap for her. She wondered, who in the village was working for them. Was it Lydia? It could be anybody, a head on a post was a mighty persuader. Something told her to seek out the priest. He helped her once, would he again? How far would his devotion go? Too many questions. They finished the second bottle, then started the third. She staggered home; the rest of the day was just a blur.

Vuk Draskovic, the priest, was haunted by demons of his own as he tried to sleep that night. They all seemed to be visiting. Evil things that lurked in the shadows, sights no man should have to witness. Suddenly, in the middle of it all, his grandfather appeared. They were standing in one of the fields where he had grown up. His grandfather, a shepherd, took him by the hand.

'Come my boy we have work to do.'

They wandered around for hours, his grandfather, shotgun at the ready, silent, not saying a word.

'What are we doing?' Vuk asked. He stopped walking, too tired to continue.

'We can't stop now. One of our sheep is missing. We must find it before the wolves do. Time is against us and we must hurry before the sun goes down.'

He looked worryingly up at the heavens. They continued searching as the sun continued to move across the sky. Every time Vuk stopped for a few moments rest, his grandfather urged him on.

'Come, my boy, come.'

They came to a place where there was a small indentation in the ground, bordered by two large rocks. From inside, they could hear the bleating of a sheep. Standing guard was a large wolf, ravenous, salivating. His grandfather did not hesitate, letting go of the boy's hand he raised the shotgun and fired. The wolf yelped, falling dead. Another appeared over one of the rocks, he fired but this time only wounding it. It bound away, the others that had gathered, followed their wounded leader. His grandfather re-loaded as they disappeared.

'Cursed luck.'

His grandfather put the shotgun over his shoulder and bent down to the opening. He reached inside. To Vuk's surprise, he pulled out Marta. He turned to the boy who had suddenly grown into an adult.

'Always look after your flock.'

With a start, Vuk awoke in his cell, covered in sweat, the dark enveloping him. A coffin appeared in the corner of the room. He wiped his eyes, then it was gone. He needed something: coffee, some hot milk with sugar, a reassuring arm around his shoulder. He dared not move from his bed. He turned his head to where the cross was nailed above the bed. Instead he saw a bloody axe! A demon appeared, smiled, then disappeared. Sitting back, leaning against the headboard, he pulled the blanket tight around him. He was about to cry.

'Calm your mind,' a voice out of the blackness told him.

He crossed himself. The voice was familiar; he couldn't place it though. Still, he felt better for hearing it. He would not move from the bed, not even if the room was on fire.

A thought occurred to him, had he saved the woman, or only delayed the inevitable? He hated these things. This other world of mysteries, darkness. His soul ached. He could ignore this, simply wake up tomorrow as if nothing had happened, yet there were consequences. The coffin, the axe, the demon, they were all warnings. He must at the very least try to save her, but how?

Then it came to him, his childhood friend Sasha, he could help. His saviour, his best friend, well ex-best friend. He would go that very day. Why did he not think of it before? The answer to that was easy, there was history there, bad history, but Sasha could help her. His cousins, his uncles if they weren't too old or dead, they could save the woman. Something, or someone, was happy with this as the mood of the room changed and he felt calm.

As the first signs of light emerged, he found the courage to rise, dress, then seek out the abbott. Breakfast was bread and salt. After a quick blessing from the abbott, he left in a hurry. Transport was a cart pulled by a donkey; the driver was paid double for waking up early. They travelled all morning; it was past noon when they reached the bus stop far below the monastery. They had not been there for more than five minutes when the big brown bus came into view, blowing black smoke and creaking from everywhere.

On the bus, he thought of Gordanna, his teenage sweetheart, her beautiful pale skin, her green eyes. He saw her naked, lying voluptuously and imagined her fully clothed, walking along a meadow carrying the milk pail, her head wrapped in a blue scarf. He could picture the three of them, Sasha, Gordanna and himself, running, playing, sixteen years old, acting like little children.

She had won two hearts. She chose Sasha's. It was the smart choice as his family had money. They were criminals who, like his father and grandfather, tended the sheep by day, then at night tended other things. Gordanna liked money. She liked jewellery and silk underpants. Vuk had little money, none to be precise. He cursed the friend of his entire life. In a drunken rage, he said many things he would regret, things unforgiveable. But love does that, especially to the young. He cursed them all and, in the middle of the night, he ran away. He would punish them all by joining the priesthood. In his mind they did not care, Sasha though, was devastated and Gordanna wept. Love was cruel.

The bus lumbered forward. It would take two days and he would then have to walk five miles, unless he could find someone to take him. The other passengers on the bus were sullen: a woman who had geese in wooden crates up on the roof, she worried about them as if they were made of gold, a man in a grey suit who claimed to be a salesman, he clutched a suitcase on his lap as if his life depended on it. When Vuk asked after the contents, he replied, 'samples,' then turning his head to the window. An old woman with grey, almost silver, hair told him she was returning to die in her father's house. She spoke with great passion about her father.

'He told me,' she said, 'you will return one day, either heartbroken, seeking forgiveness or to die here in my house.'

It was not clear to him why this was important. Once again, she was a runaway, denying her own family the opportunity of caring for her through to death, removing their right to bury her, to weep. He asked her if she had considered whether her father's house would still be there. 'Yes of course, he promised. It was his idea after all, I wonder though, if he will still be angry. I have gifts, pictures to share.'

He blessed her; they continued their journey. The check points were annoying, delays followed, The woman with the geese grew more anxious, becoming rude. The driver suggested eating them, she calmed. He felt safe in the company of these people, perhaps they had been sent to protect him, a thought that brought laughter. The sudden outburst unsettled the other passengers. They wondered if he had gone mad. The geese woman got off the bus. One by one they disappeared from his adventure, to continue their own.

Then, it was his turn. As he disembarked, a man carrying a shop mannequin and a large bag, climbed aboard. What wonders did he have to share?

Wandering down the ancient dirt road that led to the village, Vuk's thoughts once turned again to Sasha. He could see him, his uncle's holding him back, Sasha threatening to kill him, to cut off his arms then force him to eat them. An odd threat! He had dared him, having just bloodied his nose, beating his lifelong friend with his fists.

'The only way that will happen is if your criminal uncles help,' he had taunted him.

Gordanna had appeared weeping. She ordered him away. As he could not refuse her, he left, left them all. He took his vows and would never lie with another woman, never.

A man appeared, riding a horse and cart. Vuk crossed himself, then climbed on board. The man was unfamiliar to him, yet he knew the way to Vuk's father's house. They rode for a while in silence, the country becoming more familiar.

'Time passes differently here,' said the man as if reading his mind. 'Do you know Balle?' he asked.

The man nodded. 'He sent me to collect you.'

He shouldn't have been shocked, even though, as far as he knew, nobody had known he was coming.

'Your father had a dream, then he saw some lightning in the east. He called me to his house and said go and pick up Vuk at the bus stop, he needs something.'

'Do you know me?'

'Of course.'

They travelled again in silence. As they drove past a tree, he saw something: a shadow, a spectre. As they came closer, for an instant it became clear: an old woman smiling at them.

'The ghost of my grandmother,' the man said.

He pointed at the woman who waved. Vuk pinched himself, without turning around and the man laughed. The sun looked different, redder; it was high now as they turned into the yard of his father's house. The man turned his head towards him. Vuk realised he was blind.

'Be careful Vuk, the wolves come out at night. They are hungry and they smell blood.'

A crowd was emerging from the house. Vuk climbed down from the cart and the man drove off. They stood staring at one another, the crowd on one side, he on the other. The crowd consisted of his father, his uncle, his mother, an aunt. There were children he didn't know, but who reminded him of his cousins, his siblings, his grandparents, they were the echoes of letters he had received. His mother broke first, crying tears for all of them. They had missed him, they were proud, they admired their priest in his black cassock.

They ate and drank a little too much. It took care of the afternoon as years were filled in around the table. More of his relatives arrived: his brothers their wives, cousins, old friends. When he tried to speak to his father, he cautioned silence.

'Not now, sleep tonight in your room. After breakfast we will speak, it's dark and we need to close the house for the night.'

Vuk was beyond tired. Too much was happening and sleep was difficult, there were literally ghosts in his room aplenty. He called for quiet.

'Where should we go?' they shouted en masse.

Reluctantly they drifted away, still he could not rest. Sasha would know by now that he had come, Gordanna as well, he supposed. Could they deny him? It was impossible, both owed him. There were things between them that bound them together. There were secrets in this place, ancient secrets that were passed on. Then there were the secrets everyone keeps together with those shared. If Marta died, he would be cursed, that much was clear. He must do everything to save her.

Sleep remained elusive, yet when the morning came, he was in a deep one. When he woke, he splashed water on his face. In the mirror was the face of a long dead aunt, who smiled.

Breakfast was already laid on the table when he came down, with bread rolls, yoghurt, burek, cheese and coffee. Looking around, he saw many heavy heads, bleary, blood shot eyes. Everyone was eating in silence, consumed with their own thoughts. His father motioned to him; they were walking out of the door when one of the children came running into the house nearly knocking them over.

'He comes!' the child cried.

'Ah, well, you have no use of me now. Go, I will hear about it later,' Vuk's father said.

He put his arm around the boy and sent him on his way. Vuk stepped outside, almost blinded by the morning sun. Looking west, he could see a figure approaching so he walked in that direction. They stopped six feet apart, each eyeing the other. Vuk crossed himself but Sasha didn't move. He looked much the same, but the years had perhaps not been kind. There was a hardness about him now, a darkness that had perhaps always been there and had now taken over almost completely.

Vuk smiled, but was it possible to have a happy reunion, after all that had happened, all that remained between them? Like a tree, three fifths remained under the ground, only that which was tolerated came through to the surface.

Sasha broke the silence, crossing himself. 'You would see me dead, well I'm here.'

They eyed one another. Vuk started to laugh and they hugged. 'It is hot already. We cannot stay here in the sun. Let us walk.'

Neither man led the way, they walked in the same direction. In the heat and the dust Vuk's cassock felt heavy as they walked for almost an hour. There was a small stream surrounded by trees that had always been a favourite spot, where the water bubbled up through the rocks, forming natural pools.

'We should go for a swim.'

Vuk sat heavily with his back against a tree, he was feeling nostalgic.

'Come,' said Sasha.

He was being persistent. Reluctantly, Vuk stood and removed his clothes. On entering the water, he immediately felt an improvement in his health. The water seemed to purify him and he felt lighter. His mind opened as he dunked himself repeatedly.

The world was a curious place. Two days ago, he was walking through a village, now here he was swimming with his boyhood friend, a friend he had sworn an oath to kill, a friend he had never expected to see in this world again. He looked at his friend with the eyes of a young man, a young man whose lover had been stolen. He felt tears welling up inside, did he really have to kill him? Should he be forever marked like Cain? It was ludicrous, a day ago unthinkable, here in this place, time passed differently. He had not been the one to bring it up, the victim had brought it up for him, the murder he thought was forgotten, but nothing ever is. He found a shallow spot and sat down, the cool water was up to his neck, Sasha came and sat near him. 'I can't help you.'

'You have no choice.'

'It's death you are bringing to me.'

'Good.'

'I'm here, drive your knife into my heart, nobody cares. Gordanna is not expecting me to come home. Blood demands blood, our son will kill you, he will end things, there is nobody to avenge you.'

'My father and brother?'

'Will tend their sheep. I'm no miracle worker, God doesn't sit with me as he does with you. The Albanians, the Germans they hunt my kind, they...' here he tapered off. 'They are formidable, I'm not visible to them, but this will make me vulnerable.'

'How can you know until you hear the story?' 'The story is the same, it never changes.' Sasha closed his eyes, they both sat in silence.

'What's the difference, only my children's lives?' he laughed. 'These people have no morals; they kill for fun.'

They climbed out of the water sitting on a rock in the sun to dry.

Sasha gave in.

'Tell, me everything, leave nothing out. I know the story, however, I want to hear it from your lips. I want you to tell me things that seem unimportant. If you withdraw your vendetta, if you promise to look after my family, should something happen, you have nothing to worry about. We will save the woman, no bodily harm will come to her, she will live forever if that should be, but I would have forgiveness. For years I've been waiting for you to come and kill me, lying in bed at night, waiting to die. I will bring her to safety, take my word for it. Forgive me, make your promise then go back to your monastery.'

Vuk told Sasha everything. When they parted, he felt sad. It was like losing his friend all over again.

The hour was late, it was growing darker, late afternoon. As he wandered along, she appeared to his right. Gordanna stood, looking at him with an eternal longing in her eyes. The boy standing next to her looked familiar, very familiar. He did not remind him of Sasha, but the girl on the other side was the spitting image of him. He walked on without a word.

As he approached his father's house, an old man came running up to him. Vuk was surprised at the man's nimbleness for his advanced age, which he assessed to be over one hundred. He was flustered and very nervous.

'Have you seen my daughter? She's arriving by bus and is unaware that we have moved?'

Marta 1.4

MARTA SLEPT AS the dead while dreaming vividly. In the dream she was running through tall grass laughing, her husband chasing her. He was seeking the ultimate prize, a kiss. Her head scarf fell off as she ran, dodging this way and that. It gently floated to the ground marking her way. He closed in on her, then disappeared. She stopped, turning around in a circle. He was gone. She turned again and standing there was the young German officer holding Branko's head, holding it by the hair as it swung slowly back and forth, blood dripping from the neck. He looked directly at her with his cold dark eyes, his voice sending a chill down her spine.

'Another one for your collection.'

He let the head go, she caught it. The eyes stared up at her. That's when she woke, sweating and out of breath. Something was wrong; someone was in the house. A figure appeared. Marta focused, then as she started to scream, a large coarse hand clamped over her mouth.

'Silence child silence, you are safe. Help has arrived.'

His voice reminded her of the priest: kind, authoritative. Her eyes grew wide. She could feel his strength fill the room. Here was a man who would, if he chose to do so, protect you to the last breath in his body.

'Please don't scream when I remove my hand.'

She nodded. He removed his hand then lit a match. His hair and beard were long and unkempt and he wore all black. He lit the candle next to her bed.

'Come, dress quickly. Bring only what is important as you will never return here.'

Marta climbed out of bed, then quickly dressed in the semi darkness. Into a small bag she packed a picture of Branko, an old family photo album, some documents and money. There was some cheese and bread wrapped up in paper, but no brandy and there was no time to get any.

'Come now, the wolves are out and it's dangerous. We are not safe yet.'

At the open door he whistled. In the darkness, she could make out two men carrying a bundle.

'Look away.'

She obeyed the command. The two men brushed past her and once inside, they immediately went to work. The bundle was a corpse, roughly her size and hair colour. They placed it on her bed then put a shotgun directly in front of the corpse's face.

'Come quickly.'

They ran for two minutes, during which time not a word was exchanged. In the dark they met two other men who were scouring the horizon for movement. They motioned to stop. Heavy breathing was all she heard. Suddenly, there was a large bang as both barrels of the shotgun fired at once. Then, like hearing the starter pistol in a race, they were off at a run. This time when they stopped fifteen minutes later, she was exhausted, collapsing onto the ground.

When they had caught her breath she asked, 'What was that noise?' even though she already knew.

'Your salvation,' came the faint reply.

The other two men arrived. With barely a moment's rest for them, they were underway again, this time at a fast-paced walk. Dawn found them close to a large rock that was almost inconspicuous. Well hidden behind bushes was a small gap, barely wide enough to squeeze through. Inside was a vast cavern, big enough for several rooms, beds, a small place to cook and another to wash, it was a hidden oasis.

'We will rest here.'

She had expected to see Branko. When she didn't, she asked, 'Who sent you, are you friends of my husband?'

'No,' said the man who had rescued her, 'we are friends of your friends, people who want to see you live to old age, and beyond.'

That only made her more curious. 'Who are these friends of mine?'

'Good people, be happy, there are few of them in the world.'

She was exhausted, hungry, yet no longer hungover, the physical activity had cured that.

'You are dead now. That what you were, cannot be ever again. Of those things you have in your bag, only the cheese and bread is of any use to you. Put the rest in the fire, it will only cause you harm. You must become reborn. This time you have the advantage of wearing clothes instead of being naked. You must take on a new name for a new life, your old one must be left behind or one day it will turn on you and kill you. The dead cannot take anything with them.'

She wanted the things in her bag, the photos, the documents and sensing this he pointed to the fire.

'Therein lies salvation.'

Reluctantly, she opened her bag and removed the food placing it on the table. She then walked quickly to the fire emptying everything else onto it, money included. As the flames grew with intensity, she placed the bag on top as well. *My old life ends.* The thought brought the tears and they rolled down her cheeks. Life was precious. Into the ashes went her past. Feeling a sudden wave of nausea, she staggered to one of the beds falling into a fitful sleep. In her dreams she saw each of her grandparents searching for her in the cold dark night. They were unable to find her.

'Where have you gone beautiful child?' they called.

Hidden by the mist, she was no more. For ten days and ten nights

Marta and her new friends moved between caverns like the first one, hidden rooms, empty crypts in graveyards and abandoned cinemas. Branko never appeared. Why she kept expecting him to she did not understand. Hope maybe. He was the past and the past was gone, yet she did in her heart believe he was behind this, that he was her saviour. Would she ever know the truth?

On the tenth day, the rescue party did not enter the hideout with her. This one was a hidden cave next to a stream behind a large rock. Her rescuers each said goodbye, hugging her and giving some small token as a gift from their belongings: a page from the bible from one, a scarf from another, a lock of hair, they would forever remain nameless to her. Their leader was the last to say goodbye. He handed her a small cross on a leather necklace, then kissed her roughly on each cheek.

'Stay inside,' he told her. 'Do not leave, there is plenty of food, fresh water from the stream, a bathroom, beds, a table. You need nothing more. Do not leave, be patient, a man will come, he will open the doors himself. Do not open them for anyone. The smoke is hidden but be careful, only light the fire at night. Put it out before sleep and stay inside.'

He crossed himself, watched her enter, leaving the door open long enough for her to find a lamp, then she was locked in.

Time passed slowly in the dark. The only glow was from the lamp or the fire. She was scared and never sure when to light it as she wondered when day ended and night began. She had to sense it and wondered how the smoke was funnelled away. The food, as he said, was plentiful: salted meats, vegetables, fruit stored in jars. The bread ran out but she did not make more. It was lonely.

One day, she realised that to the outside world now, she really was dead. She lay in bed naked, allowing the darkness to envelop her. The cool water from the stream purified her as she washed her body. She lay for hours, days maybe weeks, everything was still. She dreamed of Branko no more, he was gone. The village, all her previous life slowly disappeared. She came to regard them as figments of her imagination.

Life had come to this, the war had claimed her, an innocent victim, a civilian. What would become of her?

She found some barber's clippers in the cave and cut off all her hair, burning it along with all her clothes. When she had given up all hope, when she was certain that she had been forgotten, the entrance opened, but not as wide as when she had entered. She hesitated but did not look back, she did not call out, she squeezed through, fighting her way out, clawing at the rocks with her fingers, She was bleeding from scratches as she emerged into the daylight, re-entering the world reborn.

She fell to the ground.

Marta 1.5

BRANKO TOOK THE death of his wife badly. He wanted sainthood for her. Only now that she was gone, did he realise how much he loved her. His course of action was clear. Revenge. The Albanians and their Nazi overlords arrived early to view her body for themselves. This obvious display of guilt she portrayed in her suicide, made them so happy in being right, that they forgot to kill Vlatko, his wife, and the other cousins. By the time they remembered, it was too late to correct their mistake. As Branko started systematically killing them, he became as fierce as any man. Now with a heart of stone, he extracted vengeance without mercy or emotion.

Marta had changed also. With her former life wiped from history, she embarked afresh, her personality altered. She now only wore plain dresses, mainly blue. She avoided black and white, anything to deflect attention. When asked where she was from, she simply answered, 'Far away.' She never elaborated. Zoran, a friend of Sasha's, had taken her into his household, promising protection. At night she still heard her grandparents searching for her, only she no longer knew who they were. Slowly their voices grew faint. She helped with the sheep, cooked lunch, sewed. There was no sadness, no longing, because there was no past.

Zoran was single. He longed to tell his story to Marta, but it always stuck in his throat. The days of hiding were slow. Patrols she crossed paths with, encountered a peasant woman, so illiterate she could barely communicate with them. Her dreams were often filled with a priest, a woman named Gordanna and a blood feud. She dreamt of strange people who traded geese, of ghosts searching for their lost loves, the ghosts of children searching for their parents and of a strange girl who had been lost forever.

When Zoran's sister married, she asked Marta for advice. 'I've never been with a man,' his sister confided.

She considered the question for some time before answering, 'I have observed men and women for some time and there are differences. As a woman, there is a price to pay, so seek your payment up front.'

'Payment?' Zoran's sister had asked.

'Yes, a price will be paid for being married. Men lie. If you are not paid up front, you will not be paid, then you will suffer twice: for being married, then for not being compensated. If not, you will suffer.'

The war continued without her. She lived, others did not. There was a house not far away where musicians lived. The place was alive with magic. One day as the musicians were preparing to leave, she happened to be walking past. A tall man holding a violin case addressed her.

'Good morning,' he said, smiling and removing his hat, then bowing to her.

'Good morning,' she replied. 'Are you ready to go?'

Without hesitation she responded. 'Yes, of course!'

He directed her on to their small bus.

'Our singer has arrived,' he said to the others, 'time to depart.' And as simply as that, the future aligned itself once again.

They played in restaurants, small theatres, anywhere. The accordion player, Bodan, the violinist, Koki, and his brother, Marko, who played guitar. They brought happiness wherever they went. The war left them alone.

She never sang a note when they were not all together, never practiced or even thought about it. When they started to play, the notes came easily. If evil was encountered, they played their instruments, happily singing as buildings collapsed around them.

One day they happened to be in Rome, fulfilling an engagement at a small restaurant. Marta was sitting outside enjoying a coffee when a face from the past walked by. Vuk Draskovic turned, unable to believe his eyes. There she was, the woman he had once helped, sitting drinking coffee.

'Good afternoon,' he said.

'Good afternoon,' she replied.

'Excuse me,' he said, 'I was walking by and I noticed you sitting here. You remind me of someone I once knew.'

There were many men like that in Rome, but she had not expected it from a priest, an orthodox one at that.

'How can I help you, Father?'

'I know you, forgive me I recognised something. We share a history.'

'I am from the old country if that is what you mean. Now we travel, my friends and I. Tonight we perform here, tomorrow who knows where we will be.'

The priest continued to stare. She shrugged, there was no longer any memory of him.

'We share something more than just heritage!' He seemed adamant. He looked onto her soul and saw it there, wrapped in cloth, hidden. He debated what to do next. The war was over, her former life was gone, that was the price she had paid.

He made up his mind. 'I am mistaken.'

'Wait,' she cried.

A longing, a deep yearning suddenly overtook her, an emotion that she didn't understand.

'Please sir, have a coffee with me.'

She signalled to the waiter. Reluctantly, he took a place at the table and the waiter placed the coffee before him.

'What brings you to Rome, Father?'

'There are people waiting for me.'

'You said you know me, that we share history.'

'I was mistaken, please forgive me.'

She looked at him, seeing through his lies. Ashamed, he blushed. 'Please,' she insisted.

'Long ago, I helped you. Your life was in danger. I sent my friend to rescue you and he saved your life. He also ended it. You died during the war. Your husband lives and you live. You sit here drinking coffee, but you are dead. Your body has a grave, only your soul is missing. It's here in this new life. Everything is possible, things don't follow directly, here time passes differently.'

'Marta!'

They looked up and saw an old man standing in front of them. 'Daddy?'

In an instant, some of her past was returned to her. She became the old Marta once again.

The geese were a gift for her former husband Branko, more of an afterthought. They were noisy. The bus brought her to the city, then a taxi to the new apartment building he now called home. It was a fitting reward for the new country's war heroes. The old was disappearing, the future, that was what they wanted, what they had fought for. The driver could wait. She saw him, he was having an argument over a jumper as a young woman was telling him off. Children were running around at his feet. The woman was pregnant and she held out the jumper that was green with a red pattern. Reluctantly he took it, they both smiled at each other. She left him to it.

The taxi took her to the station, promising to deliver the geese for her later. As she sat on the bench waiting for the train, she reflected on what might have been. She was not bitter. How could she be? Choices were made and she had lost her husband and herself a long time ago. War had taken so many things. Had it not scarred every member of her generation?

She thought of her grandparents, of the men who saved her, the priest Vuk, Sasha, Zoran, the musicians, then wondered what lay ahead.

She marvelled at the reality of the horrors she had witnessed. Was it true? Did General Branko collect the heads of his enemies?

She thought on this for a while, waiting quietly for the next chapter of her life to begin.

Tanya 1.24

THESE DREAMS WERE becoming prophetic. Tanya was living the lives alongside the women she dreamed about, along with them, absorbing their experiences. They were so vivid, so real. She also dreamt of Evan. She was still convinced he was alive. She dreamt he was safe but unable to reach out to her. She saw him stuck on the wrong side of a river, desperate to cross but unable to find a way over. Poor Evan, she had been so close to telling him that she was pregnant. It would have meant so much to her for him to know.

She made herself some tea, then sat on the window seat looking out across the gardens. It comforted her that inside her, the baby was growing. The doctor was happy with her progress, though she wanted to fly her out to a hospital to conduct tests. Tanya was uncertain what to do. She was torn between waiting for Evan and moving on with her life, while believing that one day he would return. Eventually, she told herself that she would have to go to the hospital. She pined for him, longed for his touch. She didn't want to do this without him. She was missing him so badly that it hurt. Tanya now had no choice but to get on with it and she resolved to do so and was ready to speak to the doctor. She didn't want to leave the estate though, she wanted to go on living there. She was sure her aunt would have no objection. Her plan was to hire a nanny to help, that way she could work during the day. It would help her cope with the absence of Evan. If there was light at the end of the tunnel, maybe just maybe, Tanya could reach it.

Evan 1.3

THEY HELD A small celebration for Evan's, and hopefully, what would also be the rest of their final night in the cave. It was the doctor who convinced Aman that although there was no imminent danger, the time had come for him to leave. The doctor had discovered that a British patrol would be passing by the following day. They could sneak out at first light, then traverse the five miles to reach the point where this patrol normally passed. The doctor knew the way.

The British patrolled another ravine that ran alongside a river.

They would need to cross the river to meet them. There might be some danger in doing this, but nothing was without risk. They were all so close to their desired prize. The mood was light as they celebrated. Evan was already contemplating things, jumping into the future. He would be sent home, hopefully he would never have to return. His career in the army had lost its charm, it was time to move on and he would seek a discharge, finding a way out.

The doctor, normally anxious, was calm and relaxed. Evan was their saviour as they had been his. He would miss them all, but he couldn't wait to get out of there. The cave was claustrophobic, death was waiting in every corner. That night he tossed and turned, unable to sleep. He thought of Tanya, of holding her in his arms, her long soft hair, but there were ghosts about. He kept thinking things would go wrong and was haunted by dark thoughts. They followed him as he fell into a restless sleep.

Aman woke them all, long before dawn. After a hasty breakfast, they gathered their belongings and left the safety of the cave. Evan was wearing civilian clothes but he had his weapons at the ready. The doctor had a concealed pistol, Aman was the only adult not armed. They moved quickly away from the caves, the doctor leading the way. Evan's senses were working overtime, his eyes moving constantly scanning everything. The doctor knew where he was going, leading them along the winding trails and paths. Evan was impressed with how the little boy kept pace with them. He was a seasoned veteran when it came to survival and hardly made a sound, keeping as vigilant a lookout as any of them.

By the time the sun was rising, they were over halfway to their destination. An hour later, they were there. The sun was harsh on all their eyes after spending so long hidden under ground. The doctor's plan was to arrive early, near where the patrols passed, then observe from safe places he knew until Evan could attract his comrades. Evan changed into his uniform as they took refuge in another cave. All their eyes were glued to the ravine with the water flowing rapidly below. The doctor looked concerned.

'That river is moving too quickly it's higher than usual.' His English, like Aman's, was good.

'I will swim across when we see the patrol approaching, then we can work out a way to bring the rest of you across,' Evan said, determined something as small as a river was no obstacle to him.

They had all learned patience. They sat together in their lookout and waited.

Tanya 1.25

$\mathcal{T}$ANYA WAS WORKING in the small cottage, when out of nowhere she felt incredibly tired. At the same time, the sea became rougher. Black clouds formed and it started to rain heavily. Fighting to keep her eyes open, she was staring out to sea when she thought she could make out the shape of a young boy struggling, trying to swim in the waves. She remembered the story of Karam's son, Sanjeet, and wiped her eyes. When she looked again, he was gone. Feeling nauseous as the wind whipped the rain against the bungalow, she walked over to the small lounge in front of the fire, laid down, pulling a blanket over herself as the rain continued to lash against the building. It's ferocity following her into her dreams.

Hanh 1.1

IT WAS AS if being inside a dream, she thought, as she woke and looked out across the bay from beneath the tree where they had spent the night. The vivid imagery was stunning, so beautiful that it moved her, enriching her soul. The soft morning light reflected off the still water of the bay, small fishing boats began to appear as specks far out on the water as her eyes focused.

Hanh sat transfixed, lost in the beauty of the moment, taking it all in. She remained that way for quite some time, thankful for the beauty all around her. She sat quietly reflecting on how far they had come since they decided to embark on their epic journey. She was travelling with her friend Minh, who had been her neighbour back in the village where they were from, sleeping peacefully beside her. Hanh had never been this far from home. Every day, sometimes every moment, she would see something new or see it from a different angle and her heart would lift. Her life prior to this great adventure had been very different, filled with dogma and routine. Back then, a time that seemed a lifetime ago, she had rarely, if ever, taken the time to look at the world around her, to really look at it, to take it all in. She had simply done things when they needed doing. The only time for reflection was also like everything else, scheduled and planned.

At the end of every day, along with her mother and grandmother, she would walk to the edge of the village where they lived. There they would sit, looking down the road that stretched to the valley below, in silence. It was a mediative time, a time to focus on their loved ones, for each was quietly waiting for their husbands to return from war.

Although she did not regret her life, at the same time, the thought of returning to it, or anything like it, scared her. She forced these dark thoughts away, that life as it was, had ended.

As she sat there, everything felt right in the world. She was on a journey, an unexpected one, that had no fixed destination. One where anything was possible.

It was her mother who had suggested to her that it was time to leave. One evening after they were returning to their hut from their nightly ritual, her mother unexpectedly turned to her and told her that it was time for her to go.

'Go, try to find him,' she had said.

At first Hanh had not understood what her mother meant.

'We are too old, our time is coming to a close, but you are still young. Go, see if you can find him.'

There was a long silence as she considered this. 'Where would I begin to look?'

'Go to where the soldiers are. Speak to whoever is in charge. They must have some idea of where he is.'

Hanh turned it over in her mind, then dismissed it. 'I couldn't.'

Her mother cut her off.

'Wake up in the morning, take your bicycle, take half the money, say goodbye and go.'

'What if I can't find him?'

'It's time to go. You will find him or you will find a new life. To stay here lost in your own unhappiness and grief, as we do, will condemn you to a life of loss and misery. In this way, you will find him or you will be able to move forward. All we do is stand still, trapped in time, living a life that is already over.'

Her mother had always been a deep thinker. She had obviously given this a lot of thought, then it occurred to her that her mother was sacrificing a great deal in telling her to do this. It was a selfless act that was allowing Hanh to escape. Her mother continued.

'Convince your friend Minh to accompany you. She is wasting her life here as well. Go together and never look back. If you find him, good, build a new life together. If you don't, find a new life for yourself. If all else fails, we will be here waiting.'

Hanh felt the idea start to rise up within her. It was ridiculous, yet inescapable, the temptation to go was overwhelming. Once her mother had released it, once it was off and running, it had a life of its own. Already it was too late, there was no turning back. Hanh turned to face her mother who was crying, but they were not tears of sadness, rather tears of happiness and joy. Hanh had been set free.

Alone in her hut, she ate a simple dinner, after which she visited her friend Minh, who was easily convinced to go with her. That night, sleep was difficult as she battled with excitement and anxiety and nerves over the unknown.

The following day their epic journey began. There were no long goodbyes.

Hanh's mother and grandmother watched as the two women rode away. Minh had no living relatives. There had been few words. Her mother had insisted that she take some more money and all three felt the sadness of their parting, yet the intention was a positive one and they hoped to be reunited one day. Minh, who had wanted to leave since her husband was killed, would never look back. She rode in front as the two women silently continued until the village was lost from view.

Sitting under the tree, looking out onto the bay, Hanh had the feeling that those events were a hundred years ago. She laid her feelings bare, if to nobody else, to herself, in the beautiful pre-dawn setting. When they took her husband for the army, it was the final straw, something inside her was broken.

They had become estranged from each other after marrying and starting a family at such a young age. When the children left, however, they had come back together, forming an even deeper bond. Then he was gone. He told her to wait for him, that he would find a way to come home, that one day they would be together again.

For three months Hanh and Minh had stayed in cheap rooms, moving address every few days, chasing the sparse amount of official information that may or may not exist in relation to Hanh's husband's military career. Each lead gave a slither of hope. Each ended in disappointment. The only constant was the advice to go home and wait. But she had done that, she was tired of it. They moved from city to city, but their luck didn't change. Then one day, they were told by a friendly company corporal that although he could not confirm whether he was with them, the battalion that her husband was assigned to, were close to the border, fighting the enemy in the south.

There was no discussion. The two women spent a final night in the city, then the following day, began the next phase of their journey heading south and that had brought them to rest for the night under the tree where she sat now, reflecting as the day came alive.

Hanh 1.2

THEIR DAYS EACH followed a similar path, yet all were different. They woke in their own time, usually after sleeping outside. They often picked a spot near water. Breakfast was what they were carrying with them and usually consisted of fruit and some tea. After breakfast they would bath and prepare for the day ahead. They would then cycle until they reached the day's destination. Upon reaching the next village or town, they would then make enquiries about Hanh's husband, shop for provisions then head on down the road for the next place. It was becoming more difficult the further south they were going, especially in the rural areas.

Looking out to sea, Hanh caught sight of a huge American warship.

The enormous grey vessel occupied the majority of the horizon. Watching from the safety of some trees on a small beach, they witnessed the ship as it menacingly glided through the water. Off in the distance was gunfire, helicopters. The two women, scared at their first real sight of the war, were too terrified to move. That night as they sat hiding amongst the trees, Hanh decided that the search phase of their journey was over.

They changed direction. Saying goodbye to the South China Sea, they headed east, crossing the border into Laos. It was here that Hanh had her lifetime moment of good fortune. They had been cycling all day. Tired, they had left the road following a small stream into the thick jungle, seeking a safe place to camp for the night.

They found a spot amidst some trees that they felt was suitable. Hanh left Minh to rest, then went out collecting some wood to build a fire. She had not been walking long when she came across a crashed helicopter. It must have been there for some time as it was already being consumed by the jungle. Tentatively, she peeked inside, through one of the rear doors that was open. She had expected to see dead bodies but there were none. Papers littered the floor. Unable to read English, they made no sense to her. The letters CIA were meaningless.

She spotted two khaki bags both emblazoned with a red cross. She knew the symbol and associated it with doctors and medicine. Curios, she crawled inside retrieving them. The bags were unusually heavy. It was only when she got them outside she realised why. Opening them, she found they contained, not medical supplies, but tightly wrapped packages of US money and at the bottom of the bags were six gold bars. When she returned to the camp, she decided not to say anything to Minh, not wishing to worry her friend. She simply dismissed it as some things she had found in the jungle. There was no elation in finding the money. No doubt, it would help, but money meant little to Hanh, she knew it could not bring happiness.

When Minh had fallen asleep, Hanh removed the money then carefully packed it into one of the khaki bags. It was heavy, but she could manage it on the front of her bicycle. The women were travelling light and had few possessions with them. The other small amounts of money they had, were concealed on their person.

The following day, they cycled until reaching the next large town. There, Hanh announced they were headed for Phenom Penh, Cambodia and would be traveling by bus then boat. They loaded their bicycles onto the roof of a bus. This surprised Minh, however, she was tired and on the border of becoming unwell, so she went along with it. It took five dusty days for the bus to reach the Laotian city of Pakse.

There they found a boarding house to stay and rest. Sleeping in a bed for the first time felt strange, but each of them enjoyed being off the road. They spent five days there, planning the next phase of their journey.

The plan was to seek passage on a small boat down the Mekong River. Before they left, Hanh borrowed a sewing machine from the owner of the boarding house and, with some thick white cloth she had purchased at a local market, made a custom undergarment to carry and conceal the money and the gold. She had not had a chance to tell Minh about her windfall and now felt too embarrassed to do so.

It took twenty-three days, with a mix of bus and boat trips, to reach their destination, Phenom Penh. They found lodgings at a small inn and, after some consideration, decided to part with their precious bicycles. Both women were happy they were nearing the end of their journey as soon they would be in Thailand, from where they hoped to make their way to a new life somewhere in the west.

Hanh 1.3

Pᴴᴇɴᴏᴍ Pᴇɴʜ ᴡᴀs a bustling exciting city and Hanh and Minh both enjoyed staying there. It was there that Minh visited a dentist for the first time in her life. After this both women decided to stay and have a lifetime of dental work done. Over the following months, they shopped, buying new western style clothes, visited doctors and improved their diet. After just two months, they noticed the difference. They were happy there, but the lure of the west was strong so they made plans to leave.

They hired a private car and driver to take them closer to the border with Thailand where they could cross. They were riding in the car when Hanh realised one day, how much more complex the conversations between herself and Minh had become. Although neither said so, both now wanted more out of life; their expectations and ambitions had grown.

The countryside they were travelling through was breathtaking. On one side was the river, on the other rice fields, it was very picturesque. Hanh was feeling nostalgic. When they came to a particularly beautiful spot on the river, Hanh asked the driver to stop so they could have lunch under the trees and rest.

It was a hot day and they reached for their water that they gulped down. In their western style clothing they stood out. When Minh removed her cap, Hanh noticed how her hair shone in the sunlight. Each would have to work hard to maintain their new way of life, there was no going back. They chatted about what they would do when they reached their destination as neither knew what to expect, Minh had her heart set on the US. She would somehow become a business owner. Hanh was more inclined to a life in France where she hoped her skills as a seamstress would be useful.

Minh turned the conversation in an unexpected direction. 'What about your husband?'

Hanh always had that topic at the front of her mind. 'I'll write a letter to my daughter.'

'What I meant was, you have been waiting for him for so long, what will you do now?'

Hanh, slightly embarrassed by the personal nature of the question, had not considered this.

'Will you keep waiting? Will you wait for him the rest of your life?'

'I don't really know.'

'When we were in the village, I used to watch you every night, as you went to wait for him. I wonder what would you say to him now if he suddenly appeared?'

'He is my husband. We have a relationship that is beyond words.'

'I miss the intimacy with my husband, our bed was well used, as was yours.'

'Yes, it was, privacy was difficult.'

Realising that she had embarrassed her friend, Minh set to put her at ease.

'I was your neighbour. Walls are thin, but what lies beyond it, could you go back to that? Can you go back to discussions of fields, back to the village, your old life? Can you go back to being the seamstress, that tiny world we once lived in.'

Hanh, not used to facing things, found herself unable to immediately respond.

'You are different, you are not the woman I used to watch from the darkness. The seamstress who kept working from dawn until dark. Hanh, upright, strong. You have grown into the name you were given. What if he came around that corner right now? Would you run to him? Tonight, would you lie with him? But what then? What comes when lust and the day today existence is no more? What happens when you are free to do anything? Is that what love is? You married at sixteen as your parents and his parents thought it was a good idea, a good idea for many reasons, but you were a child and he was a child. You had children when you were still a child, before you knew even who you were. Your bed was a happy one, many are not. Money, responsibility. Your husband treated you well, many do not. He was faithful, as far as we know. Familiarity, with responsibility, your marriage was based on that. Maybe you thought you knew one another, but did you?'

Hanh had never considered any of this. She understood Minh now a little better. Minh, the quiet observer, the one who saw everything.

'The men from our village visited brothels, drank in the bars when they went to the city. Was Vinh any different, do you think? What we see and what we know, can be quite different things.'

Minh did not want to go too far and decided to back away slightly. 'Have you ever asked what love really is?'

'He didn't leave me, Vinh was taken. Forced to go it was not his fault,' Hanh said.

'As I said would you now go back to that, back to him?' They sat in silence for a long time.

When they moved off again, both women could sense the difference. The afternoon car ride was quiet,. They stopped at a small inn, eating dinner in the same sombre mood. In the morning, they continued their journey.

Hanh also realised the frustration her children must have suffered living in the village and how this had affected their relationship. There were two children, both adults. Her son a doctor and her daughter a university professor, both living in Hanoi. They were peasants when her daughter finished kindergarten but she had surpassed her mother's educational achievements.

Her husband, Vinh, was cunning. He could visit the bank, sell their crops, yet she had surpassed him in education as well. Both children must have been out of their minds with frustration by the time they left. Her son was a surgeon and she felt pride in this. It replaced the anger she had felt for the regime that had taken her away. Could she have become a surgeon if the school had arrived a generation earlier? Could her husband have become a proper businessman? They had done well through hard work, building on the legacy of those who came before. For the first time, she understood that by not having an education, along with things like proper healthcare, they were at a tremendous disadvantage.

Communism had started to give these things and, in time, would deliver them. Capitalism had all those things already. That, she realised, was what was driving both the women on their journey, a better life. They travelled across the rest of Cambodia without incident.

The closer they came to their goal, the more anxious each became. The roads seemed hotter, dustier and time seemed to drag. When they finally reached the border, they had trouble making a connection to deliver them safely across. They met a woman, May Ping, who said she could arrange everything for fifty American dollars. The lady who ran the boarding house they were staying at, warned Hanh that she was a bad woman and she was worried.

Minh said they would be okay. The trip had been going so well, but Hanh said they should be cautious, suddenly seeing every stranger as a potential enemy. They waited. Hanh decided to make adjustments to her corset, changing it so it would conceal everything, even if she were forced to remove it. The money and the gold were undetectable unless it was cut open. With no other options, Hanh agreed to using May Ping as an intermediary to get them across the border into Thailand.

On the morning they were due to depart, the two women waited outside their boarding house, happy that their journey was almost at an end. Maybe her guard was down a bit in the excitement. The car picked them up and Hanh was concerned straight away as they were heading away from the border. Her protests fell on deaf ears. They drove for an hour, their bicycles and luggage piled precariously on the roof.

Finally they came to a stop at the end of a dirt road outside of a hut. Both women cowered in the back seat too scared to move. May Ping was there, as were three or four men, all armed. Reluctantly, one after the other, the women climbed out of the car. They were separated and Minh was taken into the hut. May Ping stood menacingly off to the side, holding a pistol.

'You,' she said, pointing the pistol at Hanh, 'inside.'

Clutching her bag, cowering, Hanh shuffled towards the hut, pushed open the crude door and entered. She was repelled by what she saw there. On the floor kneeling, completely naked and blindfolded, was Minh. Her heart flew up into her mouth, her pulse accelerated and her breathing became erratic. Standing behind her was a man also holding a gun, another near the window and May Ping.

'Consider yourself lucky,' May Ping said, 'you are both too old to put to work in the brothels, nobody would want you. All I want is your money. Give it to me and you can both go free, otherwise, "bang, bang!"'

She started to laugh.

'Please don't take long to decide, you have three seconds.'

'Here, just take everything,' Hanh said, offering her bag.

May Ping looked at the two men and gestured towards the door. 'Give it to me.'

May Ping still had the gun pointed at her. Hanh reached into the bag, pulled out some US dollars, her spending money. The bulk of her money was in the corset. She held them out the money, offering it to May Ping.

'Is that all?'

Hanh turned the bag upside down; the contents fell out onto the floor of the hut. May Ping came forward. Bending down, she checked the contents around with her gun. There were a few loose notes and she picked them up. She then took a $50 bill from the roll and stuffed the remainder in her bra.

'Wait here until you hear us leave. You should both be feeling very lucky that we are letting you go.'

Hanh ran to Minh the moment the door closed. She put her arm around her, undid the rope that bound her hands and removed the blindfold. She searched for her friend's clothes then helped her dress. As soon as they were outside, they moved as fast as they possibly could. Both women were in shock. Hanh knew they had to get moving.

Spotting some thick jungle on, what she thought was, the border side, Hanh pointed it out then helped Minh as they headed for it. She found a trail and they followed it. The trail branched off this way and that and after reaching a clearing under the canopy of some trees, they stopped and laid down. They had not been there for more than five minutes when a woman emerged on the other side frightening them. Seeing their distressed state, she told them to be calm and wait, she would get help.

In half an hour she returned with four young men and some cool water. They drank it down and then the men helped carry them to a nearby house. When they arrived, the woman took charge, putting them both straight to bed. All afternoon and into the evening, they remained in a semi- conscious state while they were cared for by these strangers. In the evening, a healer came to visit them. He gave them herbs to make tea, promising to return the following day.

After he left, they told their new friend their harrowing tale. When they finished, the woman, whose name was Kamira, told them to sleep, to rest in her house for as long as they needed, they would be safe there. To prove this point, she had two of her sons stand guard outside the house all night. They rested for three days.

Hanh was torn, she had done half the right thing by giving her money to save her friend, but at the same time she had the gold hidden away. She was filled with guilt. She had placed a price on human life, once more she opened herself to self-examination.

On the fifth day, after breakfast, Kamira said, 'I have a surprise for you. Today your dream will come true. My sons will safely take you across the border. A few miles across it, there is a camp for refugees. My son went there to check and they will deliver you both there.'

Hanh and Minh began to cry. Here a stranger was taking their problems to heart. That such a loving human existed, overwhelmed them. When they were leaving, Hanh turned to Kamira.

'I promise I will do something for you one day. You deserve that.'

She would always remember Kamira standing there as they left, a huge smile on her face, waving to them. She was one of the kindest and most caring people she had ever met.

True to Kamira's word, her sons delivered them across the border safely. The men had an intimate knowledge of the country and at times, they carried the women to make the journey more comfortable.

When Hanh tried to give them money, they refused. She searched for something to give them, a token, she had nothing. Both women bowed their heads, thanking them again. Hanh and Minh watched as they entered the jungle, returning to their mother.

Hanh 1.4

THEY HAD TO wait to be admitted into the camp. It was run by the United Nations with assistance from the Mercy foundation, a religious organisation that did missionary work. Hanh and Minh were interviewed by a young man who worked for the United Nations, as part of their processing into the refugee camp. They were interviewed together as it was assumed they were family. He asked them, through an interpreter, where they were from. They told him they were fleeing persecution in North Vietnam. They had been told to say this.

They had no passports and few other papers, yet the young man was optimistic those problems could be overcome. He explained they had recently re-settled people in Australia, New Zealand, the United States and Canada. He told them that there were English classes and it was a good idea to attend.

'If it is a new life you are looking for, even countries in Europe, such as France and Germany, would accept a limited number of refugees.'

He then processed them into the camp that, at any one time, had between three and five hundred refugees in residence. The camp had once been a monastery. It was old but supplies were plentiful the women could hardly believe it.

The camp always seemed to be busy and, after taking just two days to settle in, Hanh and Minh made themselves available to help in any way they could. Hanh was given the job of helping in the small school room, a job she immediately enjoyed. Minh helped in the kitchen.

They were happy, but still scarred from the experience at the border. It had changed their relationship but in different ways. Hanh was still guilt ridden for not offering everything to save her friend, while Minh felt closer to her friend for saving her. Hanh felt the secrets and a gap grow between them.

Hanh's skills as a seamstress were also valuable. When it became know that she possessed these skills, she was sought out by many of the camps inhabitants. She was especially popular amongst the nurses, who called her Mamma San. One, Dawn, a young woman from the USA, became a very good friend.

The months passed, things moved slowly, they received the documents from the UN allowing them to travel and applied to the US and France, but had not heard anything. They had been warned things moved slowly.

Hanh decided to write two letters, one to her daughter and another to her son, neither of which she would send. She also asked Dawn if she could assist with their immigration. Dawn was quick to act. She would write to people at home and tried to speed things up, she was only too happy to help.

It was only three days later that an envoy came to visit from the US Embassy to interview them. Dawn, true to her word, had phoned her father who personally visited their state's senator who had made a phone call or two and now the wheels were in motion. Dawn, a great friend to them, was a mystery. She came from, what they perceived as, a wealthy background, from a good family, yet she became a nurse, volunteered to serve in a country on the opposite side of the world. Yet there were others, who only cared about money and material possessions.

Hanh 1.5

As THEY BECAME more integrated and vital in the running of the camp, Dawn organised for the two women to have their own rooms, even though they were unofficial team members. Minh was full of ideas for her future business career. She never tired of talking about the future.

It rained incessantly which was their introduction to Thailand. The young woman's name was Kate and she was from Ohio in America. She was twenty-eight years old, full of energy and, within moments of their meeting, she and Hanh became close friends. Minh was jealous but hid her feelings. Kate and Hanh went everywhere together. She was a volunteer like Dawn and had studied at university to become a qualified teacher. She had a strong social conscience.

At first, Kate had wanted to be a nun, had recognised a lack of calling and quit. She taught in a school for a few years then, after breaking up with a man she realised she didn't love, decided to do volunteer work and see where she ended up. She had three sisters, all of whom were married and all of them in Ohio. They were starting to raise families; she did not feel drawn to that life. Hanh had discovered the value of education, never missing an English class which Kate taught and had also been learning how to read and write both in Vietnamese and

English. She held a deep respect for Kate, or Katie as she liked Hanh to call her, and valued her education, her wisdom at such a young age, her enthusiasm for life and her good heart. She also felt something deeper, but kept these feelings hidden.

Dawn encouraged Hanh to read also. The more she learned, the more voracious her appetite became. She sourced books everywhere, her mind was opening and she loved it. As time passed, she became less scared of her own feelings and emotions and began to question everything.

Why God had chosen not to speak to her, was a topic that hurt Katie to think about. Hanh, who did not understand western religion, listened without comment, whenever she brought it up. Hanh could attend, indeed had attended, western religious sermons. She was happy to stand singing along, would take part in the rituals, listen to the sermons without any real involvement beyond curiosity. Hanh smiled and nodded at the right times, bringing some to believe that Christianity touched her, but she would have been equally as happy at a concert or even better a book reading.

Both Katie and Hanh were experiencing strong emotions toward each other. Hanh though, was more concerned by their age gap than anything. Hanh, at forty-six, was eighteen when Katie had been born. Katie sometimes found herself looking at Hanh like a lovesick teenager. They worked together teaching the camp children. For them, it was not work. The children picked up on that, enjoying the classes they taught together. The refugee children, normally sullen and unenthusiastic, smiled and laughed in the classes run by the two women who made learning fun and brightened their days.

Then a large envelope arrived. Hanh and Minh would soon be leaving the camp forever; their immigration to the USA was approved and soon the final leg of their journey would be underway. Minh danced, overcome with emotion and happiness. Hanh tried to act in the same way, yet did not feel the same as her friend. Something deep inside her, told her that this was not her path. She tried to ignore it but it would not go away.

As Minh would soon be departing, Hanh decided it was time to come clean about the money. She laid it out carefully on her bed and then covered it with a blanket. She then brought Minh into the room and, after telling the story, pulled back the blanket. Minh could not believe her eyes. Hanh had expected her friend to be angry or bitter, but instead she was happy.

'That explains how we were able to travel so easily, you shared it with me.' Thankful, Minh hugged her friend. 'So, while I was dreaming of becoming rich, you already were,' she laughed. Hanh had not expected this, she thought, with the way Minh regarded money and wealth, that she would react differently.

'Half belongs to you,' said Hanh.

'No, it's all yours. You used some to help me, for that I'm eternally grateful. Without you, I would still be back in the village. You used some for my benefit already, after all you found it and carried it all this way.'

'You must take something for your new life. Take one package of money.'

'I thought we were both leaving, starting a new life.'

'Our paths are different. Yours stretches out in front of you. Your vision, what you want, all you need is to follow it to reach your destination. Mine is still uncertain, but it does not lie in the same direction.'

This saddened Minh. She hugged Hanh tightly. The jealousy she felt towards Katie began to surface; she fought hard to keep it down. She would miss the friend she had grown to love. They transcended friendship, due to their shared experiences, but deep down she knew that Hanh was right.

'I insist that you take this money.' Hanh held up the package and reluctantly, Minh took it.

It was Katie who made the discovery that would change both of their lives forever. She had been shopping for some cloth to send home to her mother, when she saw a young blond-haired boy who looked all the part like an American, one who might be from California. The child was lost in the busy market and crying. Kate took him by the hand. She was surprised to find the boy could not speak a word of English, that he was not American at all. It was only when she was closer, she saw he had Asiatic features.

She searched for a policeman. Unable to find one, she took him to the nearest police station. The boy, it turned out, was an orphan. Intrigued, she waited until someone came from the orphanage to collect him. The person who came was a nice American young man about her own age. He explained that the orphanage had been established to help the unwanted children of American servicemen. Such children faced discrimination and were often left to survive on the streets. Since the war in Vietnam had begun, with thousands of foreign troops visiting Bangkok on R & R, the problem had increased to the point it was unmanageable.

He told Katie that the orphanage building, a large old colonial mansion, was about to be sold. With nowhere to go, it meant the children faced an uncertain future. The funding was also coming to an end. Soon he would return to the US, along with the team he was working with. Unfortunately, he told her, they would not be able to find homes in the US for all the children by that time.

The story moved her. She went with him to the orphanage, wandering around the house and grounds and seeing the children's smiling faces, Katie felt she had found her purpose. She had no idea how, but knew she was going to help these children. She sought out the young man, whose name was Daniel, finding him in the office. Katie came straight to the point.

'How much would we need to buy the house and keep the orphanage running?' she asked him.

'Fourteen thousand US dollars for the building and the grounds, including taxes. You need to be a Thai citizen to purchase property, but those problems can be overcome by placing the property in a trust. The children cost roughly $10 a month to feed and clothe. There are currently fifty of them. Other expenses run to about $200 per month. If you had $1,000 a month, you could run it properly. The state department and donations would cover most, if not all, of the monthly expenses.'

The building was the problem and they had been unable to raise the money to buy it.

'The charity,' he said, 'has decided the whole project to be economically undesirable, meaning there is more money in other projects and is pulling the resources. It's political, this is a problem nobody wishes to acknowledge if you understand.

'It's too hard for them to stay here and believe me, fifty children is the tip of the iceberg. You could take in another hundred tomorrow. What we try to do is make this a temporary solution until we can find homes for them back in the States. That's the area that needs investment. There are plenty of couples crying out for children to adopt them back home. Life here is too hard for them, they become outcasts. I have to stress that point again.'

Katie understood one thing. She understood that fifty children would soon be homeless and that all future orphans, would simply be left to fend for themselves. She could not bear that thought.

The soldiers and the army were the ones to blame. They had denied responsibility. It occurred to Katie that not all victims fall on the battlefield. Ending that train of thought, she focused on the initial problem. Where could she find the money? She felt she had no choice now, knew she must act.

Back home, her church, they had money; she could get maybe a $1,000 there. Her grandmother might be good for another $500 and her parents the same. That was $2,000. She had $750 of her own savings and she could write to her congressman. But all that would take time and time was not something they had. She needed a miracle.

Hanh noted Katie's mood and asked her what was wrong. She listened to the story as they were sitting in their favourite place in the far corner of the garden under a tree. Tears flowed, as Katie spoke of the plight of the children and their uncertain future. Hanh put her arms around her in an attempt to comfort her. Katie buried her head in Hanh's side and cried, holding nothing back.

Hanh wondered. Something was stirring in her stomach. It was a sad story, some of which she did not understand, but it was growing within her, an excitement. How could she describe it? Like the way you feel on the morning of your wedding, or when you are expecting your first child: apprehensive, yet excited.

'Take me there,' she said. Katie looked her through her tears.

Hanh continued, 'Come let us go now, right away. Wipe away your tears, you have cried enough.'

When Kate looked up, she was met with the most loving eyes she would ever see. Hanh brushed some of her hair away from her face, beautiful blond hair, soft to the touch. She leaned in and kissed her. It was only a kiss on the cheek, but it was wonderful.

They called for a taxi. As they rode through the streets, Hanh was becoming more anxious, as if something could easily take away the feelings she was experiencing. Katie was becoming concerned about her so they held hands in the back of the taxi. They arrived at the orphanage. For Hanh it was a moment she would never forget. Speaking years later, she said that it felt as if her heart was opening up. They sought out the young man, Daniel, who Katie had met earlier.

'You two wait here,' Hanh told them.

She walked around the entire compound. The children started to follow, feeling her excitement. She picked up a small boy and carried him; he was dark skinned with the deepest green eyes. When she returned to where Daniel and Katie were standing, she had the biggest smile Katie had ever seen. There was something serene about the way she looked.

She looked directly at Katie. 'Together?'

Kate wondered what she meant.

'Together, you and me, we run this place, care for the children. You stay in Thailand with me.'

Katie smiled.

'Yes of course, but how?'

'Understand, this will take many years, lots of hard work, no going home, only maybe to visit. Think about your family.'

'Yes, we will stay together, but how?'

'What about you?' Hanh had turned to face Daniel. He looked at her closely. *Who was this crazy woman?* But something he could not describe was happening, it was something magical, he dared not say "no" to her.

'Yes, yes I will stay,' he said. 'Let's go inside.'

They went into the small office that served as the orphanage's administration area, where Hanh started to remove her clothes.

'Hanh, what are you doing.'

'Don't be embarrassed.'

She was wearing a white corset that resembled a bathing suit. As they watched, one by one from within the corset, she removed four yellow bars and placed them on the desk. Kate struggled, but Daniel recognised them right away.

'Bloody hell.'

Katie could only manage to say her name. 'Hanh?'

She then pulled out two packages and opening one. It was full of US dollars. She placed it onto the desk also. Daniel recognised the CIA markings, but he said nothing.

'Call the people selling this home, buy it today. You,' she said pointing to Daniel, 'you run things, look after the money. We will care for the children, the three of us. We will help each other. Together, we will work together.'

Hanh was the only one not in shock.

'Hanh where did you get all of this?' asked Katie.

'Not important, I found it in the jungle.'

Hanh looked at the other two still standing with open mouths. 'Come on we have too much to do.'

Daniel counted the money only after Hanh and Katie had left.

The packages contained $50,000 American dollars in each, a

fortune. He kept the gold bars in a safe. They would come in handy one day. He marvelled at how fantastic the world was, while burning the CIA wrapper.

That night, Katie stood shivering in Hanh's room. She had crept inside without being heard. Slowly, she removed her clothes in the darkness. Without hardly a sound, she moved across the room and into the bed. She was surprised to find Hanh naked, then she smiled, realising if her visit was not expected, it was at least desired. She moved in behind her and, for the first time, felt naked skin against naked skin. Hanh smiled in the darkness.

Hanh 1.6

TEN YEARS LATER, Minh was sitting at her kitchen table. A letter from her friend, Hanh, was open, lying flat in front of her. So much had happened in the previous decade after they said their goodbyes in Thailand. The world was changing, not always for the better, according to Hanh who seemed to be still in the thick of it. Her letter was full of news from across the border in Cambodia. Bad things were happening there, refugees were fleeing in their thousands. Kamira and her sons were at the front of Hanh's thoughts; she longed for news of their safety. She was, as she stated in her letter, willing to do anything to help, but did not know what to do or if help was needed. She had considered paying some men to go across the border to find out for her.

Katie and Daniel, who helped her run the orphanage, were still with her. Daniel had fallen in love and married a Vietnamese girl he had met and had just returned from a honeymoon back home. Hanh was prepared for them to tell her, eventually, that they were leaving. She could not expect, as she put it in her letter, that they would stay forever. Maybe another year.

Not to worry, she had said. There was now a steady flow of young people arriving to work in the orphanage every year as volunteers. Katie was happy. They shared a nice life together, but Hanh said, she felt one day she would also leave. Minh had suspected the relationship between Hanh and Katie, though Hanh was not aware. If she was, it had never been discussed. She was sad that Hanh felt Katie would leave her. Perhaps she was right.

A young man named Tavanah, a lawyer, had joined them. He helped Daniel handle the orphanage's business affairs. She had started the letter with a sad resignation, that young people have their own lives to live. A year after the last Americans had left Vietnam, there was still no news of her husband. She felt he must have fallen. She had written to her daughter and son, neither had replied. She was now resigned to the fact she may never see either of them again.

The influx of new refugees from Cambodia had overwhelmed the UN camp where they had once stayed. Hanh still volunteered there, even though she was busy enough at the orphanage. She seemed happy, yet there was something that still haunted Minh. Was it the way she spoke about her husband or the relationship with Katie? It seemed that her past was still tying her down, stopping her from experiencing the happiness that she deserved.

Minh concluded that there were things unsaid in the letter, confirming her earlier thought that Hanh still waited for her husband to return, even if she was now committed to someone else. She wondered if she still sat at the entrance to the orphanage each evening, a habit she had fallen back into. If she did, how did it make Katie feel? Did it cause problems between them? she wondered.

The letter had concluded with a request for Minh and Dawn to visit. Could they both come? Could Minh persuade Dawn to take a short visit? Hanh had something to discuss that could only be done in person. Minh wondered what it could be.

Both Minh and Dawn had assisted in fund raising over the years. This had started small, collecting donations, to now holding major fundraisers that contributed most of the capital required to run the orphanage. They had petitioned the government and the army for assistance and had also helped set up a new adoption network to bring the children out of Asia and resettle them with families in America, Canada and Europe.

Minh, through an enormous amount of hard work, commitment and perseverance, had become a successful businesswoman in the relatively short time, since arriving in America. She had proved to be extremely shrewd and a visionary. Unable to find steady work after arriving, she had learned how to drive and purchased a cheap station wagon. With the assistance of Dawn's family giving advice and showing her how, she purchased some basic cleaning equipment, placed ads in the local paper, in every window and on every noticeboard she could find. At first jobs were slow to find, but she took them all, regardless of how small, doing them all with the same dedication and high level of service.

Word soon spread and before she knew it, she had more work than she could handle. She hired others. One person quickly turned to three, then five, then ten. She trained everyone. Customers came to expect and receive the same level of service, regardless of whether it was Minh or a new employee doing the job. Those that did not measure up, and there were few of them, were quickly moved on. Those who remained, received good benefits. She looked after her people. Dawn and her family received a ten percent interest in the business. They had refused it at first. When Minh continued to insist, they accepted with the idea of passing it on to the orphanage and other charities.

After three years, Minh put the next part of her plan into action. She purchased outright, an old, abandoned supermarket in a rundown part of the city, a building that she fell in love with the moment she laid eyes on. She saw potential where everyone else could only see a boarded up, wreck awaiting demolition.

It was huge, ideal for what she had in mind. It had its own parking lot with a solid fence surrounding it. At the rear, above the old storerooms, were a series of offices. this, Minh decided, would be her home. She set about having it converted into an apartment on one side, retaining some of the office space to run her business, on the other. Downstairs, in what had once been the entrance with cash registers still in place, was transformed into a foyer, with a fountain on the righthand side and a bar where people could enjoy a drink before dinner.

The middle of the building was dug up and an oriental garden installed, complete with koi pond and wooden decking, where tables and chairs were placed. Those looked out into the garden where there was a small stage and dance floor, that could be seen from wherever you sat.

Hand painted screens on the left side formed, to make private dining rooms that were popular. They were so positioned that you could open a screen and look out into the garden. The storeroom became the kitchen, where chefs prepared a mixture of cuisine based on recipes Minh had learned from her home in Vietnam and places from her travels through Cambodia and Thailand, and some shown to her by others from Japan and Korea, all altered and adjusted to meet western tastes. As dishes from different cuisines were represented, she named the restaurant, *Flavours of the Mysterious East.*

It was a huge success and reservations were difficult to come by. It not only added to her own wealth, but revitalised a section of the city that had been dying for years. Minh received awards and accolades from the public. Dawn's family still received their ten percent. She was still looking to the future and had researched other cities where she might be able to open more restaurants. She had a short list: Santa Monica and San Francisco in California, Las Vegas, Chicago and New York.

She would like to open in all those cities, but she remained cautious and decided she would open one, move there, run it for a year herself, then see. If it failed, she would return to the original and, in a year or two, try again. If it was a success, she would appoint a manager and move to the next one. She had already chosen somebody to run the first restaurant and had recently agreed to sell the cleaning business to another one of her employees.

Although the banks would happily lend her money, she was reluctant to borrow and was a good saver. She had used her own money feeling more at ease. Her risks were calculated. They were only taken if she could afford the losses.

Minh had never been able to study. That dream remained unfulfilled. All her time was consumed by work. She would like to see her old friend, perhaps persuade her to move to the US now the orphanage was established. Feeling compelled to do so, she pushed all doubts aside and decided to go, perhaps she could visit California on the way. She picked up the phone that sat amongst papers and notebooks on the chaotic kitchen table and phoned Dawn. Dawn was reluctant, but eventually agreed to accompany her.

Outside, it began to rain, there was no time like the present. She phoned the manageress of her restaurant and explained she would be away on business for two weeks; Susan was a young woman she had trained herself and was immensely proud of her. A college graduate, eager to learn, with a strong commitment to the business and a family friend of Dawn's, she had earned her complete trust.

Minh packed her bags, booked the tickets and along with Dawn, left for San Francisco that same afternoon. It was fun traveling with Dawn. Two days later, they stepped out of the plane and into the sweltering heat of Thailand. She had forgotten how hot it was.

The orphanage was very different to the one they had left behind. The dirty concrete walls were now painted white, the red roof tiles shimmered in the sun. At the entrance, Hanh and Katie welcomed them warmly, all three embraced. Inside was an explosion of colour with every wall brightly painted, where there had once been nothing but dirt. The courtyard and grounds had been transformed for the children. Everywhere you looked, there were sandpits, climbing frames and swings; trees and flowers had been planted, along with a fine grass lawn where children could play. Minh and Dawn were impressed. The pictures they had seen did little justice to how it looked in real life.

'The plumbing and all of the electricals have been replaced also,' Hanh said, waving her hand around the compound. 'A courtesy of the US Army. Guilt is sometimes a powerful motivator.'

Their bags were taken to their rooms and all four women sat at a small table beneath one of the trees. The children were having lessons so they would not be disturbed.

'You have done a marvellous job here Hanh and Kate, the orphanage looks spectacular,' Minh said.

'We can't take all of the credit; we have a lot of helpers. It would also not be possible without the help we receive from yourself and Dawn. Without the two of you, the government and the army would not help us. The money, the volunteers, without these things we would not be able to remain open.'

Minh was touched. She felt Hanh's warmth and the setting took her back to the days when they were traveling across Cambodia.

'Our life here is fulfilling. Of course, Daniel is married now. He has been invaluable and, although he will always be a part of our family, it will soon be time for him to leave us.'

Minh was impressed. Hanh had always been wise, yet now she was displaying more maturity.

'We are prepared for it; we have a replacement already working here. I cannot ask more of Daniel; he has been the backbone of our organisation from the beginning. I am resigned to this and it should be. This is not a country for outsiders to build a life. They don't like us, yet they accept that they must allow us to do our work. We are an embarrassment to them, although the women that provide services to the men fuel their economy. Our main job remains unchanged: to raise the children, care for them, then see them successfully adopted abroad. 'Our reputation has grown. We have seen children in similar circumstances arrive from Saigon and Phenom Penh. They will never be accepted into society, either here or back home, they are outcasts. I asked you all here because we need to plan for the future. One day, I will no longer be here; we will all grow old, have other commitments but the work here needs to continue beyond us. We are only the beginning. I need all of your help to make sure that it does.'

Dawn took Minh's hand in hers, then Hanh's in the other. Katie linked herself in, then Dawn spoke, 'I promise, to do everything in my power to ensure that this orphanage not only continues, but grows across the world forever. I propose we establish a foundation to guide the organisation and govern it.'

'Does everyone agree?' asked Hanh.

They answered all at once, 'Yes.'

A bell rang and children came running from everywhere. Their bright smiles told Minh the quality of life they experienced in the orphanage. The older children sat under the veranda chatting and playing board games, the younger ones ran wild from one thing to the next. A boy, small for his age, who Minh judged to be eight or nine, cautiously approached them.

'This is Jimmy,' Hanh said, beckoning him into her arms.

She hugged him lovingly, then brushed his fringe out of his eyes. Jimmy had blond hair, blue eyes with Asian features that were somehow familiar.

'He is a very special boy. Run along and play now Jimmy.' Hanh sipped some tea before continuing, 'You know his mother, Minh.'

Minh was alarmed, her expression changing.

'How would I? I've never seen him before in my life.'

'His mother robbed you and threatened to kill us both.'

In an instant, Minh was transported back to the tiny shack, stripped naked, hands tied and forced to kneel on the rough dirty ground.

'May Ping arrived as a refugee and I found her when I was working at the UN Camp. She had suffered greatly. Jimmy was the result of a brief liaison with an American. She was reduced to poverty caring for him as her family and her friends all turned their backs on her and she was forced into... well she needed to make a living. She fled when the Khmer Rouge decided to exterminate her, barely making it across the border.

'She recognised me. I forgave her for what she had done to us as she was a changed woman, then she contracted typhoid. just like that in two weeks Jimmy was an orphan.'

Hanh clicked her fingers as she said the last part. Minh was stunned.

How could this be? The strange series of events that had brought them back together.

'I promised his mother on her death bed, that I would take care of him, that I would take responsibility for his future and now I need to ask a favour of you.'

Without another word, Minh understood. As her brain screamed "no, now is not the right time", she heard herself say, 'He can live with me; I will take care of him.'

Hanh stood and embraced Minh. For the longest time they stood holding each other. Hanh then spoke from the heart, 'We are a family now; we must take care of each other, we are all that is left, all that we have.'

Minh said all she had to say with the embrace.

MINH DECIDED THAT what she needed was a fresh beginning. With Jimmy in tow, she moved to California, buying a big house on the beach in Malibu. It was a beautiful home, set on a cliff with a downstairs room that opened onto the beach. They were surrounded by water. Upstairs was a sparkling swimming pool that looked out over the ocean. Minh employed a local man, Dan, a surfer who ran a pool cleaning business, to look after it. Dan was tall with rugged features. He was friendly and they chatted often. He had served two tours in Vietnam.

After hearing that Jimmy couldn't swim, Dan offered to teach him.

It was while she sat watching him patiently, getting Jimmy to float on his back, slowly building his confidence, that she decided she loved Dan and then and there, was going to find a way to marry him. Life was once again turning on its axis.

These were the times you lived for, Hanh reflected, as she sat near the gate to the orphanage one evening. Kamira, the woman they owed their very lives to, had been killed. Her only surviving son had delivered the terrible news. Hanh had given shelter to him, his wife and young son and the wife of his brother, the only survivors. The entire family murdered on the orders of a teenage girl who forced them to watch the strangulation of their mother.

It was a horrible story; he had never told her how they had escaped. To be able to help others was the supreme honour of humanity. Minh, Dan and Jimmy continued to visit every few years, as did Daniel, Dawn, and their families. The years passed and Jimmy went to university, then ran the business empire Minh had started. Minh retired earlier than she expected, to finding solace in the garden and spending time with Dan. Jimmy, Dawn, Daniel and Katie ran the foundation. They were only custodians. Each would see to that when their time to depart arrived. They would seek out the right people to replace them.

Hanh's own children had never visited, she had regrets. Her daughter had told her in a letter that their father was honoured as a fallen hero, an unknown soldier in the great struggle. It was their final correspondence. She had received awards from the Thai royal family and Thai government, the United States and United Nations.

Hanh, always secretive, had kept from everyone the diagnosis and treatment for the cancer that was ravaging her body. As the illness overtook her, the nightly trips to the gate became difficult. Still, she insisted that the ones she loved, other than Kate, remain ignorant. Katie escorted her to the gate every evening. She never stayed, respecting Hanh's privacy and the sanctity of the ritual. Hanh's prediction was wrong, Katie remained her lover until the very end.

One evening, while Hanh was sitting quietly waiting, a young man approached the gate. She did not recognise him at first, then she ran to him, holding on to him through the gaps in the closed gate's bars. As he beckoned her to open the gate and come with him, she turned. There, standing behind her, were hundreds of souls; the souls of children, abandoned, lost. They surrounded her. The young man smiled, turned and began to walk away. Although her heart longed to follow, she stayed with the children.

The waiting for Hanh was finally over.

Tanya 1.26

LIGHTNING AND THUNDER welcomed Tanya as she woke from her sleep. While these dreams were emotionally draining, they were also empowering. How long had women like her endured this torture? It seemed as if, since time began. Men had felt compelled to go to war, leaving behind everything and everyone they loved. She kept coming back to this, then there was the other question. Now there were female soldiers, what were they thinking? Was there no better way to settle things? Were there ever any winners?

She remained hidden beneath the blanket, even though the fire was getting low and she needed to visit the bathroom. She didn't want to leave the safety of the blanket. It was the phone that finally roused her. Her aunt was calling, asking if she was okay. She assured her that she was, then added some wood to the fire, visited the bathroom, followed by the kitchen, putting the kettle on and toasting some crumpets.

With no desire to venture outside, she returned to her desk. The rain was beating down hard, the thunder was like artillery fire and the wind howled. To take her mind off things, she picked up another of Karam's journals and returned to that world.

Karam 1.6

$\mathcal{T}$HE MONEY MEANT nothing to her, though it came more easily to her than it came to many. Some years were leaner, but they never took a step backwards. Karam found no joy in it. Since the death of her son, nothing really mattered, the meaning of these things diminished. The business grew, the bank accounts overflowed, she invested in art. Sculptures became a favourite medium. She sponsored artists, writers, funding all manner of things.

There was some joy in watching Dilbagh's new family grow. She suspected he was her brother, but without her father's confirmation, it remained a mystery. News from New York was always welcome. She looked forward to visiting her eldest son, but always found a reason to delay the trip. Hours were spent staring out to the ocean. Sometimes she felt she could see her little boy, Sanjeet, bobbing up and down in the waves. She commissioned a statue of him, and then another, the intention was to have one made of gold. She placed them around her estate, spending more and more on the gardens that surrounded them. She felt that his soul dwelled there and wanted it to be comfortable for him.

She reflected on things, found it odd that men would blindly follow their queen and yet not allow their wives, their own wives, to open a bank account. She had met Queen Victoria both publicly and twice in private. Whatever was discussed at those meetings remained secret; there was no record. Tanya wondered if the women, united in grief, Queen Victoria for her husband; Karam, her son, had bonded, had consoled one another in some way. Did the women, who both outwardly conveyed a message of strength, in private share their true thoughts and feelings? Karam had opposed the shipment of arms by their company, but had allowed herself to be convinced to do so in the interest of the nation. Her days were spent trying to remain busy. Sanjeet was always there whenever she closed her eyes. She had failed him and lived to atone for that sin.

Her father's passing was painful. The news was slow to arrive and her brother's letters emotionless. Aprajeet's retirement was the event that would reluctantly bring her home. Dilbagh needed to remain with his family and, even though the transition of power to Aprajeet's sons was but a formality, it deserved a senior member of the firm's attendance.

Aprajeet had done something near impossible just a generation before. Through hard work alone, he had helped save them; he had become rich and prospered along with them. Now at seventy, a wealthy man, he could enjoy his final years.

Retracing her steps on her own private vessel, she rarely left her cabin. As her life had become, she always remained in the shadows. It was possible, entirely probable, that Karam was the wealthiest woman in the world at that time, yet official documents showed she had no income or assets. All her affairs were in the hands of male relatives.

Albert Syme, another to whom they owed so much, had also been promised retirement. Upon her return, he would divest all his holdings to the family. Heirless, he had decided to bequeath most of his assets, upon his death, to charities and the arts. His desire was that his enormous estate in Kent become a university, that his two London homes become a gallery and a hospital. The millions of pounds in cash, stocks and other investments would become a foundation with a multitude of endowments and scholarships.

Karam asked him once, if he had ever experienced love. His response was typical of the man, 'Only so far as was practical.'

Although she suspected more, she left it there. An only child, he was at the very least, leaving the world a better place than he had found it.

A railway replaced her journey from Calcutta to her old home. Before she knew it, she was riding through the town of her birth and much had changed. She stayed at her brother's home, which had grown substantially since she had last seen it. Her father's estate was the same as she left it; the beautiful gardens, where she had bathed, washing away the remnants of her previous life, remained intact.

Although she sought nothing of her husband, amidst the celebrations, it was Aprajeet who bore the news of his fate. Jasleen and her father had swindled him. Where he had believed true love awaited him, instead, a careful trap had been laid. Over the years, they had drained his wealth, selling his assets and keeping the money for themselves, which had been largely squandered. He was now heavily in debt. There were rumours that creditors were to evict him from the home they had once shared. Jasleen had gone to join her father. She had not even taken her own children. Aprajeet was sombre, she could tell that he somehow felt sorry for him. He had wondered if perhaps she would visit him.

A thought crossed her mind, a wicked thought. How would he react? She wondered if he had contacted Karminder. She dismissed it, her son would have told her. The way he felt towards his father, having been told the truth when he was old enough to understand, he would not have given him the time of day. Aprajeet promised to make the arrangements for the visit, it would be his final task.

Two days later, her carriage drew up at the front of her former home. Harmeet was waiting in the same room where she had seen him last. Was it really so long ago? How old and sorry he looked. Neither knew how to begin. Suddenly, she realised they had not seen nor heard from each other since Sanjeet had perished. A rush of sadness crossed her face and he noticed it.

'Come sit,' he offered, 'please join me.'

They sat facing each other. He called for tea and she could tell there was no money in the house, that there had not been for a long time.

'We have both entered our final stages, I see. Is it true what they say, that you prosper?' Harmeet finally asked.

What a shame, she thought, *he really is a servant to money.* And then it dawned upon her, money, that was the one thing that would bring his true love running back to him. Even now, having robbed him, the fool still yearned for her. Was the feel of her flesh in his bed that enticing? Had she been built to such a position in his mind? For an instant she was jealous, no man had ever desired her in such a way.

'My dear husband, I am only a woman. I do not prosper but live at the mercy of my male relatives. My father and, now my brother and son, provide for me, since you decided to abandon your family.'

She was as smart as ever, he thought.

'Is it not true, you live in huge mansions and control vast business interests?'

'I have no such interests, husband; I live purely from the benevolence of others. Even the clothes on my back do not belong to me; the cottage I live in would fit inside this parlour.'

He changed the subject.

'Our son does not acknowledge me; my letters return unopened.'

'You made a decision long ago, in this very room, as I remember.'

No, it was in the garden. You decided to follow your heart, abandoning those who were dear to you. Now you feel the consequences of that decision.'

This wounded him. She was surprised, he could be so easily hurt.

'I have no such desires anymore. I live now as a monk. I desire one thing only, to care for my children and grandchildren, to see them taken care of before I depart this world.'

Karam eyed him suspiciously. 'And Jasleen?'

'A regret. I would rather not look upon her black heart again.'

For some reason, perhaps the sincerity of his words, Karam believed him.

'I cannot tell you Karam, that I loved you. That you were the one I should have stayed with. Of course, I regret hurting you, but if I told you that, it would be a lie and I have told enough lies.'

A small face appeared from the garden. It was Sanjeet, cheeky adorable, no it was not him, but it reminded her of him. In an instant, things changed.

'Go now, run along and play,' said Harmeet. 'My grandson,' he told her.

Karam nodded, smiling for the first time. In that moment, she put aside her grievances. *How such a small thing changes everything,* she thought. What if this little boy had not shown himself? *But he had, and now, well things would be different,* she thought. Karam stood, her mind made up.

'I will visit our eldest and speak to him on your behalf. Not this year though. Write to him in the new year, he will respond. It was nice seeing you, I must go now. Goodbye Harmeet. I cannot remain here another moment, there is much to do.'

As always, when her mind was made up, she acted. What did she care? The child didn't deserve the fate of those who should've been wiser. A young lawyer whose name was Carter, was traveling with her party. She summoned him at once, along with Aprajeet and his sons. Karam spoke with great authority. There was no arguing at these times, one was simply compelled to listen to her and obey. Carter seemed distracted, but she would deal with that later.

'I have decided to assist my former husband, though I do not want his new wife, who has left him, or her family to benefit. You will sort the details between you to ensure this does not happen. First, Aprajeet, we need your services one last time. Along with your sons, make enquiries and find out the name of each of my husband's debtors, then pay them. Then allocate him an allowance, generous, but not overly so. Restore the house, ensure the children and grandchildren are well provided for.

Place any assets in trust for the children and grandchildren, ensuring succession, but not to the woman or her father.'

Aprajeet spoke, remembering days of old. 'It will be an honour.'

'Carter, return here tomorrow, I wish to speak to you further.'

After they had departed, she collapsed onto her bed, wondering at the peculiarities of life, her life in particular. At least, it was never dull! If Harmeet ever thanked her, she would never hear it. She did not want anything more from him. She would pave the way for a relationship with Karminder, if that was what he wanted, but to her it was finally over.

Carter arrived just after breakfast. Karam liked this young man and had insisted he accompany her. He had a sharp mind, yet there was more about him. He appreciated things, he understood the moral implications, he cared about the world around him. They walked through the garden; something was bothering him and Karam, a friend of his mother, felt obligated to help if she could.

'Tell me Carter, are you enjoying your time here?'

'Yes, very much so. It is different to how imagined it.'

'I've noticed you've been distracted.'

Carter blushed. He was glad they were outside. 'Come now there's no need for embarrassment.'

'Have you ever been in love? I mean of course you have. I'm afraid, I don't know what I mean.'

'I thought I was once; I was happy, happier than I ever felt possible, but it was just an illusion. Tell me, does your heart miss a beat when you see her.'

The young man looked as if he would burst under the strain. 'Come tell me, who is the object of your affections?'

'Your great niece, Athena.'

'Then we must move with delicacy. She may already be promised to somebody else, have you spoken to her?'

'We have exchanged words.'

'Leave it to me, you have work to do. Concentrate if you can.'

Karam knew far more than she had revealed. Athena was considered difficult, headstrong and had refused every attempt to find her a suitable match. Educated by private tutors, she was a favourite of Karam's already, though they had only just met. There were stories of her dominating her grandfather's beloved cricket, a rejection of what was accepted as normal. So why did Karam want to marry her off to Carter? She understood how the world worked, there was only so much she could do. If Athena had feelings for Carter, then that would be a better life than here, and one day, slowly she stopped, or could she do something more, could she make some real changes. Karam did not seek her brother, nor did she seek his son or anybody else. She sought Athena.

Convincing the young woman to accompany her to visit her father's old estate, where she had bathed in the garden so many years ago, it was also the place where she had learned the truth about her marriage and decided her future.

'Athena.'

'Aunty.'

'If you could do anything, anything at all, what would that be?' Athena considered the question.

'I would like to move away from here, I would like the opportunity make a life of my own, a life of my own choosing.'

'Wouldn't you miss your family, all of this, the things, the houses, the money? It's an easy life.'

'Yes, but it is not my life. It's the dreams of another. I am smart, I can make money. I can have things, the things I want, things that are beautiful to me.'

'Life is unfair, Athena. The young man who accompanied me, Carter.'

'Yes, Aunty I have noticed him.' Athena blushed.

'Learn to control your emotions. If you want to master your destiny, you must learn to control your emotions and not be controlled by them.'

Athena bowed her head, accepting the admonishment.

'Carter has similar feelings. Come with me when I leave, live with me in my house, get to know him, you can work in our firm. I'll tell your father I need you to travel with me to New York. If something develops, perhaps the two of you can build a future together.'

Athena was overcome with joy. A world of opportunities had suddenly opened up for her. Without hesitation, she accepted.

'I will come.'

'Good, now go and see the young man. He waits for you in the house and remember what I have said to you. Only you can obtain the things you truly desire.'

Karam was only happy when she returned to the cliffs at Land's End. It was there she decided not to visit New York, indeed, she decided to only leave her home on the rarest of occasions from that day forward. Karminder visited with his family. They finally made peace, reconnecting in the beautiful gardens where they spent hours together. He had turned into a wonderful, thoughtful man that she had always hoped he would be. They enjoyed the time they spent together, so much that Karminder returned each year up until Karam's death.

Athena flourished, though she often felt homesick. With Carter, she had a good life, living there by the cliffs when Karam was no more. By then, a new century had begun and a horrible war had come and gone with another on the way. Karam gently slipped from this world while sitting in her beloved gazebo, looking out to sea. They found her with a peaceful expression on her face.

In her will, it was revealed that, although everybody assumed her estate to be enormous, it totalled less than a thousand pounds, and this was only after her jewellery was valued. She did legitimise Dilbagh as her brother. True or not, he was more family to her than many of the relatives who shared her blood. The necklace Tanya had worn on the night of the dinner at the hotel, the gift from her mother, had passed to Athena. She was surprised to see listed, the blue diamond necklace, also given to Jasleen. She wondered where it had ended up. All the other assets were either trusts or owned by others.

A large party had been planned for Karam's ninety-fifth birthday. Instead, a celebration of her life was held, attended by more than two hundred people, with hundreds more visiting to pay their respects, while thousands of cards and letters of condolence arrived for years after her death. For a woman who died with nothing, she had led the richest of lives.

Tanya 1.27

TANYA HAD NO sooner placed the diary down, when her phone rang again. She answered it. Time stood still as she listened. A lightning strike hit close to the bungalow, followed by a deafeningly loud clap of thunder. It snapped her out of it. Scared, she dropped her phone and ran for the safety of the lounge, cowering under the blanket as another lightning strike hit nearby. She braced herself for the following blast of thunder as the rain fell with increased ferocity and roared around the bungalow.

A primal instinct told her that bad things were about. The doors were locked, but would a lock stop them? Paranoia crept into the room as she felt her stomach churning. The phone was ringing again, but it was distant. She dared not venture out to retrieve it. Opening her eyes, she peered out from beneath the blanket.

She was now looking up from the lounge and seemed to be sinking. Then suddenly, as though she was dreaming, she was thrown into a dark cold room where she huddled, shivering on the cold floor. Two creatures entered, foul things, they each took an arm, forcing her to her feet then almost dragging her up some stairs. They emerged into bright sunlight and were standing on a huge barge in the middle of an ocean. Attendants were scattered about. It was something old, ancient and Tanya was scared as a man appeared.

'Why have you brought me here?' she demanded.

'All in good time. Follow,' he commanded.

They led Tanya to a covered pavilion where there was a luxurious day bed, surrounded by cushions.

'Here, sit.' Tanya did as she was told.

A creature arrived, a demon, dressed in rich fabric covered in gold. It was female, or had taken that form, and she reclined on the day bed. 'I've been waiting to meet you again, Tanya, do you remember me?' Before Tanya replied, she continued, 'We have met before in your dreams,. You probably never believed that I was real. Perhaps, this will jog your memory. Sanjeet.'

A little boy appeared, bowing to her, smiling.

'Hello, Aunty.' His bright little voice melted her heart. She needed to be strong.

'Why have you brought me here?' Tanya demanded, the tone of her voice bordering on anger.

'To do a little bargaining of course. You see, we need new energy like this little one here. Run along and play, Sanjeet.'

The boy obeyed, leaving them with a bow. 'Why would I need to bargain?'

'You will see.'

More creatures appeared. Carrying a large mirror, they placed it in front of her. It was cloudy at first, but slowly an image started to come into focus. Tanya watched in horror.

Evan 1.4

Evan heard the patrol before he saw them, lumbering along the other side of the ravine. He had left his weapon in the hands of the doctor and already stripped down to his shorts for the swim across the tumultuous river. Anxious to get moving, he ran across the rocks from their vantage point and made it to a point where he could enter. He slipped into the water, breaking out for the opposite bank,. The water was deep, the current strong; it bubbled and frothed around the rocks, attuned as he was to taking risks. He did this, without a thought to the obvious dangers. It was only thirty metres or so, yet seemed longer. Before he knew it, he had reached the opposite side. He climbed up the small ridge and started down the track to where the patrol was passing.

Aman, the doctor and little Farrah anxiously followed his progress. The patrol spotted them and they held up their arms to show no threat, while pointing to Evan on the other bank, who was running with his arms raised. The patrol then spotted him. The doctor and Aman stopped running, but the little boy kept going, following Evan from the other side of the river. Evan was yelling, the troops started towards him. They were cautious and yelled at him to stop, which he did, placing his hands on his head. At that moment, the little boy, close to the edge, also stopped, lost his footing, slipped and fell into the raging waters below.

Aman screamed. Evan looked up, just as the little boy fell into the water. He ran to the edge and dived in without thinking. Evan swam like he was being chased by the devil, racing against time as the fast-moving water washed the helpless boy further away from him. He swam with total abandon, every fibre of his being committed to the task, only glancing up momentarily to see if he was getting any closer.

On either side of the bank, both parties ran after them. The soldiers were shouting as one of them, Eddie Taylor, recognised Evan and started shouting his name. In the din and panic, his head in the water, Evan didn't hear him. Eddie yelled at the others. Evan looked up; he had almost reached the boy. He stayed above the water, putting everything into the last few strokes. He reached out and grabbed Farrah, his heart filled with joy. He held him tightly as they bobbed along, Evan strong, powerful, keeping them afloat. Farrah felt safe in his tight grip. Death had been avoided and the emotion overwhelmed them both as he was saved. Evan spotted a place where they would be able to climb out of the water and headed for it. Taking refuge in an eddy, the soldiers on the opposite side caught up to them, Evan decided to get Farrah out first. Mustering all of his strength, he threw the boy out of the water, up onto the bank just as his mother and the doctor arrived. They grabbed the young boy. Evan turned away, heading for the opposite bank, where the soldiers had found some rope to help get him out. When Evan reached the opposite bank, they were waiting for him. There was cheering and the crowd was ecstatic. They threw the rope down to him. He was climbing out in a space between two rocks where the bank was much higher.

Evan was almost out, the smiling face of Eddie Taylor waiting for him, when suddenly one of the soldiers slipped. He bumped into another and they both fell over losing grip of the rope. Evan fell backwards. Just before he reached the water, he hit his head on one of the rocks below. Instantly he lost consciousness, blood flowed from the wound as his body washed downstream. Eddie started to remove his clothes and equipment, but by the time he was ready to jump in, it was too late.

Tanya 1.28

TANYA WAS HORRIFIED. Through tear-streaked eyes, she had no idea of what to do or even think. This was an incredible series of events. How could it be happening? She tried to speak.

'I, what can I–'

'Do you want to barter for your husband's life?'

'I, I, what would–?'

'Hurry and make up your mind, he is fading fast, we need to act quickly.'

Tanya was unmoved, lost, unable to deal with the situation. The demon grew impatient.

'Look at you, pathetic, alone, nobody to offer assistance or counsel. Oh well, prepare to say goodbye.'

'She is not alone; I stand with her.'

Tanya looked up. There was a familiarity with this woman. She held out her hand, helping Tanya to her feet. That smile, I know that smile. It was Helga, one of the women from her dreams.'

'I stand with her.'

Another woman appeared. It was Stella. One by one, each appeared, along with the statement, 'I stand with her.'

Side by side, they closed ranks behind her. Even Kamiko, the woman whose story she could not recall from the first dream, appeared. Kamiko, Stella, Helga, Marta and Hanh all locked arms. Tanya felt the strength of the women flowing through her.

'Save him, my family has already given much.'

'Not so quickly, I will save him, but what you have given has already been spent. Just give the word and he is saved.'

'Wait.'

Another woman stood forward; it was Karam.

'Tell her first what you will take in return, then she can make her decision.'

'His life is already mine; you need to offer me like for like, or better. I will accept the child you carry.'

'How can you ask me for that?'

'Choose. This man is the love of your life. You can have a life with him, you can always have more children or lose him forever.'

'I offer myself for him and for Sanjeet, but not for my child.'

'Sanjeet has passed already.'

'Yes, but his soul remains trapped here.'

The demon considered the proposal. Smiling sardonically, it spoke, 'It's not enough, you are not worth that much. I wonder what your husband would say, if he knew how little you valued him.'

Evan appeared.

'It doesn't involve him; he gets no say, this is between you and me,' Tanya yelled, her anger rising.

Evan ran to Tanya and they embraced. 'What is this place?' he asked.

'I'm bartering for your life, but I'm afraid the price is too high.'

'What's the price?'

Tanya took Evan's hand and placed it on her stomach. A broad smile appeared on his face as he realised what she meant; it was a flicker of happiness.

'I offered myself for you, I would do anything.'

'But what of the baby, if you give yourself for me, you are also giving the baby? I refuse, return me to the river.'

'Wait, I can't live without you, Evan,' Tanya cried.

'It's the only way, raise our child, carry our love forward, always remember me.'

'You promised me forever.'

'No, my love, I never did.'

Tanya was desperate. The demon spoke, 'As you wish.' They were embracing as Evan faded away.

'Now I have his soul for eternity.'

'That was not the agreement. You gave nothing.' The demon laughed.

'You offered yourself without thinking, he offered himself for you and the baby. He is mine now, forever.'

Karam spoke up, 'No, not this time. You have fooled us for the last time.'

The women all joined hands to focus their energy. It was magical as their inner strength and resilience was transformed into a power to fight the demon. It laughed at the feeble attempt. The sky turned black, a storm brewed and the sun disappeared. The calm ocean became violent, waves formed, smashing against the barge. The women stayed resolute, bowing their heads as they continued focusing all of their combined energy.

Sanjeet re-appeared. 'Mama, please help me.' Karam ignored him knowing he was not the little boy she had once loved so dearly.

Slowly, the strength of each of the woman's energy became too powerful, as the demon's own power wilted. The storm began to die down and the demon screamed out in frustration.

Evan reappeared momentarily, surrounded by light, as he faded away again. Tanya broke down. Little Sanjeet was the next to fade away. She looked over to where the women were still standing, hands joined. One by one, each faded away, smiling, when only Karam remained. She stepped forward and embraced the distraught Tanya.

'Go now wake up from this nightmare.'

'What will I do without him?'

'You must find the strength to keep going. Honour the man you loved by raising your child. He was a good man and he deserves that.'

'I'm not strong like all of you. I can't do it.'

'Then they win, all of them, the people who make war, the evil forces, everyone. That's why we all kept going, us and the millions of others over the ages.'

Tanya felt stronger, emboldened by her words. Karam smiled at her. 'How can I ever repay you all for what you have done for me?' asked Tanya.

'Tell people about us, you know all of our stories. Let us live through your words. By telling our stories, you will make us eternal. Be strong Tanya, be strong. Remember all you have learned.'

Karam faded away. The rain stopped.

Aman 1.2

IT WAS A solemn party that followed the body down the river; the soldiers on one side, Aman, her son and the doctor on the other. They found him on Aman's side, where the river became wider as it flowed down onto the plains. He was floating face down, the horrible wound, on the back of his head, exposed. Aman hid Farrah from the sight, burying his head in her side.

When the doctor turned him over, Evan was smiling. Although he was obviously dead, the doctor still went through the motions of checking for any signs of life. Back at the British base, Aman told the entire story to the regiment's commander. She was concerned that they would not believe her, but she needn't have worried. When they were going through Evan's belongings, they found a letter he had written, confirming everything she had said. It also asked that they fulfill his promise to assist the doctor, Aman and her son in immigrating to a country where they could live in peace. He added that if any money was needed, his wife, Tanya, would assist.

The regimental commander would take personal interest in their re-settlement, beginning the process of obtaining clearance to travel as refugees to England, but first he said he had a difficult duty to perform. Picking up the satellite phone he dialled a now too familiar number.

Tanya 1.29

TANYA WOKE BACK in the bungalow; the storm had subsided. As the fog of her mind cleared, she could make out the sound of somebody knocking at the front door, while softly saying her name. She climbed off the lounge, almost collapsing as she stood. Slowly, she crossed the room, opening the front door. It was the general, he was alone. He had come to check on her and was wearing a raincoat and holding an umbrella.

'Tanya, sorry to bother you, but we were concerned.'

'Come in, warm yourself by the fire.'

He entered the bungalow and sat himself down in an armchair; Tanya took her place on the lounge.

'Can I get you something? A whiskey?'

'I'll get it, I'll pour one for you as well.'

'I really shouldn't.'

'Just the one won't hurt, I insist.'

The general poured two whiskies, handed one to Tanya, then returned to the armchair.

'I'm afraid Tanya, I have some very bad news.'

She knew instantly that it hadn't simply been a bad dream, that it was real.

'I know.' She dropped her eyes, accepting the fate that awaited her. 'Evan has been killed, drowned in a river in Afghanistan.'

'How on earth, did–?' he paused. 'They contacted you?'

'No, nothing like that. I don't think you would believe me if I told you.'

'I don't know about that; I've seen some incredible things in my time.'

A feeling of calm washed over her. She was upset beyond words but still, at that moment, she felt, no knew, that everything would be okay. There were tough times coming, yet she knew she had the strength to get through them. Perhaps it was shock, at that moment she was at peace. In the back of her mind, the thought that she had, when she tried to reconcile Karam's experience, came to her. Was the bartering with the demon, just a coping mechanism? She told the general everything, true to his word he didn't judge.

'Well, you know even more than I do. I can't ask you how you feel?'

'Sad beyond words, but at the same time resolved to have this baby and raise it in his honour.'

'You never know Tanya. You are young, although it seems impossible right now you might fall in love again one day.'

His smile, as he said this, was weak, apologetic.

'Evan and I were soulmates, there can never be another.'

'Never say never, Tanya. Never say it and never think it.'

'I just want to also say, how sorry I am. I can't help but feel that I could have prevented this, I should have pushed harder for him to take the job with Harry.'

'You offered him a safe job?' The realisation of this hit her hard. 'He never said anything?'

She nodded.

'I suppose he had his reasons; I couldn't convince him. Your mother and I both tried, more than once.' He stood up. 'Come on, we had better get you back to the main house. We need to show the others that you are alright.'

'Give me a moment I just need to use the bathroom.' As she closed the bathroom door, she burst into tears. 'How could he?' she said softly. 'How could he?'

As he was waiting, the general spotted Tanya's phone lying on the floor. He picked it up. The screen was still open. A call was showing and he recognised the number straight away. Then without really thinking about it, he closed the screen and placed it onto the coffee table.

It took only a few days to bring Evan's body home. They wasted no time in organising the funeral, burying him in a plot on the estate. It passed in a blur for Tanya. She was determined not to succumb to depression, remaining focused on the light at the end of the tunnel: the child she was carrying. She thought of all she had learned. She longed for Evan, but it could not be. Fate was cruel but perhaps the General was right. Perhaps somewhere out there, there was another, but how could that be? Still, she refused to completely dismiss it out of respect for him, and also out of hope. One afternoon, two weeks after the funeral her aunt came to visit her in the bungalow. They wandered over to the gazebo, where they sat staring out at the sea.

'How are you feeling?'

'The days all meld together. I don't know where I'm at only I know I have to keep going, for this one's sake.' Tanya touched her stomach as she said this.

'I've been doing some soul searching also and I have come to a decision,' said her aunt. 'I have decided to turn Land's End over to you, if you want it. I want you to make your home here. Perhaps, now, you can bring it into the new century, but do it in the way that it should be done.'

'That's very nice of you, but Evan wanted us to live in the sun. I'm going to live in the house we bought together in Ibiza.'

Tanya could see her aunt's disappointment.

'My time here is done,' she said. 'I suppose I could employ an estate manager, selling it is out of the question of course. Is there no chance you might re-consider? I thought, well it just seems like you fit here.

Something tells me that it's a part of you, that more than any of us, you should be the one to look after it.'

Tanya hadn't considered this. It was true that it had grown on her, even more so after learning Karam's story. An idea formed in her mind, then another thought occurred to her. Was moving to Ibiza running away? When Karam ran away, she had little choice. Tanya, on the other hand, had no reason to run.

'Perhaps, I could do both, live in the sun, and live here. Yes, I will do it. Thank you, Aunty. I'm thrilled, gratified that you would have that much faith in me.'

They hugged. It was a huge undertaking. The responsibility alone was enough to overwhelm her, but she would do it and do it with pride. The legacy, she was determined, would continue.

She stayed sitting in the gazebo, long after her aunt had left, staring out to sea. It was calm, flat, as she sat deep in thought. Karam's words came to her. *Honour us, let us live.* She stood up, patted her stomach, then went into the bungalow for the first time since Evan had passed away. She started her laptop, then began to type.

The story begins at the end. History repeats.

About the Author

JUSTIN FOX IS a writer who lives in Sydney, Australia at the foot of the Blue Mountains. A born lover of storytelling, he never tired of hearing the stories of others and began creating his own at a very early age. Justin's writing shows a deep understanding of emotion. Readers are given insight into his character's inner thoughts, feelings and emotions as they come to life. The stories that have been building up over a life spent living, are finally ready to come flowing out. Justin's 'desire' is to bring enjoyment too as many people as possible, by sharing his stories.

RICHFOX BOOKS Pty Ltd

www.justinfoxauthor.com